Stephen Martin-Leake

Life of Captain Stephen Martin, 1666-1740

Stephen Martin-Leake

Life of Captain Stephen Martin, 1666-1740

ISBN/EAN: 9783337075965

Printed in Europe, USA, Canada, Australia, Japan

Cover: Foto ©Raphael Reischuk / pixelio.de

More available books at **www.hansebooks.com**

LIFE

OF

Captain Stephen Martin

1666—1740

EDITED BY

CLEMENTS R. MARKHAM, C.B., F.R.S.

PRINTED FOR THE NAVY RECORDS SOCIETY

MDCCCXCV.

INTRODUCTION.

THE life of Captain Stephen Martin embraces the
period from 1666 to 1740, and his active service in
the Navy from 1686 to 1714, having previously
served for some years in the merchant service. His
journal is not that of one of the leading worthies of
our navy during that period, and cannot claim the
interest that would attach to a personal record of
the commanders of our fleets, such men as Sir
George Rooke, Sir John Leake, or Sir Clowdisley
Shovell. Such interest as it possesses is that which
belongs to the career of an active naval officer in
stirring times, who saw a great deal of service;
while there is some special interest in the close professional and family connection between Sir John
Leake, one of the leading admirals of that period,
and his devoted flag captain, Stephen Martin.

There was an old friendship between the families
of Martin and Leake, and when the future admiral
was commanding merchant vessels during the peace
which preceded the Revolution, he took his young
friend, Stephen Martin, to sea with him. Again,
when the boy was discharged from the Montagu
for jesting at the ceremonies of the mass introduced on board by James II., he was befriended

by Captain Leake, who took him on board the
Firedrake as a midshipman.   Martin again served
a commission on board the Eagle under Captain
Leake, and saw much service, including the battle
of La Hogue.   It was during this period that the
ties of friendship between Martin and Leake were
strengthened by a family connection, when they
became brothers-in-law.   Martin married a sister of
his captain's wife, and he was Sir John Leake's
flag captain throughout the reign of Queen Anne.
When the admiral was dismissed from his employments on the accession of George I. his flag captain
retired with him, and continued to be his constant friend on shore.   On Sir John Leake's death,
having no surviving descendants, he left his fortune
to his flag captain, who assumed the additional name
of Leake, the two names having been used by his
descendants ever since.

The eldest son of Captain Martin began life in
the Navy Pay Office, and afterwards became a
herald.   Stephen Martin-Leake was eventually
Garter King of Arms.   He was the biographer of
Sir John Leake, and also the editor of his father's
journals, which took the form of a life of Captain
Stephen Martin.   The ' Life of Sir John Leake ' is
a work of considerable merit, and is now very rare.
It was written by Stephen Martin Leake out of
affectionate gratitude to his uncle-in-law, and at the
particular desire of his father, and was prepared
from a large collection of journals and other documents of Sir John Leake, most of which are still
preserved by the family.   It is an octavo volume of
463 pages, and is of great value as an authority for

the naval history of those times. It was printed in
1750, when Stephen was Clarenceux King of Arms,
but only fifty-one copies were struck off for circulation
among private friends, and it was never published.
The Garter's son, also Stephen Martin-Leake, presented the volume to the British Museum, together
with thirteen volumes of documents relating to Sir
John Leake's services in the navy.[1] The Garter
also **wrote** an essay comparing the services and
merits of Sir John Leake with those of his contemporaries, which is still in manuscript.[2]

Having printed the life of Sir John Leake, the
Garter King of Arms[3] thought it necessary to
add a memoir of the life and actions of his father,
Captain Stephen Martin, for the use and information of his children. It was compiled from his
father's journals, his plan being ' to be very brief in
the relation of transactions to be found at large in

[1] Original commissions, order and letter books, weekly
accounts, papers on naval affairs, minutes of courts-martial, list
of admirals who were commanders-in-chief in the Mediterranean
from 1676 to 1689, with their respective allowances, list of
captains from 1688 and of the ships they commanded, orders
respecting half-pay, tables of wages and rates for pilotings, a
general state of the navy from 1688 to 1698, prices of slop-clothes
established in 1704, and monthly abstracts of ships and vessels in
sea pay 1701–1710.

[2] The same manuscript volume contains a list showing to
whom the fifty-one copies of the life of Sir John Leake were
presented, beginning with nine copies to Stationers' Hall. There
were fourteen left in stock. The author's own copy, with fifteen
maps and plans, is now in the possession of his great-grand-
daughter, Mrs. Lowe, of Sherwood, near Guildford.

[3] Stephen Martin-Leake became Garter in 1754 in succession
to John Anstis, and held the office until his death in 1773.

Sir John's history, and to enlarge only upon such as may be called his own, whereby it will appear how well he merited Sir John's favour as an honest man, a faithful friend, and a brave captain.' This ' Life of Captain Martin ' has remained in manuscript until now. It is compiled from the captain's own journals, from 1690 to 1712 inclusive, which are still preserved by the family ; and it will be found to contain records of events which cannot fail to be interesting to naval readers. Captain Martin was seriously wounded at the battle of Bantry Bay in 1689. He was not at Beachy Head, but was busily engaged in strengthening the Plymouth defences, when the French fleet held the Channel immediately afterwards, and he was at the siege of Cork. He was at the battle of La Hogue, and was actively engaged in the boat work, of which he gives a capital account. He performed a good deal of difficult service with credit during Rooke's abortive attack on Cadiz, and also took part in the battle of Vigo Bay. At the battle of Malaga, where he was in the van led by his brother-in-law, he relates several stirring incidents, and he was at the capture of Barcelona in 1705, afterwards seeing a great deal of service in the Mediterranean and the North Sea.

If Captain Martin had his share of battles, he certainly had his share of storms. The captain being in the sick list, he saved his ship as first-lieutenant in the furious gale near Gibraltar, when Sir Francis Wheler's flagship went to the bottom. Coming back from Newfoundland in the Blast bomb, he encountered heavy weather in the Atlantic, was dismasted, and was given up for lost, but he brought

his vessel safe into Tenby. He was in the Downs
during the great storm of November 1703, and rode
it out when so many other ships were lost. Again,
on board the Russell, in 1711, his ship was dismasted
and in great danger, but his good seamanship was
the means of saving her, and bringing her safely
into Portsmouth.

The narrative is indeed full of stirring incidents,
and if it does not contain the more general views of
strategy and of tactical arrangements, the negotiations and political considerations which would be
found in narratives of the lives of commanders-in-
chief, it has an interest of a different kind, bringing
us somewhat nearer to the actual events, and in
closer touch with officers and men who actually conducted the details of the work. It is useful to be
able to follow the services of an officer who was
deeply engaged in the regular work of the navy, as
well as to study the lives of those of higher rank,
whose proceedings are more connected with politics
and with the course of general history.

Captain Martin survived for twenty-six years
after his retirement on the accession of George I.,
and the latter part of the narrative shows us
how the old sailor fell among land sharks, in the
form of South Sea directors, Treasury clerks, and
lawyers ; and how his impulsive and generous
disposition, and his inexperience in dealing with
shore-going people, led him into all sorts of trouble
and embarrassment. This part of his life-story is
far from being devoid of interest to the naval
reader. It will be found that the biography gives
a vivid picture of the career of a naval officer in

the days of William III. and Queen Anne, of the position he held in the various ranks, especially in those of flag captain and captain of the fleet, of the work he had to do in peace and war, and of the internal economy of a ship of war in those days. Nor would the picture be complete without the final touches which show him stranded at last and the prey of land sharks. The position of his son led to the old sailor receiving an honourable funeral, in strict accordance with heraldic rules and customs, which is not an unfitting conclusion to the story.

The end of the seventeenth century is one of the periods in our naval history which deserves special study. The end of the sixteenth century found England entering upon a desperate struggle with Spain, on the result of which not only our liberties but our very existence depended. It was to our fleet that we owed our deliverance from danger. Again, in the end of the seventeenth century England had to enter upon a struggle for existence with a still more formidable opponent in some respects. France was then in the height of her greatness and prosperity. Her king was preparing to invade and conquer this country, and to force upon us the expelled James II., thirsting for vengeance, and ready to accept the position of a tributary and creature of Louis XIV. Our defeat at La Hogue would have been as disastrous to England as the success of the Spanish Armada. Again we were saved by our fleet.

It may be convenient very briefly to give an abstract of the military history of the period comprised in the quarter of a century of Captain

Stephen Martin's sea service, for facility of reference. The expulsion of James II. and the accession
of William III. and Mary II. at the opening of the
year 1689 led inevitably to an immediate rupture
with France ; for the revolution substituted a vigi-
lant enemy for a subservient pensioner on the
throne of England, and threatened the success of
the ambitious projects of Louis XIV.

The war commenced in the spring of 1689,
when James II. landed in Ireland, summoned a
parliament of his adherents at Dublin, and the
whole island fell into his hands, except the Presby-
terian town of Londonderry, which was closely
besieged. On April 30 the English fleet, under
Admiral Herbert, gained a slight success over the
French at Bantry Bay, and on June 22 Captain
Leake cut the boom, threw supplies into Londonderry, and raised the siege. William III., having
landed in Ireland with a well-disciplined force, won
the battle of the Boyne on July 1, entered Dublin
on the 6th, and James II. hastily fled from the
country, landing at Brest on the 9th. But in the
meanwhile a large French fleet, under the Comte
de Tourville, had sailed up the Channel, and
encountered the combined English and Dutch
fleets, under Herbert, who had been created Earl
of Torrington for his success at Bantry Bay, off
Beachy Head, on June 30, 1689. The action was
partial, and Torrington, feeling that a hardly
contested battle would so cripple his ships as to
leave them helpless in the event of an attempted
invasion, wisely retreated into the Thames with
scarcely any loss. Thus Tourville was for the

moment in command of the Channel. William III.
returned to England on September 6. In the same
month the fleet conveyed a force, under Marlborough, to Ireland, and after a short siege Cork
and Kinsale capitulated to him. In the following
year the subjugation of Ireland was completed by
the capitulation of Limerick on October 1, 1691.

Louis XIV. then determined to invade England,
and force their expelled king upon an unwilling
people. He assembled an army at La Hogue; the
fleet, under Tourville, was to convey it across the
Channel, and James II. had arrived from St.
Germains, and was ready to embark. Never had
England been in such danger since the rout of
the Spanish Armada. The English fleet was
scattered in three squadrons, but, fortunately, they
succeeded in forming a junction, and with eighty-
two sail of the line Admiral Russell sailed across
to the French coast on May 18, 1692. The first
action with Tourville was fought on the 19th, and
was desperately contested, although Russell, with
his centre squadron, was alone engaged. It was
calm and foggy, and the French ships retreated, but
were again engaged with the blue squadron. On
the 20th the French fleet was chased to the westward. Some of their ships escaped to St. Malo, but
three were run on shore at Cherbourg and burnt,
including the flagship, Soleil Royal. The portion
of the French fleet which had not escaped to St.
Malo took refuge in La Hogue, while the great
army ready to invade England was encamped on
the hills above, round St. Vaast. Rooke was sent
in with a light squadron and the boats of the fleet

on Monday, the 23rd, **hoisting** his flag on board the Eagle. Thirteen of the enemy's **ships** were burnt in sight of their army, and the danger was over. This great victory saved England from invasion. The French fleet never again attempted to cope with us until the end of the war, operations being confined to cruises in **the** Mediterranean and to the West Indies and Newfoundland. The Peace of Ryswick was signed **on September** 10, 1697.

This **peace** did **not** last quite five years. The **cause of the outbreak** of hostilities was the question **of** succession to the Spanish throne. England, Holland, and the Empire were resolved **to** resist **the** accession of a French prince. Charles II. of Spain was childless. His next heir was **Joseph** of Bavaria, grandson of his **sister,** the Empress **Mar-**garet, and his **succession** would not have **been** disputed. **But, unfortunately,** Joseph died in 1699, and **the succession question** was opened again. The **nearest heir** after Joseph **was** the Duke of Anjou, grandson **of** Maria Teresa, another sister of Charles **II. of Spain,** but also a grandson of Louis XIV. The allies were determined to resist **the** accession of a French prince, by which the whole power of Spain would be at the service of the French king. They advocated the succession of the Archduke Charles,[1] a grandson of the Empress Maria, the same lady after whom our Charles I., as Prince **of** Wales, went courting to Madrid. She was **a sister** of Philip IV. and aunt

---

[1] He subsequently became Emperor of Germany as Charles VI. **in** 1711, and was the father **of** the Empress Maria Theresa. After a reign of thirty years Charles VI. died in 1740.

of Charles II. of Spain. Nothing happened until
the King of Spain's death in 1700, but as soon as
Charles II. was buried, Louis XIV. proclaimed his
grandson Anjou as Philip V., King of Spain. War
then became inevitable. The allies declared that
the Archduke was the rightful King of Spain as
Charles III. ; while Philip V. was sent to Madrid,
and acknowledged by most of the Castillian nobles.
Catalonia was in favour of the Austrian prince.
James II. had died at St. Germains on September 17, 1701, and his daughter Anne became
Queen of England on the death of her brother-
in-law, William III., on March 8, 1702.

King William was making preparations and
maturing plans for military operations at the time
of his death, and on May 2, 1702, Queen
Anne declared war with France. The first naval
enterprise, which had been carefully planned by
William III., was an attack on Cadiz, with Sir
George Rooke leading the fleet, and the Duke of
Ormonde in command of the land forces. It was a
disgraceful failure, but Rooke retrieved himself by a
great success at Vigo on October 11, 1702, when the
French lost fifteen ships and two frigates, while
seventeen galleons were sunk or taken.

The Archduke Charles, called King Charles III.
of Spain by the allies, was conveyed to Lisbon in
March 1704, and the Prince of Hesse Darmstadt,
with 6,000 men, accompanied the fleet ; for an
assurance had been received from Catalonia that the
people were ready to proclaim the Austrian prince
as Charles III. if a sufficient force was sent to
protect them. The fleet proceeded to Barcelona,

but the force was too small to attempt a siege, and
it was, therefore, resolved to make some attempt on
the coast of Andalusia in order to divide the enemy's
forces. An attack upon Gibraltar was decided upon.
Sir George Rooke sent in an attacking squadron
under Admiral Byng, and the Prince of Hesse
Darmstadt was landed with his troops on what is
now the neutral ground. But the capture of this
famous stronghold, which took place on July 24,
1704, was due to the gallantry of the seamen under
Captains Jumper, Whitaker, and Robert Fairfax,
who landed at the new mole.

The battle of Blenheim was won by Marlborough
on August 13, 1704. In the same month the
French fleet, under the Comte de Toulouse, a
son of Louis XIV. by Madame de Montespan, sailed
from Toulouse, consisting of fifty ships of the line,
several frigates and fire-ships, and twenty-four galleys.
The van was commanded by the Marquis de Villette.
The allied line, under Sir George Rooke, consisted of
fifty-one English and Dutch ships of the line, besides
frigates ; the van being led by Sir Clowdisley Shovell
and Sir John Leake. It was on the day of Blenheim, August 13, that Sir John Leake engaged the
French van, and a hotly contested action ensued off
Malaga. The battle was indecisive, no ships were
lost on either side, but the French fleet retreated to
Toulouse, and Gibraltar was saved from re-capture.

In 1705 a fleet sailed from England under the
joint command of the Earl of Peterborough and Sir
Clowdisley Shovell, and the Archduke Charles was
taken on board at Lisbon. The Prince of Hesse
Darmstadt, who had been Governor of Gibraltar

since its capture, also embarked. Barcelona was the destination of this expedition, and the siege was commenced on August 27. Lord Peterborough captured the fortress of Monjuich by assault, on September 17, and in October Barcelona surrendered. The Archduke then made his solemn entry into the city, and was proclaimed King of Spain as Charles III. The next expedition despatched from England took out a large land force under Lord Rivers in 1706. But it proved abortive. The troops were eventually landed at Alicante, and suffered severely in the great defeat of the allies at Almanza, by the Duke of Berwick, on April 25, 1707. Peterborough had been recalled in the previous March.

Meanwhile Marlborough had been leading the allies from victory to victory in the Low Countries. Ramillies was fought on May 23, 1706, Oudenarde on July 11, 1708, and Malplaquet on September 11, 1709.

But a change of Ministry in June 1711 led to a reversal of the policy of Godolphin and Marlborough. Robert Harley, the new Lord Treasurer, negotiated a peace by which all the objects of the war were abandoned, our allies were deserted, the brave people of Catalonia were left to their fate, and the French nominee, Philip V., was acknowledged as King of Spain. The Peace of Utrecht was proclaimed on May 4, 1713, just eleven years after the breaking out of the war. Queen Anne died on August 1, 1714, after a glorious reign of twelve years, and, in accordance with the Act of Settlement of June 12, 1701, the Elector of

Hanover became King of England as **George I.**
He landed on September 18, and **was** crowned
on October 20, 1714. One of his first acts
was to dismiss Sir John Leake from all his employments, and his flag Captain Stephen Martin's
active service came to an end at the same time.

During this long period of a quarter of a century,
from 1689 to 1714, the navy once saved England
from invasion, and manfully maintained her supre-
macy at sea during the whole time.

It is, therefore, with more than common interest
that we should inquire into the constitution of the
navy, the state and condition of the fleet, and the
efficiency of officers and men during the reigns of
William III. and Queen Anne. Such an inquiry is
a necessary introduction to the perusal of the narrative of Captain Stephen Martin's life. It should
commence with the civil branches of the navy,
and their direction and superintendence by the
Admiralty.

The ancient office of Lord High Admiral was
held by James II. himself during his short reign,
with the veteran Mr. Samuel Pepys as secretary.
After the Revolution there were Lords Commissioners of the Admiralty, except from 1702 to 1708,
when Prince George of Denmark was Lord High
Admiral, acting by the advice of a council, and for
a year after the prince's death, when the Earl of
Pembroke filled the same exalted position. Mr.
Pepys was dismissed at the Revolution, and, after
a short interval, his clerk, Mr. Josiah Burchett,
became secretary of the Admiralty in 1695, and
filled the post with diligence and ability for many

years.[1] The Admiralty regulated and superintended
the executive work of the navy, and transacted its
business in a house in Duke Street from 1689 to 1695,
afterwards at Wallingford House, on the site of the
present Admiralty, which was built in 1725.

The Commissioners of the Navy administered
the civil branches, with their offices on Tower Hill,
and afterwards in Seething Lane, Crutched Friars,
whence they moved into Somerset House in 1780.
There were eight commissioners, all receiving
500*l.* a year, except the treasurer, who had 3,000*l.*
The others were the comptroller of accounts,
the surveyor, the clerk of the acts, the victualler,
the storekeeper, and two commissioners, who had
charge of the dockyards at Chatham and Portsmouth ; the other dockyards of Deptford, Woolwich,
Sheerness, and Devonport not having a resident
commissioner in those days. The total cost of the
civil branch of the navy was about 22,000*l.* Phineas
Pett, the shipbuilder, was commissioner at Chatham
in 1688.

We next come to the ships, detailed lists of
which are in existence for several periods during
the two reigns. The oak for building was obtained,
for the most part, by contracts with timber merchants at Danzig, Riga, and Hamburg, only a fifth
of the annual consumption of oak timber being of

---

[1] From 1695 to 1742. He was M.P. for Sandwich from 1705
to 1713, and from 1721 to 1741. He was author of 'Memoirs of
Transactions at Sea' (1703), and the larger 'History of Transactions at Sea' (1720). Mr. Burchett and Captain Stephen
Martin were almost exact contemporaries. Born in the same
year, Burchett survived Martin by six years.

home growth. The ships of the navy were divided
into six rates, besides fire-ships, yachts, hoys,
sloops, and smacks, and at the time of the Revolution there appear to have been nine first-rates and
fifteen second-rates not in commission, thirty-nine
third-rates, forty-two fourth-rates, eleven fifth-rates,
nine sixth-rates ; altogether 125 vessels, besides
seven fire-ships, eighteen yachts, and fourteen
smaller craft.

The Britannia, built at Chatham by Phineas
Pett in 1682, was a good example of a first-rate of
that period, and she was at one time commanded
by Captain Stephen Martin. She was, in fact, the
largest ship in the navy in 1688, being 146 feet long,
47 feet extreme beam, 19½ in depth, and drawing
22 feet. Her tonnage was 1,739. Her armament
consisted of twenty-eight 42-pounders, twenty-six
40-pounders, twenty-eight 18-pounders, fourteen
6-pounders or sakers, four 16-pounders, a total of
100 guns. Her complement of men was 710.
Cost 21,000*l.*

The Victory, also built at Chatham by Phineas
Pett, was an example of a second-rate. She was
114 feet long, 42 beam, 20 draft of water, and 1,029
tons.

As examples of a third-rate we may take the
Exeter, a ship in which Stephen Martin served
during a whole commission ; or the Suffolk, Sir
Francis Wheler's flagship, which went to the
bottom with all hands. They were 124 feet long
and 40 extreme beam, drawing nearly 18 feet, and
1,070 tons. Both were built at Blackwall in
1680, at a cost of 10,900*l.* They carried twenty-six

63-pounders, twenty-six 41-pounders, twenty-six 20-pounders, and 10 sakers.

Fourth-rates varied from 400 to 700 tons, and a length from 85 to 116 feet; fifth-rates from 200 to 350 tons, and sixth-rates from 79 to 200 tons.

The heaviest guns were the 42-pounders, the shot supplied being cast, hammered, and in tin cases. The muskets were matchlocks and snap-haunces,[1] and among the gunners' stores were musquetoons, blunderbusses, pistols, pikes long and short, halberts, hatchets, swords, and hangers.

The long boats were thirty-six feet long, pin-naces thirty-three, and skiffs twenty-seven. The ships were not fitted with davits, the boats being hoisted inboard.

A full-rigged ship had a spritsail and sprit top-sail as head sails, one on a yard under the bowsprit, and the other on a mast fitted to the bowsprit cap. Jibs were not then invented. There were courses, topsails, and topgallant sails for the fore and main masts, and a mizen topsail and course, main mizen and fore staysails, main and fore topmast staysails, and maintopmast studding sails. Cables were each 100 fathoms long of 21-inch hemp, and the bower anchors were 74 cwts. for a first-rate, 66½ cwts. for a second, and 58 and 49 for a third-rate.

Turning from the ships themselves to the officers and men, we find that a great reform was effected when the Stuarts were expelled. After the Revo-lution the admirals were professional seamen, with a few exceptions, and the captains had invariably

---

[1] The 'snaphaunce' was a flint lock.

been brought up to the sea as a profession. The three ranks of full, vice, and rear admirals were established, and the practice of having red, blue, and white ensigns and pendants, the different squadrons, which had been introduced in the time of Charles I., was continued. The ensigns of the three colours, shown on an ensign staff, each had a cross of St. George on a white field in the upper canton. The jack, flown on the sprit topmast, was blue with a white saltire, and a red cross with white fimbriation over all, representing the union of Scotland and England.

Signals were made by changing the positions of flags, and not by combinations of flags. The system of Admiral Russell (afterwards Earl of Oxford) was to hoist red, white, or blue pendants at the different topmast heads and yardarms and in the lower rigging, when he wished to speak with any captain in any of the three squadrons. In this way he was able to make signals from twenty-five different positions with three differently coloured pendants, thus to make signals to seventy-five different ships. His order to this effect is dated May 6, 1691. He also made a number of other signals on the same principle. If he wanted any particular ship to chase to windward or to leeward, he made the signal for speaking to her captain, and also showed a red or a blue flag in the mizen rigging. When he desired that the boats of the fleet should come to the flagship manned and armed, he hoisted a pendant at the fore topmast head and fired a gun. A union jack at the mizen peak and one gun was a signal to form line ahead, and it was to be repeated by all the flagships. For line abreast, a union jack and a pendant at the mizen peak and one gun. To move in **succession, a yellow** flag at the mizen peak and one gun, and **so on.** When the fleet was in line of battle and hove **to,** and the admiral wished the ships to fill and stand on, he hoisted a yellow flag at the fore topmast head and fired a gun. By these devices a very considerable number of signals could be made, and fleet manœuvres were possible.

The admiral was assisted by a first captain, **equivalent to the more** modern captain of the fleet, and he **also had a flag captain,** then called second captain, who was **captain of the** ship. Captains received instructions **from the** Admiralty, **which were** printed and delivered to them with **their commissions.** These instructions enjoined the reading **of** daily prayers, a weekly muster of the men, inspection of rigging and cables, and superintendence of the shipment of stores. A captain was always to sleep on board, to keep the key of the powder room in his own cabin, and to see that the gunners' stores were duly accounted for. He received minute instructions respecting the entry and treatment of the men, and punishments for various offences were specified. Instructions as regards salutes were very precise, and a captain was strictly enjoined to make sure that his salute would be returned with the same number of guns before firing one in any foreign port. A commander-in-chief received eleven guns, an ambassador the same number, a vice-admiral nine guns, a rear-admiral, a knight, or a gentleman of quality, seven guns. Captains were strictly forbidden to carry bullion or merchandise, or to receive any gratuity for convoying merchant ships. A captain was to make frequent reports to the secretary of the Admiralty on the state and condition of his ship, and to keep a journal in a prescribed form.

There were three or four lieutenants in a first-rate, and two in a second and third-rate. The master, examined and selected by the Trinity House, was responsible for the navigation, and for all stores except ordnance and provisions. In battle he conned and worked the ship, placing her in positions desired by the captain. In a first-rate he had under his orders six master's mates, four quartermasters, the boatswain, who belonged to the ship permanently, and his mates. Young gentlemen, in Queen Anne's days, were admitted as volunteers between the ages of 14 and 16, and after serving four years as volunteers they became midshipmen. After two years as midshipmen they were examined, and when they had passed they were capable of receiving lieutenants' commissions. There were usually from ten to twenty volunteers and midshipmen on board each ship, according to the rate.

The instruments used for taking celestial observations were the back staff or Davis's quadrant, and an improved astrolabe. The log and line had been in use since 1622, and the use of logarithms had greatly facilitated computation. Hadley's quadrant was as yet unknown, but rapid progress was being made in improving instruments and methods of observation. The Greenwich Observatory had been founded in 1676, and from that time until

1719 John Flamsteed, the Astronomer Royal, was working at fixing the positions of stars, and at his chart of compass variation. The provision of charts in those days was a private speculation, for there was no Admiralty hydrographer until 1795.

The gunner received his ordnance and other stores from the department of the master-general of the ordnance at the Tower, under orders from the Admiralty; and under the master-general was the master-gunner of England, who had the duty of instructing and examining in the art of gunnery, and of certifying to the competence of gunners. The gunner had under **his orders a** quarter-gunner for every four guns, **gunner's mates, armourer,** gunsmith, and a **yeoman** of the **powder-room.** The part of the ship called the gunner's **room or** gun room was allotted to the gunner and his mates.

Every ship carried gentlemen volunteers, as well as the regular staff of executive officers, who were anxious to obtain commissions. Their certificates testified to their diligence, sobriety, and obedience to orders, and also to their application to the study and practice of navigation.

The civil branch afloat consisted of the purser, his steward and mates, the surgeon and his mates, and the cook and his mates. The position of the chaplain was dependent on the captain, and was usually a very wretched one, as we may gather from the diary of the Rev. Henry Teonge.

It was seen in the days of Blake how splendidly the English sailors fought, and of what good stuff they were made. **They** were worthy successors of the generation which repulsed the Spanish Armada, and the successors of Blake's sailors, in the days of Queen Anne, had certainly not degenerated. They were indifferently fed and very irregularly paid ; yet they appear to have been hard-working, contented fellows, with great powers of endurance, well acquainted with the mysteries of their craft, and fighting with indomitable pluck. Their ratings were yeomen of the sheets, quartermasters and their mates, boatswain's mates, the coxswain and his mate, the yeoman of the storerooms, carpenter's crew, sailmaker, cooper, able seamen, ordinary seamen, grommets, and boys. Ordinary seamen were between 18 and 20, and grommets[1] were the first-class boys of later times.

The scales of pay, which were established in the reign of Charles II., and continued nearly the same until the end of the last century, have been previously published. From July 1700 the captains of Her Majesty's ships were allowed four servants for every hundred men, a very large allowance ! But numerous ratings of captain's servant were given to young volunteers who were sons of the captain's own friends or relations. Previously, from 1693 to 1700, a captain of a first and second rate was allowed six, and of a third and fourth rate five, and of a sixth-rate four servants. Flag officers had a retinue of eight servants.

Soldiers had always been borne on board ships of war—at Sluys, at Gravelines, and under the Commonwealth, but they were disbanded at the end of each great war. In 1702 six regiments

[1] From the Spanish word *grumete*, a cabin boy or any well-grown lad on board ship.

were allotted for sea service, as it was considered that soldiers would be very useful on board ship, as well as serviceable on every occasion of landing on an enemy's coast. This was the commencement of the marines, that gallant, loyal, and most valuable arm of the service. But in 1749 the marine regiments were disbanded, and it was not until Lord Anson's time, in 1755, that the corps of marines was established on a somewhat different footing, and they have not since been disbanded.

The men and boys were divided into messes, four in each. The daily allowance of food was 1 lb. of bread, 1 gallon of beer, 1 lb. of beef or pork with pease, or else one side of salt fish with 7 oz. of butter, and 14 oz. of cheese for two days in the week instead of the beef and pork. In 1703 leave was given to the pursers to issue tobacco, to be smoked over tubs of water on the forecastle, and nowhere else, the allowance being 2 lbs. a month for each man. The scale of victualling would have been sufficient if the provisions had always been good, and if care had been taken to serve out fresh provisions whenever opportunities offered. But this was very far from being the case. The surveys ordered, especially on the beer and cheese, frequently disclosed a very disgraceful state of things, and outbreaks of scurvy resulted in numerous deaths. Mr. Burchett, the secretary of the Admiralty, was quite aware of the faults in the victualling arrangements, and of the remedial measures that should be adopted, but he was not sufficiently influential to obtain a reform of abuses.

There were, however, special commissioners for

sick and wounded seamen until 1705, when Greenwich Hospital came into working order.

Clothing was supplied by a contractor or slop-seller at prices fixed by the Admiralty. The purser received the slops and sold them to the men, receiving one shilling on every pound from the slop-seller, as a gratuity for keeping the accounts. The bedding was supplied by Government, consisting of hammocks, then called *hammacoes*, mattresses 5 feet 8 inches in length by 2 feet 2 inches, made of 'Hommels' cloth, and containing 11 lbs. of clean flocks, pillows of the same material, and coverlets 6 feet 2 inches by 4 feet 9 inches.

The scale of prices for slops [1] was as follows :

	£	s.	d.
Kersey waistcoat of Welsh red with brass buttons .	0	5	6
Grey jacket lined with red cotton, 18 brass buttons, and button-holes stitched with gold coloured thread	0	10	6
Drawers	0	2	3
Red breeches of either kersey or shag, and leather pockets, and thirteen white tin buttons . . .	0	5	6
Blue shirt	0	3	3
Grey woollen hose	0	1	9
Double soled, round toed shoes with brass buckles .	0	4	3½
Leather cap faced with red cotton	0	1	2
Blue woollen mittens	0	0	6

So that we may picture to ourselves Queen Anne's sailors in red waistcoats and breeches, grey jackets, grey woollen stockings, and round-toed buckled shoes, and a leather cap faced with red cotton. Naval officers had no regular uniform until Lord

[1] See order to the captains of H.M. ships, signed 'George' and 'J. Burchett,' and dated July 12, 1706.

Anson's time in 1750. In the days of Queen Anne the admirals and captains wore stately flowing wigs and three-cornered hats, laced blue coats, and breast-plates when in action.

The service was one in which officers and men took a pride, and there were greater facilities for men of ability to rise from before the mast than exist now, which must have increased the popularity, and probably the efficiency, of the navy. The stories about Clowdisley Shovell having crept in at the hawse-hole are clearly apocryphal, but Admiral Sir David Mitchell was certainly a case in point. He shipped himself as an apprentice on board a Leith trading smack, he was pressed into the navy when serving as a mate in a Baltic timber ship, and his good conduct and abilities soon obtained for him a commission as lieutenant on board the Defiance in 1678. This is not a solitary instance. It rather closely resembles the case of Captain Cook. But there was quite enough difficulty in obtaining advancement, jobbing was very prevalent, and deserving officers without interest were constantly passed over. There is something of this kind in the history of most of the officers of those days, and Captain Stephen Martin was not at all singular in his causes of complaint. His friendship and con-nection with one of the leading admirals of the day were not always sufficient to secure him fair play.

Those were days when every nerve was strained at first to enable England to hold her own, just as in the days of the Spanish Armada. But confidence and strength were gained as the war proceeded.

The position was very different from the first year when Tourville held the Channel, during the short breathing time of the Peace of Ryswick ; and when Queen Anne's Government resumed the struggle, success after success attended the British arms by land and sea. The main facts are well known, and in the journals of a naval officer such as Captain Martin we find them illustrated in a most interesting way by the stirring incidents of his own sea service.

The Appendix contains lists of ships in the navy in 1685 and 1699, taken from Sir John Leake's papers, and a statement of gains and losses between 1688 and 1698. I have also included letters from Captain Stephen Martin's son, who was in the Navy Pay Office, describing Portsmouth and its defences in 1729, which are interesting.

In my editorial work I have to acknowledge most valuable assistance from Lieutenant Francis Martin Leake, R.N., who transcribed some of the letters, revised all the transcriptions with great care, made lists of letters and other documents, prepared indices, and made some very helpful researches in the British Museum. He is a descendant of Captain Stephen Martin[1] in the fifth generation. My best thanks are also due to Mr. Laughton for some valuable suggestions, and for revising the proofs.

[1] The most distinguished members of Captain Stephen Martin's family have been his son the Garter, and his great-grandson Colonel William Leake, R.A., F.R.S., the learned and accomplished topographer of Greece and Asia Minor. Colonel Leake was one of the first Vice-presidents of the Royal Geographical Society, and was for many years an active member of its Council. He died at the age of 84 on January 6, 1860.

CONTENTS.

CONTENTS xxxvii

xxxviii *CONTENTS*

CONTENTS xxxix

APPENDIX.

ILLUSTRATIONS.

LIFE

OF

CAPT. STEPHEN MARTIN

HAVING wrote the life of Sir John Leake for your benefit, that you might be truly informed of the actions of an uncle whose name and arms you are to transmit to posterity with your own,[1] I thought it necessary to add some memoirs of your own family, and particularly of the life and actions of your grandfather, Captain Stephen Martin Leake, which, though of an informal nature, are not less interesting, as from them more immediate honour is derived to you. I shall, however, be very brief in my relation of transactions to be found at large in Sir John's history, and enlarge only upon such as may be called his own, whereby it will appear how well he merited Sir John's favour as an honest man, a faithful friend, and a brave captain. And I shall likewise insert some domestic occurrences, that you may not be wholly ignorant of what passed during

---

[1] Printed in 1749; only fifty copies, but never published. The writer is addressing his son, John Martin-Leake, Somerset Herald and Clerk in the Treasury, who was born in 1738, and died, aged ninety-seven, in 1836.

B

that time in your own family, having often wished
my father had done so.

Captain Stephen Martin, the son of Captain
Thomas Martin, by Eliza his wife, the daughter of
Ely Boream, of Hadley, in the county of Suffolk, was
born the 21st of September, 1666 ; his mother died
whilst he was about four years old, and some years
after he had a violent fever which he hardly overcame.   It seems he was to have this fever, if there
be any truth in astrological predictions, for his father,
being skilled in that science (then much in vogue),
foretold at his birth that at such an age he should
have a violent illness, which if he overcame he would
live to be old.   And certain it is, he recovered and
lived to old age.   But having overcome this fit of
illness, he could not so easily get the better of an
aspiring temper, which prevented his engaging in the
way of business he was designed for.   He had a relation, an eminent tradesman in London, in good circumstances, who, having no children of his own, his
father was for putting him apprentice to him.   But
Stephen could not be brought to like it, for it is observed there must be a certain languor of spirit in
the dispositions of persons adapted for trades, without which they seldom succeed ; and even among
those of the learned professions, which require a
sedentary life and close application, there must be a
coolness of temper and calmness of mind adapted to
their speculations ; whilst those of more fire cannot
be fixed till, by infinite danger and fatigues, they are
brought to a proper temper.   To this sprightliness
and vivacity in some above others it is we are
obliged for our military persons both by sea and
land ; and this natural propensity prevailed in young
Stephen to follow his inclinations and leave the rest
to fortune.   In short, he had too high a spirit and
notions of gentility to debase himself, as he thought,

with a trade. However, it is not unlikely the prospect of advantage and the advice or command of his father, who was a rough, stern man, might have induced him to proceed contrary to his inclinations if it had been insisted upon ; but his father having married a second wife,[1] who proved a very mother-in-law, Stephen had been so ill-used that he begged he might go to sea, not only to see the world, but because it would carry him the farthest from home. The old man, conscious of his ill-treatment, was the more willing to consent, especially as he had an acquaintance to whose care he could safely commit him.

This acquaintance was Mr. John Leake, the son of his friend Captain Richard Leake,[2] who was then master of a ship in the merchant service. Stephen likewise knew him, and was very desirous to go with him.

[1] Her Christian name was Sarah. Her surname is not given in the pedigree. She survived her husband, and was executrix of his will, dying on January 27, 1720.

[2] Richard Leake was born at Harwich in 1629, and was the son of another Richard Leake, who was bred to the sea, and held an appointment on board the fleet of the Parliamentarian Earl of Warwick. The son was serving under him, but deserted and joined the Royalists as a volunteer. At the end of the war he went to Holland, entered the Dutch artillery, and became an excellent gunner. He afterwards returned and got command of an English merchant ship, in which he made several voyages to the Mediterranean. During this time his son John was born. At the Restoration he became a gunner in the Royal Navy, serving in several men-of-war. He was in more than one action with the Dutch, and in 1677 received the appointment of Master Gunner of England and Storekeeper of the Ordnance at Woolwich, where he passed the rest of his life. He was an expert in the preparation of explosives, and was gifted with much inventive talent. His son, John Leake, was born at Rotherhithe in June 1656, and was well instructed in gunnery by his father. He entered the navy as a midshipman, but at the end of the Dutch war, seeing little chance of promotion, he took command of a merchant ship. Returning to the navy, he became one of the

With Mr. Leake he made several voyages to
the Straits, till Captain Richard Leake (then commander of a yacht), being made Master-Gunner of
Whitehall, and soon after Master-Gunner of England, his son John thought it advisable to quit the
merchant service, not doubting but by his father's
interest to get preferment in the navy, and he had
good pretensions to it, having been a midshipman
at the conclusion of the Dutch war. Mr. Leake,
upon his father's promotion, was presently appointed
one of the Master-Gunner's mates, and soon after
gunner of the Neptune,[1] a second-rate, at Chatham,
a post at that time of much more reputation than
it has been esteemed since, for then they wore their
swords, appeared like gentlemen, and kept company
with their captains, and were frequently preferred
from gunners to be commanders ; and it was the best
preferment he could expect at that time, it being
peace, and no half-pay for commission officers, whilst
gunners were in constant pay ; and, indeed, from
the time of his being made a gunner he had the
prospect of a command at Chatham. In the year
1686 it was thought necessary to send some ships
to cruise upon the Algerines, and a small squadron
was appointed for that service under the command
of the Lord Berkeley.[2] Mr. Leake took the opportunity to get his pupil on board the Charles

Master-Gunner's mates ; and in September 1688 he received
command of the Firedrake, to give a trial to a piece of ordnance
invented by his father, called a 'cushee piece.' His only brother,
Edward, was killed at Woolwich by the explosion of one of the
'cushee' shells. From that time Leake and Martin frequently
served together.

   [1] The Neptune was a second-rate of ninety guns, with a
complement of 680 men.

   [2] The ninth Lord Berkeley was created Viscount Dursley and
Earl Berkeley in 1679. He died in October 1698. The Lord
Dursley whose name occurs further on was his grandson.

galley [1] as a volunteer, to walk the quarter-deck, whereby he might be in the way of preferment. He entered on board this ship on August 16, 1686. They sailed from the Nore October 11, and two days after anchored in the Downs. The 28th they sailed from thence, and on November 12 arrived at Lisbon, but left that place the 24th following. This is all the particulars I have met with of this voyage, only that they continued at their station, on and off, at times for two years, suffering great hardships by want of provisions. During this time Mr. Martin behaved himself so well that he came home a midshipman.

As he was desirous to go to sea again as soon as possible, by the assistance of Mr. Leake he got a midshipman's berth on board the Montagu,[2] and entered August 29, 1688. The ship was one of the squadron appointed to be under the command of Sir Roger Strickland,[3] in order to oppose the Prince of Orange, but the squadron was afterwards augmented and put under the command of Lord

[1] The Charles galley had thirty-two guns and 155 men, a fifth-rate.

[2] A fourth-rate of sixty guns and a complement of 360 men.

[3] Roger Strickland belonged to the Sizergh family. He entered the navy at the Restoration, and was captain of the Plymouth in the battle of Solebay, re-taking the Henry from the Dutch, for which he was knighted. In 1678, when in command of the Mary, he captured a large Algerine corsair of forty guns. In 1688 he was Rear-Admiral of England, a Roman Catholic, and a staunch supporter of James II. In August 1688 he received orders from the King respecting the disposition of the fleet to oppose the landing of the Prince of Orange. He had twenty-six ships in the Thames, and thirty-five more were ordered to be fitted out with all possible speed. He found that the great majority of his officers held liberal opinions. He took the fleet to the Downs. But even James was struck by Strickland's imprudence in having priests on board to say Mass, and in October he was superseded by Lord Dartmouth. He followed James into exile.

Dartmouth;[1] and the better to effect King James's designs, many Roman Catholic officers and popish priests were put on board the ship, and all possible encouragement given to those that professed themselves Papists, and those that did not were discouraged; a strict command was likewise exercised over the seamen, and many were punished every day for quarrelling with their officers and ridiculing the priests who publicly said mass on board; but all could not restrain the rough seamen, who were set on by the Protestant officers; and Mr. Martin, having too openly made a jest of some of their popish pageantry, was discharged. This gave him very little concern, for his friend Mr. Leake being approved captain of the Firedrake fireship, and then just come at the Nore, he went and entered immediately on board of him, where there were neither priests nor Papists. The Firedrake was appointed to go with the squadron under the Lord Dartmouth, and as soon as the ships were all joined at the Nore they proceeded to the Gunfleet to intercept the Dutch fleet in their passage; but the Protestant wind that favoured *them* kept the English fleet fast at anchor; however, they followed as soon as they could, but the same adverse wind drove them out of the Channel, whilst the Prince of Orange landed in safety with all his forces, and the face of affairs being soon after wholly changed, the Roman Catholic officers in the fleet were dismissed. The fleet joined

[1] George Legge, first Lord Dartmouth, went to sea at the age of seventeen with Sir Edward Spragge. In 1667 he commanded the Pembroke, and the Royal Catherine in 1672. He was wounded in the Dutch war. In 1677 he was Master of the Ordnance, and was created a peer in 1682. In that year he was sent out to Tangiers to demolish the fortifications and withdraw the garrison. James II. made him Constable of the Tower; but William deprived him of all his employments, and he was committed to the Tower, where he died in 1691, aged forty-three.

in an address to the Prince and Princess of Orange, and being soon after ordered into harbour, the Firedrake proceeded to Chatham.

In the meantime, whilst the fleet was in harbour for the winter, the King of France, having resolved to restore King James, despatched him with a body of troops to Ireland to secure that kingdom. As soon as King William had notice of this design, a squadron was ordered out in haste under Admiral Herbert,[1] to prevent their landing, but too late.

Mr. Martin, upon the fitting out of this squadron, procured a midshipman's berth on board the Edgar, a third-rate of seventy guns, commanded by Captain Clowdisley Shovell;[2] Mr. John

[1] Arthur Herbert was born in 1649 ; and entering the navy at an early age, he became a lieutenant in 1667, captain in 1668, rear-admiral in 1676, and was a Lord of the Admiralty from 1684 to 1687. He took an active part in inviting the Prince of Orange to come to England, and commanded his fleet in October 1688. First Lord of the Admiralty, 1689–90. After the battle of Bantry Bay he was created Baron Herbert of Torbay and Earl of Torrington on May 29, 1689. He fought the battle of Beachy Head on June 30, 1690. In December he was tried by court-martial for retreating before the French fleet, and honourably acquitted. But he was most unjustly dismissed by the King, and died childless on April 13, 1716.

[2] Clowdisley Shovell's parentage is uncertain. He joined the navy at the early age of ten years, on board one of the ships of Sir John Narbrough. His first act of heroism was to swim through the line of the enemy's fire with despatches in his mouth. At Tripoli he volunteered to destroy the enemy's ships under the guns of their forts ; and, going in command of the boats, he was completely successful. He was rewarded with the command of the Sapphire, and he assisted in the defence of Tangiers against the Moors. In 1688 he was in command of the Dover. He was knighted for his gallantry at the battle of Bantry Bay in 1689, and conveyed William III. to Ireland. At the battle of La Hogue he served in the central division, which bore the brunt of the French attack. He was at Vigo and at the battle of Malaga, and afterwards on the coast of Spain in joint command with Lord Peterborough. The story of his shipwreck off the Scillies is well known ; it was on October 23, 1707. His funeral

Norris (since Sir John and Admiral of the Fleet) was a midshipman on board the same ship. The fleet came before Cork on April 17, 1689, and finding they were too late for the purpose they were designed, they went in search of the French fleet, and the 29th discovered them off Kinsale; they followed them, and on May 1 came to an engagement in Bantry Bay, being but eighteen ships to twenty-eight of the enemy.[1] This made the battle, which lasted from daybreak till five in the afternoon, very sharp on the side of the English, though the French first drew off, leaving them the honour of the day. In this engagement Mr. Martin had his left thigh broke by a cannon ball, which, passing through the side of the ship, had taken off a man's legs before it came to him. After this, which happened towards the conclusion of the battle, he was carried down as unfit for further service, and almost insensible; and as upon these occasions they are in too great a hurry and confusion to consider properly the circumstances

took place in Westminster Abbey on December 22. He died in his fifty-seventh year, Rear-Admiral of England and Governor of Greenwich Hospital. His wife was the widow of his old chief, Sir John Narbrough. His stepsons, the two young Narbroughs, were drowned with him. His daughter married Lord Romney.

[1] On the news arriving of James having embarked at Brest, Admiral Herbert made for the coast of Ireland. When he arrived before Cork on April 17, 1689, he heard that James had landed at Kinsale two months before. He sailed over towards Brest, returned to the Irish coast, and sighted the French fleet off Kinsale. He followed it all day, and saw the enemy's ships— under Admiral Château Renault, twenty-eight men-of-war, five fire-ships, and a fleet of transports—standing into Bantry Bay. The English fleet of eighteen ships of the line, the Dartmouth frigate, and the Firedrake, lay off the Bay all night, and next day, May 1, stood towards the French. Château Renault bore down, avoiding close quarters, but maintaining a distant fire until 5 P.M., when he stood into the Bay. The English fleet was temporarily disabled and could not follow. The loss was one captain, one lieutenant, and ninety-four men killed, and 250 men wounded.

of every patient, so the surgeon had determined to cut off his leg, and prepared accordingly ; but Mr. Martin coming to himself, and perceiving what they were about, he would by no means consent to it, declaring he would live or die with his legs on, and by this resolution he saved his leg. The thigh-bone was set after he had lain a considerable time in great pain, and then it was so unskilfully performed that if it had not been new-set afterwards he had never had the use of it. This accident made his left leg sensibly shorter, and altered the position of the legs ; but by custom he so well humoured it, that it became very little inconvenience to him. As soon as there was an opportunity he was put on shore with the wounded at Portsmouth,[1] and continued there a considerable time before he could stir abroad. His captain, Sir Clowdisley (for he was knighted for his behaviour in this battle), was very kind to him, gave him an ample certificate of his good behaviour, and told him that if he would return to him as soon as he was able, he would prefer him to be a lieutenant ; but the affection he bore to Captain Leake made him determine rather to follow his fortune, though he was but lately made a captain, than to return to Sir Clowdisley, who, being an old officer and in expectation of a flag, certainly had it in his power to serve him more effectually. In pursuance of this resolution to follow the fortunes of Captain Leake, his thigh being well united and fit for travel, he left Portsmouth to go for London, not knowing certainly where to meet with him ; all that he knew of him was, that after the battle of Bantry Bay he had been appointed captain of the

[1] When the fleet arrived at Portsmouth, King William came down to visit it, being much pleased that the war should have opened with this slight success. He created Admiral Herbert Earl of Torrington, and knighted Captains Shovell and Ashby.

Dartmouth, a frigate of forty guns then upon the coast of Ireland.[1]

At London he had the satisfaction to meet his father, whom he had not seen for above a twelve-month. He found him preparing to go with the army to Ireland, so his coming was very opportune and gave his father great pleasure, it being very uncertain amongst military persons, in times of war, when they part, whether they may meet again. He was particularly pleased at his son's behaviour in the Bantry engagement, as fully appeared by the certificate Sir Clowdisley had given him, which he looked upon as a sure earnest of future preferment. With his father he likewise paid a visit to old Captain Leake, who received him very kindly, and advised him, as the most certain means to find his son, Captain John Leake, to go to Liverpool, at which place he was ordered to attend the embarkation of the troops and supplies for Ireland. Without making any stay he took post-horses to Liverpool, but Captain Leake was gone from thence. He stayed some time in hopes of his return to that place, till, being impatient, he embarked on board a vessel to go in quest of him. In the meantime Captain Leake, having performed that remarkable brave action at Londonderry, returned to Hylelake, near Liverpool, where he stayed a few days, and then sailed to join the fleet under Sir George Rooke off Cork. There Mr. Martin had the good luck to meet with him, continuing cruising with the fleet, till, being in want of provisions, they repaired to the

---

[1] Captain Leake commanded the Firedrake at the battle of Bantry Bay, and set one of the French ships on fire with his 'cushee piece.' Two days after the battle Admiral Herbert gave Leake the command of the Dartmouth frigate, and sent him to Liverpool to hasten the embarkation of troops for the relief of Londonderry.

Downs, and arrived there on October 13; from thence the Dartmouth was ordered to Chatham, and paid off the 25th following.

As soon as Captain Leake was paid off in the Dartmouth he was commissioned for the Oxford, a fourth-rate, at Portsmouth, and Mr. Martin was entered as midshipman. On December 5 they ran out to Spithead, where, soon after, they met with a violent storm that put them in great danger, by a large Dutch man-of-war driving on board them, and the Oxford received so much damage, she was forced to go into the harbour to be repaired. Afterwards they went with the fleet under Admiral Killigrew [1] to the Mediterranean, and in their passage met with such extreme bad weather, that two Dutch men-of-war foundered, and the fleet lay by four days under their mizens. On April 8, 1690, they arrived at Cadiz, and May 5 at Gibraltar. Here Captain Leake was removed from the Oxford to the Eagle, a third-rate, and Captain Myngs [2] succeeded him in the Oxford. Mr. Martin continued there till May 22, when he likewise removed into the Eagle. In the meantime he had been ordered on board the St. Elizabeth prize, to take charge of her, on April 21, and continued in that charge till June 8, when he went on board his proper ship, the Eagle; so that, in fact, he was not on board the Oxford at all after Captain Leake left her, though he continued upon the ship books. Soon after this the fleet made the best of their way for England,

[1] Henry Killigrew, grandson of Sir Robert Killigrew, of Harworth, entered the navy in 1666. He was dismissed from his command after Rooke's disaster with the Smyrna fleet in 1693, and died in 1712.

[2] Son of Admiral Sir Christopher Myngs, who fell gloriously in the war with Holland. Captain Myngs was afterwards severely wounded at the battle of Malaga. He was superintendent of Portsmouth dockyard from 1708 to 1717, and died in 1725.

and arrived at Plymouth on July 14. Here the admiral received letters of advice from the Admiralty, of the defeat of the English fleet under the Earl of Torrington,[1] whereupon proper measures were taken to secure the fleet from any attempt of the enemy. The ships went into Hamoaze, and a battery of cannon was raised chiefly by the direction of Captain Leake, to defend the entrance. Mr. Martin, who was very forward upon this occasion, was appointed to command some seamen employed in this work, as well as the party which was afterwards detached from the Eagle to defend it. But these apprehensions being soon blown over, on August 18 they sailed from Plymouth, and the 29th anchored at Spithead. After this they joined the fleet under the command of the joint admirals,[2] bound to Ireland to assist the army in the siege of Cork. On September 21 they arrived before the place, and the next morning, it falling calm, they towed into the harbour. On the larboard side there was a platform of ten guns which fired upon them to hinder their passing, whereupon the ship's boats, manned and armed, were sent to drive them from the battery, which they effectually performed, dismounting the guns and setting fire to the works. Mr. Martin, at his own request, went in the Eagle's boat upon this occasion, was one of the first that landed, and was slightly wounded in the arm by a musket ball; after this the soldiers were landed, and the town was immediately besieged. At the siege Mr. Martin met with his father, and was with him most part of the siege. The attack was briskly carried on on that side, and Captain Martin had the mis-

---

[1] Off Beachy Head, on June 30, 1690.
[2] Sir Richard Haddock, Sir John Ashby, and Admiral Killigrew. Their fleet escorted Marlborough and his troops to Cork in September 1690.

fortune to be desperately wounded by the bursting of a cannon—he was, indeed, all over wounds, but none of them mortal, though he never perfectly recovered the hurts he received by it. His son had not been long gone from him, otherwise he would have shared the same danger. The day after this accident, being the 29th,[1] the town capitulated ; and the fleet leaving that harbour on October 2, the 8th following they arrived in the Downs, and the Eagle from thence was ordered to Chatham for the winter.

February 13, 1690-91, Mr. Martin received a commission appointing him second lieutenant of the Eagle ; March 7 he brought that ship to the Nore ; the 14th they sailed from the Nore to the Downs, and the 23rd weighed from thence, but were put back and detained there by tempestuous weather till June 9. They then sailed, bound with the Grand fleet, under the command of Admiral Russell, to the westward ; soon after they got off of Plymouth, but were forced back to Torbay on the 22nd. They stretched over for the coast of France to intercept the French fleet, but had not the fortune to meet with them. September 2 they were surprised by a violent storm that dispersed the whole fleet ; a second-rate foundered, a third-rate bulged, and two more sailed ashore, and the rest were miserably shattered. The 15th the fleet joined again and sailed for the Downs, from whence the Eagle was ordered to Chatham, where she continued all the winter. During this interval from the sea, a match was concluded between Lieutenant Martin and Miss Elizabeth Hill, sister to Mrs. Christian Leake, Captain Leake's wife, and they were married the latter end of January 1691-92, to the great satisfaction of Captain

---

[1] September 29, 1690.

Leake and his wife, who had very much promoted the match.   Being thus united together by the band of affinity, it cemented that friendship which from this time became inviolable.[1]

Though Mr. Martin had leave to be absent from his post on account of the wedding, nevertheless, the Eagle being ordered out early in the spring, he was obliged to go to his ship the middle of February, and the 20th of the same month they joined a squadron at the Nore under the command of Sir Ralph Delavall.[2]   From thence, April 28, they sailed

---

[1] 'Miss Christian and Miss Eliza Hill were the daughters and co-heirs of Captain Richard Hill, of Yarmouth, in the county of Norfolk, an eminent seaman, and for that reason much esteemed by the Duke of York (afterwards King James II.), which was the occasion of his death ; for, attending that Prince on his voyage to Scotland, on board the Gloucester, in the year 1682, on Friday, May 5, early in the morning, the ship struck upon the Lemon and Oar Sands (though there was an experienced pilot on board) and was lost, whereby several persons of distinction, some of the Duke's servants, and about 130 seamen were drownded.   Captain Hill did, indeed, escape drounding, being driven ashore upon a grating, but died the next day; whereas, had he trusted to his swimming, being an excellent swimmer, he had probably saved his life, for his hurts were chiefly owing to the bruises he received by the grating.   Though he resided at Yarmouth, yet he was born at Youghal, in Ireland, but of English parents, they having some estate in and near that town which had induced them to go thither ; but at the Revolution somebody else got possession of it, and the father being dead, and the mother an easy woman, and not knowing how to assert her right to it, it was lost.   But she was allowed a pension for the loss of her husband, with which, some small matters she had besides, and some houses in Nightingal Lane, Limehouse (in one of which she lived), she brought up her daughters very decently.'—S. M. L.

[2] Ralph Delavall was a son of Sir Ralph Delavall, Bart., of Seaton Delavall, co. Northumberland.   He entered the navy when very young, and was captain of the York in 1688.   He was knighted for his gallant conduct at the battle of Bantry Bay, and led the van at Beachy Head.   Sir Ralph was president of the court martial which tried Lord Torrington.   He was at the battle of La Hogue, and drove the French flag-ship Soleil Royal on shore.

for the Downs, and the next day were upon the
coast of France, and after a cruise, May 10 came to
Spithead. During this cruise, and a great part of
the last summer, viz. from July 1, 1691, the first
lieutenant of the Eagle being either sick on board
or sick ashore, Mr. Martin had acted as first lieutenant, and now, May 16, received a commission to
be so. The 18th they sailed with the Grand fleet
under Admiral Russell,[1] and the next day discovered
the French fleet, which brought on the famous
battle of La Hogue. The whole engagement fell
upon the Red squadron commanded by the admiral,
and the Eagle was the third ship ahead of the
admiral's ship. The fight began about eleven in the
morning, and lasted till four in the afternoon. None
animated the seamen by his example more than
Lieutenant Martin; but he had like to have paid
severely for it, for getting upon the booms to give
some orders, a cannon ball shot the boom which he
stood upon from under him, and besides the danger
from the shot, he escaped another no less imminent
of falling down the hold. The seamen who saw him
immediately cried out that Lieutenant Martin was
killed, which (like ill news) soon reached Captain

Sir Ralph was joint admiral with Killigrew and Shovell at the
time of the Smyrna fleet disaster. He was accused of mismanage-
ment and disaffection. He retired, and died in 1707.

[1] Edward Russell was a nephew of the first Duke of Bedford,
and cousin of Lord Russell, who was judicially murdered in 1683.
He entered the navy at an early age, and on the death of his
cousin he warmly espoused the patriot cause. One of the first
to join the Prince of Orange, he became an Admiral and Treasurer
of the Navy in 1689. His jealousy of Admiral Herbert is a stain
on his character, but the accusation that he was ready to betray
his trust to James is false. The battle of La Hogue was his
answer. He became First Lord of the Admiralty in 1694, and in
1697 was created Viscount Barfleur and Earl of Orford. He
was First Lord of the Admiralty in 1709, 1714 to 1717, and died
childless in 1727, aged seventy-four.

Leake upon the quarter-deck, and was a great shock
to him ; but Mr. Martin, who was only hurt and
stunned by the fall, soon got upon his legs, and
immediately went upon the quarter-deck to let his
captain and brother-in-law see that he was living,
and to receive his commands.   But even this compliment was not paid but with equal hazard, for as
he was going up the stairs to the quarter-deck, a
shot carried away the rails, and passed so near his
legs that they were so numbed with the wind of
the shot, that he could hardly stand, but, after a little
pause, he passed on, and after Captain Leake and
he had given each other a hearty embrace, they both
resumed the fight with greater cheerfulness.   At
length, after a sharp engagement, all their topmasts
shot, and mizenmast being shot away so that it fell
upon the deck, their mainmast much damaged,
seventeen guns disabled, seventy men killed, and
twice that number wounded, they were judged by the
admiral to be so disabled, that he ordered them out
of the line to refit, which, however, they did not do,
the French bearing away ; and having stopped their
leaks they soon after joined in the pursuit.[1]   About
four o'clock, a fog arising, the enemy could not be seen,
but clearing up in a little time, they were discovered
bearing away to the northward.   It was foggy all
night, but at eight next morning they were seen

[1] Russell had his flag on board the Britannia, and was in about
the centre of the fleet, receiving the attack of the French ; the next
ship ahead was the St. Andrew, a first-rate, then the Chester, of
fifty guns, and then came the Eagle.   Tourville, the French admiral,
led into action on board the Soleil Royal, of 110 guns, at eight
o'clock on May 19, 1692.   The battle raged with great fury from
11 A.M. to 4 P.M.   The van and rear squadrons of the allied fleet
were idle spectators of this desperate attack on the centre by a
largely superior French force, for it had fallen a dead calm.   At
last the French ships ceased firing, and were towed off by boats,
their retreat being favoured by a dense fog.   The English ships
were diligently repaired, and began the pursuit.

again, the English fleet chasing without order. About four, the tide of ebb being done, both fleets anchored, but weighed at ten at night, and chased till four next morning, then anchoring again. At four in the afternoon eighteen of the enemy's ships hauled in for La Hogue, where our ships anchored about ten at night, but in the morning stood in nearer, and in the afternoon plied in close with La Hogue, where they found thirteen of the enemy's ships very near the shore. On Monday, May 23, Sir George Rooke,[1] vice-admiral of the blue, was ordered with a squadron, some fireships, and the boats of the fleet, to go in and endeavour to destroy them. For this purpose he came and hoisted his flag on board the Eagle in the afternoon, and about seven in the evening weighed, and went in as near the enemy's ships as possible, but they had run themselves so far in, that none but the small frigates would come near enough for service ; nevertheless, the boats being sent in, destroyed six of their capital ships that night, and came away by the light of

[1] George Rooke was the son of Sir William Rooke, of an old Kentish family, and was born in 1650. He served with distinction in the wars with Holland and at the battles of Bantry Bay, Beachy Head, and La Hogue. In June 1693, Sir George Rooke was ordered to convoy the Smyrna fleet of seventy sail. The fleet under Admirals Delavall, Killigrew, and Shovell accompanied him a short distance beyond Ushant, and he then proceeded with a small squadron of Dutch and English ships. Off Lagos he was attacked by a greatly superior force of French ships. He lost four men-of-war, three Dutch and one English ; forty merchant vessels were captured and thirty destroyed. This great disaster was visited upon the Admirals Delavall and Killigrew for not continuing in company. Rooke appears to have escaped all blame. He was afterwards sent on an expedition to Copenhagen by William III., which called for diplomatic skill and address, as well as the qualities of a seaman. His attack on Cadiz was a failure, but the Vigo action was a great success, and he was in chief command at the taking of Gibraltar and battle of Malaga. He died in 1709.

C

them.   Lieutenant Martin commanded some boats
upon this occasion and found it a difficult under-
taking, the ships they attempted to burn having still
some of their crews on board and all their wounded,
and some of the soldiers to defend them, who made
a sharp fire from the galleries and gunroom ports ;
besides the small shot from the soldiers on shore,
where the whole army were encamped, and could
only be spectators of the destruction of their fleet.
In this attempt many in the boats were killed and
wounded, and Mr. Martin was attacked in a particular manner, which had like to have cost him his
life, and all his boat's crew, with some others ; for
seeing a ship which lay very far in, not easy to be
destroyed, he therefore had a mind to make the
attempt, which he hoped to effect the better because
the night was very dark.   For this purpose, at the head
of a few boats he went in very silently, and prepared
the combustibles to set her on fire ; but the tide being
low and the night dark, they were insensibly aground,
and being discovered by the soldiers on shore, they
were fired upon, and a party of horse attacked them,
riding up to the very boats.   This was a sort of
battle they little expected, and so close that the bow-
man of the Eagle's barge, where Mr. Martin was,
pulled one of the troopers off his horse with his
boat-hook.   However, they repulsed the enemy and
made a brave retreat, but not without the loss of
some men.   The next morning the boats were sent
in again, and six more of their men-of-war were
destroyed, and going up a creek they burnt fourteen
sail of merchant ships designed for transports.   In
all these attacks of the boats Mr. Martin was concerned, and behaved with great forwardness ; and
besides what he contributed in general, himself set
fire upon the first attack that was made to a great
ship of the enemy of three decks, after a very smart

skirmish. Sir George Rooke having thus entirely
executed his orders, rejoined the fleet, which sailed
the 25th, and arrived at St. Helens the day following. Here they stayed no longer than to repair the
damage they received in the late fight. As the
Eagle had suffered much, she was one of the last
refitted, but nevertheless joined the fleet July 2 on
the coast of France, and cruised some time off the
Isle of Batz, and August 9 came to St. Helens ; here
the Eagle was obliged to go into dock again, but
anchored at Spithead September 7. The 18th Sir
John Ashby [1] hoisted his flag on board the Eagle,
and the next day sailed with a squadron bound to
the westward. They cruised off the Ushant, and
October 10 returned to St. Helens. November 3
Sir John Ashby struck his flag, and soon after they
sailed, and the 14th arrived at Chatham, where they
continued all the winter ; but Captain Leake left
the Eagle the last of December, being commissioned
for another ship, and Captain Lestock [2] succeeded
him in the command, and so continued all the time
Mr. Martin was first lieutenant. June 15, 1693,
Captain Lestock came on board the Eagle, and
July 9 they sailed to the Nore, at which place they
continued all the summer.

On June 20, Lieutenant Martin's father, Captain
Thomas Martin, died at his house in Southwark,

[1] John Ashby, the son of a merchant at Lowestoft, entered
the Navy in 1665, and was captain of the Defiance in 1688. Being
a warm supporter of the Prince of Orange, he led the van at the
battle of Bantry Bay, for which service he was made a rear-
admiral, and knighted by William III. at Portsmouth. He was
in the van at Beachy Head, and commanded the Blue division at
the battle of La Hogue, which, however, was not engaged but
joined in the pursuit of the French fleet. Sir John Ashby died
in July 1693.
[2] Richard Lestock was captain of the Cambridge, and went
with Rooke to Cadiz. He was an old officer of the time of
Charles II., and, retiring in 1694, he died in 1713.

in the forty-eighth year of his age—a brave
soldier, a good engineer, and an honest, generous,
good-natured man, and what the world calls a
good companion, whereby he impaired his health ;
but this was chiefly after his second marriage,
as an opiate to his domestic troubles, which
too often attend a second venture when there is
issue by the first.   But what more immediately
hastened his death were the wounds he received at
the siege of Cork, in Ireland, of which he was never
thoroughly healed.   His free temper and profession,
and the sufferings of his father with the Royalists in
the unhappy rebellion, made it impossible he could
leave any considerable personal or acquired fortune.
What estate he had he left to his wife for life (who
survived him almost twenty-seven years), making
her whole and sole executrix, and after her death to
his son, together with a small legacy and a part of
his personal estate.   To his daughter, who had
married meanly against his consent, as a mark of
his displeasure he left one shilling.   It was a great
satisfaction to him that he had lived to see his son
married, and to Mrs. Leake's sister, as well because
he knew her to be a virtuous and prudent woman as
because it cemented a friendship between his son
and Captain Leake, his friend, who he saw was a
rising man.   By this match he likewise saw the first
child born, named Hannah, which gave him great
hopes that there might one day be a son.

The Eagle remained, as I said, at Chatham and
Portsmouth all the summer, Captain Lestock being
appointed commander and Mr. Martin continuing
first-lieutenant.   On December 27, 1693, they sailed
from Spithead, bound for the Straits with the fleet,
under the command of Sir Francis Wheler,[1]

---

[1] Francis Wheler, of a good Kentish family, went to sea when
very young. From 1678 to 1683 he was serving in the Mediter-

and January 19 anchored in Cadiz Bay. Here, having heeled and scrubbed their ships, they sailed with the fleet February 10 following, and six days after anchored at Gibraltar, but made no stay, for they sailed the next day, and the 18th, at night, were taken by a most violent storm of wind, accompanied with thunder, lightning, and rain in so extraordinary a manner that the like had not been known in those seas in the memory of any man. About two o'clock they were forced to cut away their long-boat; at five they lost their main topmast and sprung their mainmast, broke their chain plates to windward, one of their gun-deck beams, and a standard, and, being in the utmost danger, made the signal of distress; but there was none to help them, for all were in the like condition. The vice-admiral of the Dutch hove out his colours and bore away, and all the fleet were dispersed, every one having enough to do to take care of himself. Captain Lestock was at this time so ill of the gout as to be confined to his bed, and, though he could not possibly be a proper judge what was best to be done, very positively gave his orders. It was therefore at the discretion of Lieutenant Martin to do what was right, and, considering their present circumstances, he made no scruple to act directly contrary to his captain's orders. Though he threatened to confine him for it, Mr. Martin insisted that, though the captain was on board, yet being confined to his cabin, and in that situation it being impossible for him to give orders suitable to the emergency (as

ranean, under Herbert and Narbrough, and fought some actions with Sallee rovers. In 1688 he was captain of the Centurion and was knighted. At the battle of Beachy Head he commanded the Albemarle. Rear-Admiral in 1692, when he received command of a squadron in the West Indies, and made an unsuccessful attack on Martinique. In 1693 he was appointed commander-in-chief in the Mediterranean.

those which Captain Lestock gave were not), he
was accountable for the safety of the ship. This
was the 19th, in the evening, which being very hazy,
and the storm still continuing with great fury, all
the squadron were in confusion, not knowing where
they were. Some at last discerning the mouth of
the Straits, stood away for it ; others, having the
Bay of Gibraltar open, and mistaking it for the
Straits, put in there, not being able to see the land
westward, and these were either lost or drove on
shore ; and this had been the fate of the Eagle if
Mr. Martin had not had resolution enough to pursue
his own judgment and disobey his captain, who was
for standing after those ships that were lost when
he should have took the entrance of the Straits.
But Mr. Martin was morally certain of the contrary,
and swore he would pursue that course unless his
captain came upon deck and took the command
from him. The success approved what he did, and
his captain afterwards acknowledging that, under
God, the preservation of the ship was owing to
him. In this storm the admiral's ship, the Sussex,
foundered, and, out of 550 men, two Moors only
escaped by swimming to other ships.[1] Four days
after the storm they had the good luck to find their
long boat (which they had cut away) among the
wrecks. March 22 they sailed from Gibraltar, and
the next day arrived at Cadiz.

The Eagle being careened and refitted for the
sea, sailed from Cadiz June 29, 1694, and the next
day joined the grand fleet under the command of
Admiral Russell ; July 21 they anchored in Altea
Bay and watered the fleet ; the 26th they sailed, and
three days after came before Barcelona. They
stayed at Barcelona till August 16, and September
10 anchored in Alicante Road, and the admiral,

[1] The body of Sir Francis Wheler was washed on shore. He
was an able and gallant, but a most unlucky officer.

being ill, went on shore, and left the fleet under the command of Mr. Aylmer; [1] three days after they sailed from thence, and after a short cruise returned, and the admiral, being recovered from his indisposition, resumed the command again, and sailing with the fleet, arrived, October 7, in the Bay of Cadiz. November 14 they had a storm of wind at Cadiz, wherein the Eagle broke her small and best bower, and tailed ashore with her sheet anchor ahead, but soon after got off and rode fast. It was intended to order her home, but on a survey of carpenters it was judged she was not fit to go home to England till she was careened. During the winter this was done, and being in a condition for sea by February 27, they sailed from Cadiz upon a cruise, with a squadron of five English and four Dutch. In this cruise they touched at Gibraltar, Malaga, Alicante, Barcelona, Finale, and Cagliari, till they joined the grand fleet in the attempt on Palamos,[2] where they anchored August 6. Some troops were landed and the town bombarded, but with little effect, only to say they had attempted something; whereupon they weighed the 17th, and the 30th arrived in Altea Bay [3] and watered the fleet. Here Mr. Martin was discharged from the Eagle, and had a commission appointing him fifth lieutenant of the admiral's own ship, the Britannia. From Altea Bay they sailed the 9th, and the 23rd arrived

[1] Matthew Aylmer was the second son of Sir Christopher Aylmer of Balrath, co. Meath. He began life as a page to the Duke of Buckingham. In 1678 he was lieutenant of the Charles galley, and served continuously until 1688. He was at the battles of Beachy Head and La Hogue, attaining flag rank in 1693. He retired when Admiral Churchill went to the Admiralty, but had his flag up again in 1709. In 1718 he was created Lord Aylmer of Balrath, and in 1720, the year of his death, he was Rear-Admiral of England.

[2] On the coast of Spain, between Barcelona and the gulf of Rosas.

[3] A small Spanish port between Alicante and Cape St. Martin.

at Cadiz. From thence, October 2, they sailed for England with twenty-one sail of English and seventeen Dutch men-of-war, and arrived in the Downs November 7, when the admiral struck his flag and went for London, the Britannia proceeding to the Nore, and so to Chatham, where she was paid off December 4, 1695.[1]

Whilst Mr. Martin was abroad he had a daughter born, July 10, 1694, named Mary. A few days after Mr. Martin was paid off as fifth lieutenant of the Britannia, he was appointed fourth lieutenant of the same ship by a commission dated December 24. January 22 he sailed from London with the Mayflower tender, a cruising to the westward to impress seamen for the fleet. The next day he anchored in the Downs, and was detained there by hard blowing weather and contrary winds till February 17; however, in the meantime he got some men out of the homeward-bound merchant ships, which having put on board the admiral's ship in the Downs, he sailed, but met with such untoward weather that he was forced to run into Dover pier. March 8 he joined the fleet in the Downs, and April 8 went on board the Britannia. The 20th they sailed to the Nore, the 23rd got into the Downs, and the 30th arrived at Spithead. May 7 Sir George Rooke hoisted the Union flag on board the Britannia, and sailed with the whole fleet. The 14th they were off Ushant, and the 23rd anchored in Torbay. June 1 Sir George Rooke struck his

[1] 'Whilst he was Lord Orford's lieutenant he was offered the command of a bomb ketch, but refused it, because the other admiral's lieutenants had been preferred to post ships, and, he being the only one unprovided for, he thought his lordship would do him the same favour. By this mistake he had the mortification to remain several years longer a lieutenant, and to see a junior officer who accepted the command of the bomb ketch become a post-captain long before him.'—S. M. L.

THE LONDON.

flag, and the Lord Berkeley, from the London, came and hoisted his flag on board the Britannia, and bringing his own officers with him, those of the Britannia were removed to the London, which was likewise a first-rate. Mr. Martin had a commission to be third lieutenant, but Lord Berkeley was so ungenerous as to put a younger officer over his head, one that had married his housekeeper. This, after his former disappointment, made him so angry, that he wrote a complaint to Lord Orford,[1] challenged the lieutenant, and had obliged him to fight him if it had not been prevented. Lord Orford was likewise much displeased at it, and bid his brother Leake write to him to be easy, for he would take care of him, but he was so unlucky as to have nothing to offer immediately.

A few days after Captain Munden[2] was appointed to command the London. On June 24 they sailed with the fleet from Torbay, and on July 4 came to an anchor in the Belle Isle road in the Bay of Biscay. All the barges and pinnaces in the fleet were sent on shore, with detachments of seamen from

---

[1] Admiral Russell was created Viscount Barfleur and Earl of Orford in 1697. He was at the head of the Admiralty in 1694, 1709, and 1714 to 1717, when he finally retired. He died in 1727.

[2] John Munden entered the service in 1677, and he distinguished himself when in command of a Mediterranean squadron during the peace, by successfully negotiating a liberation of Christian slaves with the Emperor of Morocco. He was selected by Sir George Rooke, for his known conduct and courage, to command the first naval operation of Queen Anne's war, and hoisted his flag on board the Russell on May 9, 1702. His orders were to intercept and capture a French squadron known to be off Coruña, commanded by M. du Casse. But the French outsailed the English and got safe into Coruña. Sir John Munden was tried by court-martial for not having captured the French fleet, and honourably acquitted. But the Government, cowering before the ignorant clamour from a mob, dismissed him from the service a few days afterwards. He went on shore a broken-hearted man, lived in strict retirement, and died in 1718.

every ship, to destroy the enemy's settlements upon
the adjacent islands, called Cardinals.   Lieutenant
Martin commanded a party of seamen from the
London upon this occasion, and going ashore upon
one of the islands called Houat, they burnt the town
and brought off several boats and 300 head of cattle.
The next day a larger detachment was made, with
all the tenders and long boats, to another island
called Groix, where they burnt the villages and
brought off a great number of cattle, and the following day they did the like to another island called
Hoedic.   Having done all the mischief they could
here they sailed on July 10, and the 22nd anchored in
Torbay.   Whilst the fleet lay here, Mr. Martin received a commission to be second lieutenant of the
London, dated August 8, 1696.   The 29th the fleet
weighed from Torbay, and two days after came to
Spithead.

The 16th following they arrived with a squadron
at the Nore, where four days after Sir Clowdisley
Shovell hoisted his flag as admiral of the blue on
board the London, but struck it the next day, and
the 23rd Admiral Aylmer hoisted the red flag on
board at the foretopmasthead as vice-admiral of the
red, and the next day struck it again, and they sailed to
Blackstakes, and afterwards to Chatham ; from thence
Lieutenant Martin (November 26) set out with leave
for London, and returned no more to his ship, but
was not discharged from the London till February 9
following, in order to be a commander.   At the same
time he was welcomed by another daughter, born on
August 25, and named after her mother and grand-
mothers, Elizabeth.

On February 10, 1696, the day after Mr. Martin
was discharged from the London, he had a commission appointing him commander of the Blast
bomb ketch at Deptford, being now under a ne-

cessity to accept of the same preferment which he had refused a year and a half before. As soon as he had received his commission he went to Deptford to enter with the clerk of the cheque there, because from the time of his entry, and not from the date of his commission, he commenced pay, and having dispatched what was necessary and taken in his stores, the 24th he sailed to Woolwich, where he took in his provisions, guns, and mortars. Leaving Woolwich he came to the Nore, the 28th, and on March 15 he sailed from thence in company with the Monk, and anchored short of the gun fleet. But they were forced to anchor, and it blew so hard that their boat sunk astern, and it was with much difficulty they saved her. The 17th he got into the Downs, and soon after a vessel brought him his shells and bombardiers, whereupon he sailed, and on April 1 arrived at Spithead. Here he put his fore-mortar and bed on board the Suffolk hag-boat, according to the usual custom when they are designed for a foreign voyage, which otherwise, in these small bomb ketches, would endanger their foundering; at the same time he received on board twenty soldiers of Colonel Gibson's regiment who were going with the squadron designed for Newfoundland. The 16th all the squadron joined at St. Helens, and the next day they sailed, consisting of the Monk, Captain Norris,[1] commodore, and seven sail of frigates, two fireships, and two bombs and some storeships. The

[1] After his Newfoundland service, Sir John Norris went with Rooke and the Duke of Ormond to Cadiz. He was so quick-tempered, that he drew his sword on Sir George Rooke's first captain, Ley, on his own quarter deck. He was put under arrest. He was released on the intercession of the Duke of Ormond, and Captain Ley died soon afterwards. Norris was at the battle of Malaga, and was knighted for his gallantry at the assault of Monjuich. Rear-Admiral, 1706; and escaped shipwreck when following Sir Clowdisley Shovell. He was commander-in-chief

20th they anchored in Torbay, but sailed the 29th, and off of Plymouth were joined by several merchant ships. They pursued their voyage with fair weather till they arrived in the latitude of 49° 22', when they had squally weather and a great western sea, which lasted several days, in which time the Blast bomb broke her main topsail yard in the slings, but they soon got up another. On May 9 they had hard gales in gusts, and shipped a great sea. It continued squally, hazy weather for several days, but the 16th they had a good observation, and found themselves in the latitude of 46° 6', longitude 27° 35'. After this they had hazy, squally weather, with rain, and the 19th they shipped much water, which filled both their boats upon deck several times. As they drew near the land the hazy weather increased. The 24th it was so foggy they were forced to fire guns, beat drums, and ring their bells to keep clear of each other. The 27th they had hazy, squally weather, blowing hard, with much rain, and sounding, they had ground at eighty fathoms, whereupon a ship was sent ahead to look out for the land ; but the foggy weather continued so bad for five days they could not see each other, and then, clearing up a little, they discovered six of the fleet. On June 4 they sounded, and thirty-five fathoms upon the Great Bank, and in an hour's time they caught on board the Blast bomb twenty-four great codfish. The next day it blew hard, and they broke their main topsail yard in the slings, not having anything to make another ; but the Suffolk hag-boat being near, they got one of her fore booms and made a yard of that, most of the rigging being ready to come down

in the Mediterranean in 1710, and was sent to the Baltic four times, once as envoy to the Czar Peter. Lord of the Admiralty, 1717 to 1730. He went with a fleet to protect Lisbon in 1732. Sir John Norris died in 1749.

about their ears. But the following day in the morning (being the 6th) they discovered the land, and the day after anchored in St. John's harbour, having been forty-six days from the Land's End of England.

Soon after their arrival at St. John's, Colonel Gibson's regiment of soldiers, which they brought on board the ships of the squadron, were put on shore, and Captain Martin took his mortar on board from the Suffolk hag-boat; and the commodore, having stayed a few days, till the soldiers had got all their materials on shore, and were in some condition to defend themselves in his absence, he sailed with the squadron June 14 a cruising, except the Suffolk hag-boat, and the Blast and Comet bombs, which he left behind for the defence of the harbour. The 16th they began to drink water; the 21st the commodore returned with several prizes, and having received advice of the enemy's designs to attack them with a superior force, he called a council of war, and it was concluded to secure the harbour's mouth, which was accordingly done by a boom of cables. To defend this, the commodore, with the rest of the ships, placed themselves in a line before the mouth of the harbour, and the two bombs were placed within, in order to throw their shells over them. The 27th the Portland and Fortune, with three merchant ships, arrived from England. The next day a council of war was held of sea and land officers, and it was agreed the men-of-war should go to sea for twenty-one days, till the land forces had fortified the harbour, leaving the hag-boat, the two bombs, and the storeships behind. July 1 the engineer broke ground for the intended fortification. The next day the commodore sailed, and they boomed up the harbour mouth again. The following day a boat came in with five deserters, who were soon after tried and condemned. July 4 a small ship and brigantine came in from Placentia with prisoners—men, women, and children, giving an account that ten days before sixty men more made their escape, and were coming by land to St. John's ; that four men-of-war and a fly-boat sailed from Placentia four days before. The 7th the Dunwich came in, and the next day the Portland with a prize laden with wine and brandy, and the following day the commodore arrived with four sail. The day after this a rich prize of twenty-two guns was brought in, and some others of the squadron came in with three merchant ships from Ireland. The same day, being under apprehensions of an attack by a superior squadron, they got all the top chains of the ships across the harbour's mouth and boom them up ; having now two booms, one of cables and one of chains, at some distance from each other. The 13th a general council of war was held at Colonel Gibson's quarters, where, taking into consideration the intelligence they had received of a French squadron, consisting of four seventy-gun ships, eight from sixty to fifty, four fireships, and one bomb, commanded by Monsr. Nesmond, it was resolved to send every day four hundred seamen ashore to assist the soldiers in getting ready the fortifications, and to keep themselves in a readiness to defend themselves if they should be attacked by the enemy. The 14th a runner came in with a French banker they had taken. Two days after a ship from the Madeiras arrived, and the following, two runners went for England. From the 20th to the 30th inclusive, I have no account of what passed, a leaf having been torn out of Captain Martin's journal. The 31st they heard at least one hundred guns fired, and at night were informed the French had taken Carboniere. In the meantime several French bankers were taken and brought in by the cruisers and runners, and August 9 the Mary galley came in from cruising with a French banker, giving an account that two days ago she fell in with fifteen sail of French men-of-war off the Banks, two of them three-decked ships, who gave chase to him, but he soon left them. The 11th Captain Desborow was broke by a court-martial for disobeying orders, and two days after the Dunwich was dispatched to England with a packet. The 17th the commodore held another council of war, and the next day, in the morning, fifteen sail of French appeared before the harbour, with an admiral and rear-admiral, ten of them great ships ; whereupon the commodore with his squadron put themselves in a line expecting their coming, but the wind veering to the E. and N.E. with dirty weather, they stood off again. The 22nd twelve sail appeared again in the offing, whereupon the ships took their stations, and two more guns were mounted on the north battery, making in all six guns, there being on the other side a battery of ten guns, and the two bombs hove short in order to go without the men-of-war, to bomb the enemy as they came in, if they attempted it. In the intervals of time between these alarms, the seamen were very serviceable in cutting stockades and sods for the fort, and otherwise assisting the soldiers in their work ashore. September 5, according to the resolution of a council of war some days before, the soldiers were taken on board the ships, it proving too cold for them on shore. The 13th the ditch of the fortification was finished, and the north-west part of the fort was sodded. The 17th a council of war was called, to consider if they should leave a ship behind when they went for England, but it was not thought convenient by reason of the shortness of provisions. The 19th the seamen, having finished their part of the fortification, a four-oared yaul was filled with flip and given them to make merry. The

23rd Captain Martin put out his after-mortar and bed on board of the ships of the squadron, the better to enable him to return to England, and two days after he heeled his ship and gave her a pair of boots tops.[1]

The next day one of his fireworkers died. The following day several runners and merchant ships sailed, and Captain Martin put out his fore-mortar and bed on board another ship of the squadron. The day after, seven sail of merchant ships came in. On October 1 it blew a mere fret of wind at S. and S.W., insomuch that the men-of-war as well as merchant ships drove, with three or four anchors ahead, and seven or eight drove ashore; but at night the wind came up at W.S.W. and put them off again with little or no damage, except one which sunk and another which lost her foremast and bowsprit. The next day after this storm, the rendezvous, signals, and line of battle was delivered to the several ships, in order for their return to England; and the day after three hundred soldiers were put on shore that were to remain there under the command of Major Handyside, the governor. Nevertheless, the new fort, called King William's Fort, and intended to mount sixteen guns, was not quite finished; but the harbour's mouth was provided with a good bomb, and a platform of ten whole culverins on the south side and six more on the north, with two small mortars on each side, the entrance at the batteries being but eighty fathoms wide. On October 7 Captain Martin discharged his bombardiers from the Blast bomb to go on board some of the ships of the squadron; and everything

[1] The manuscript has 'booterstops,' the *r* having come in through an error in transcription. 'Bootes tops' was a scraping or scrubbing along the water line. They then daubed the water line with a composition of tallow and rosin which, presumably, gave it the colour of boot tops.

being now prepared for their return home, the same day the whole squadron, with the merchant ships for England, Portugal and the Straits—in all about sixty sail—made sail from St. John's about six in the evening.

But before I prosecute the voyage with them I think it necessary to say something more than I have yet had occasion to mention, touching this Newfoundland expedition, for which the commodore suffered in his reputation with many people, and which may by consequence reflect upon every commander concerned in it. The case was this : the French Admiral Pointis, who had taken and plundered the city of Cartagena, being in his way home to France, by a misreckoning (as himself confessed) got to the eastward of Newfoundland, when he thought he had been to the westward, and was obliged to go into Conception Bay for water. Besides that his ships were foul and in a bad condition, his men were very sickly, not above half (as he says) fit for action. The news of their arrival and the circumstances they were in was carried to Commodore Norris at St. John's, and though he had only four fourth-rate, two fifth, two sixth, two fireships and two bombs, it was generally the opinion of the sea officers to go and attack him ; excited, no doubt, by the prodigious wealth he must consequently have with him, and encouraged by the bad condition of his ships and men ; for otherwise it would have been a vain and rash attempt, they being equal in number of ships and so much superior in force. Lediard[1] says the commodore was overruled in the council of war, upon a pretence there was another strong squadron under Monsr. Nesmond, and a resolution

---

[1] See Lediard's *Naval History*, vol. i. p. 720 (note *k*), who quotes the passage from Burnet given in a note on the next page.

was taken to secure themselves in the harbour, which he calls an ill-timed caution, if not worse, of our own officers ; endeavouring to excuse the commodore by accusing the captains.   Burnet[1] likewise censures the action and condemns the Admiralty board for passing it over, calls them partial, and charges our marine with corruption and treachery. Both these authors seem to charge the officers with cowardice or treachery, or both ; but I think the latter can hardly be imagined, since no corruption could have balanced the prodigious advantage they then had to enrich themselves.   It can only be supposed, then, that they had not the courage to take it ; but except one or two of the captains, there was not, perhaps, a set of braver men at any time in the navy, as their behaviour upon other occasions demonstrated.   The whole, then, of the scandalous insinuations is founded in ill-nature and ignorance of the facts.   It appears they had advice of a French squadron   under   Monsr.   Nesmond of   fifteen   sail soon after their arrival, and thereupon, on June 21, took measures to secure the harbour.   On July 4 they had certain advice of four French men-of-war that were at Placentia, and this was long before Pointis arrived.   On the 13th it appears they had further intelligence of Nesmond's squadron, which they so much depended upon, and expected would

---

[1] Burnet says that when the French sailed towards Newfoundland we had a squadron lying there, which might have fallen upon the French and would probably have mastered them.   But as the English had no certain account of the strength of the enemy, and were out on another service, they did not think it proper to hazard attacking them.   So the French got safe home, and the conduct of our affairs at sea was much censured.   'Yet,' adds Burnet, 'our Admiralty declared themselves satisfied with the account the commanders gave of their proceedings.'   He goes on to say, 'it was generally believed that there was much corruption, as it was certain there was much faction, if not treachery, in the conduct of our marine.'—Bishop Burnet's *Own Time*, i. 195.

attack them, that they thought proper to add another boom of chains, and two guns to the north battery. After this Carboniere was actually taken by a squadron of the enemy the last of July, which they were informed of the same day, and a few days after they had certain information of a squadron of the enemy of fifteen sail, and of their strength, by the Mary galley (one of their own cruisers) that fell in with them, and whereby it appeared the enemy were very much superior to them ; and this was put beyond all doubt on August 18 when they appeared off St. John's harbour, with a design—as was thought—to force the place, had not the wind and weather prevented them.

There was therefore no need of a pretence (as Mr. Lediard insinuates), it was a matter of fact, nor any overruling of the commodore, when the enemy thought themselves strong enough to attack them in their harbour ; so that their resolutions to secure themselves in St. John's against their attacks was a well-timed and not an ill-timed caution. If there had been no squadron under Monsr. Nesmond, and they believed there was from the intelligence they had received, and which must govern in all cases, they were sufficiently justified. Even though Monsr. Nesmond had not been there with his squadron, Mr. Pointis was much superior ; but as both were there, their precautions were little enough. If, despising the intelligence of Nesmond, they had gone out to attack Pointis, how would they have been disappointed to have found both much superior in strength, when perhaps they could not have retreated. Would not the commander and all the officers have been condemned for rashness and folly ? Could they have been justified going to attack Pointis on equal terms ? Might it not have been asked very properly what they were sent to Newfoundland for ? Was it

not to make a settlement and secure the harbour
of St. John's? and would not the design by these
measures have been wholly frustrated?   It must
likewise be remembered that all the councils of war
were composed both of sea and land officers, and
the latter very rightly judged their preservation
depended upon the safety of the squadron.   And
when, upon the first intelligence of the arrival of
Admiral Pointis, it was proposed to attack him, upon
a supposition he was much weaker (and much richer
too) than he really was, the land officers would
by no means consent to it, for they considered the
success as doubtful ; and though they should succeed,
yet the land forces would want their assistance in
the meantime to carry on their work, as well as
their protection, and if they were worsted, the
designed settlement with the whole island would be
lost, and they should all be made prisoners, both
soldiers and inhabitants, having no asylum to fly to ;
so that though the sea officers had resolved to
attack Pointis in spite of all opposition, they could
not have done it without abandoning the soldiers,
and all our footing in Newfoundland, to the chance
of war, and manifest breach of their orders.   But it
proved very fortunate they did not do so.   Nevertheless the bait was so tempting, that could everyone
have pursued his own inclinations they would probably have run all hazards.

To return now to the squadron, which, as I
observed, left St. John's harbour on October 7, on
their voyage to England.   The day after they sailed
they had hazy weather (as they had on and off all
the summer) with rain, and it blew so hard they
went under their bare poles for the most part, and
mainsail in the brails.   The following day they had
more moderate weather ; but the next day the same
weather as before, blowing a mere fret of wind, which
split their mainsail in the Blast bomb, but at night

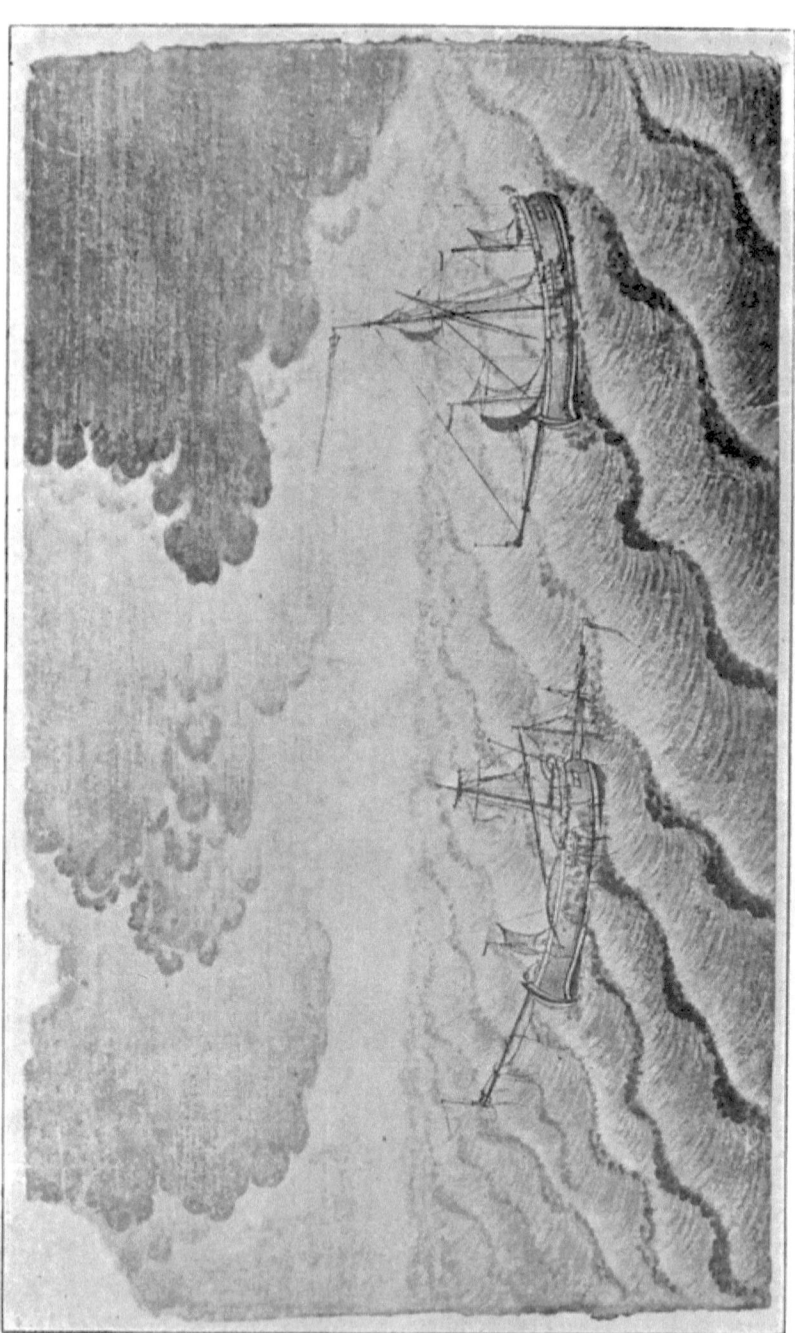

THE BLAST BOMB, CAPTAIN STEPHEN MARTIN, IN A STORM, RETURNING FROM NEWFOUNDLAND IN NOVEMBER 1697,
AND WITH HER JURY MASTS.

having mended it they got it up again, the weather
being then something more moderate, but a prodigious great western sea that rolled the muzzles of
the bomb's guns in the water. On the 12th the
same hazy, rainy, blowing weather returned, which
sent their mainsail to shivers, leaving nothing but
the bolt rope, so that they were forced to go with
bare poles for six hours, during which time they lost
sight of the fleet. Upon this occasion, Captain
Martin ordered a spritsail to the main stay, and ran
with that till three in the afternoon, then bent
another mainsail and set it with both reefs in. The
next morning they broke three of their main chain-
plates to windward, and one to leeward, with one
of their topmast back stays; but at the same
time had the good luck to see the commodore with
the rest of the fleet to windward, and soon after
joined them. In the afternoon he got up three chain-
plates to windward, and set up his shrouds and
catharpins. At night it blew very hard at W.S.W.,
and they scudded away with a mainsail. The next
day (the 14th) the bad weather returned with more
fury than it had yet done. All the fleet were
dispersed and shattered, and Captain Martin having
lost his mainmast and mizen topmast, being almost
foundered, was left like a wreck at the mercy of the
sea, for he saw none of the fleet afterwards. Here
my journal having lost a leaf, I cannot particularise
what happened during this dismal scene. It may
easily be imagined that being thus encumbered with
their masts, rolling impetuously, and the sea making
a free passage over them, they could do nothing but
cut away the mast till the fury of the storm was
over, which was not till twenty-four hours after ; and
had it been any other than a bomb ketch, which
vessels are made remarkably strong to sustain the
shocks they are designed for, she must inevitably
have foundered.

On the 15th, the weather being more moderate, Captain Martin got up jury-masts in the best manner he was able, in order to prosecute his voyage home, which in the condition he was in, the bad weather he must expect at this season of the year, and long, dark nights, afforded but a melancholy prospect. The 16th, in the morning, it was hazy, with rain, and blowing hard brought his jury-masts by the board, so that he was forced to lay by under a mizen, having no other sail aboard for some time. He then got up a broken topsail-yard for a fore-mast, with a crossjack-yard for a fore-yard, and two main studding-sails sewn together made him a complete foresail. The same day his steward died, and two days after another of his ship's company died, all the rest being sickly. The two following days were hazy, with rain, and the day after he had a good observation. The 20th it was fair weather, and he began to new rig the ship. He got his broken mizenmast out of the step, and, setting up a pair of shears, fixed it in the mainmast step and hoisted the mizen-yard and sail upon it, and a main-studding sail boom was made to serve for a mizen-mast, with a boat's mainsail for a mizen, so that now from a ketch he was converted to a pink. It continued hazy, moderate weather till the 24th, when, the wind blowing fresh at E.N.E., he was forced to hand his spritsail, maintopsail, and mizen-staysail, not being able to carry them upon a wind. The three following days it blew hard, and he had the misfortune to carry away his maintopmast and the foremast main chain-plate on the larboard side. The two following days it continued hazy, blowing weather. The 30th he had an observation, and found himself in the lat. of 49° 38′ ; whereupon, at noon, he sounded, but had no ground ; but in the evening, sounding again, he had ground at 110 fathoms, to their great joy, having no more than two men in a watch, besides officers, the rest being sick. The following day he buried another man, which made the fifth that died in the passage from Newfoundland; and, being now in soundings, he put his men to whole allowance of provisions, to strengthen those that were yet upon their legs, and bent his small bower and sheet cables. The 4th November, by his soundings judging they were near the land, he brought to and lay by all that night. The next morning he made sail again, having hazy, blowing weather, as had been all the voyage, and about two o'clock in the afternoon made the land between Milford and Tenby, in Wales.

In the meantime it was generally believed at home that Captain Martin was lost, not only because of the distress he was seen to be in after he lost his masts, but because a commander of one of the squadron reported he saw her sink. It seems Commodore Norris, observing his distress, had ordered a frigate to his assistance to stay with him, which, however, the commander did not endeavour to do; but whether he really believed she sunk, or gave out so only to excuse himself, is uncertain. However that be, most people thought the Blast bomb was lost; only Commodore Norris himself declared he believed the contrary, because the commander was so good an officer that if there was any possibility of saving her he would certainly do so. Indeed, he did use the proper means, and held out with great resolution, whilst all his company were sick and desponding, for courage and presence of mind in time of danger never failed him. But these were but human endeavours, the event was the work of Providence. In fine, after a dangerous and tedious passage of twenty-eight days, as has been related, they arrived at Tenby and ran into the pier.

This was November 5, at night, which being a day of public rejoicing for the remarkable deliverance of the nation **twice** from popery and slavery, Captain Martin was resolved to celebrate that festival **and** his own happy arrival together. All **hands went to** work to prepare what was necessary; even **the sick** and the dying revived upon this occasion. A great bonfire was prepared on shore with the billet wood of which Captain Martin had brought a great quantity from Newfoundland, and crowned all with a tar barrel. They had likewise three dozen of rockets on board, which they fired upon this occasion, besides some other fireworks prepared in haste. These, with the firing of guns, alarmed the whole country and **brought down many people to** know the meaning of it, such rejoicings not having been known in those parts. At the same time, being pretty well stocked with liquors from the prizes that had been brought into St. John's, he entertained the whole place. In short, he made the 5th of November more remarkable at Tenby for his arrival than it had ever been before for the public benefits that day was designed to commemorate. Indeed, they could not have happened upon a fitter time or place to forget their late dangers, for besides that Christmas was coming, when good cheer abounds everywhere, the gentry of Wales are at all times very hospitable, more especially to strangers, who seldom are seen in those parts. The next **day, therefore,** after this public notice of his arrival, which was taken as a compliment to the country as well as in honour of the day and joy of their own safe arrival, he had numerous invitations from the gentry to spend his time at their houses during his stay in those parts, and some of them would not be denied; so that, having secured his ship in the harbour and wrote to the Admiralty to acquaint them of his late distress and safe arrival at that place, and to satisfy his family and friends (now almost hopeless) that he was alive, he accepted their kind invitations, and for two months that he stayed there was one continued round of feasting and merrymaking, the very contrast of their late voyage. Nor was the ship's crew neglected in this general scene of mirth and jollity; they had their part of the good cheer, and, forgetting their late danger, rather looked upon the disaster that brought them to such an hospitable country as a fortunate accident. Thus it is that seamen, having escaped drowning, drown their cares; and thus it is necessary that it should be, else no man would persevere in that kind of life.

In the meantime the Admiralty, having received Captain Martin's letters, ordered masts to be sent to him as the first thing necessary to enable him to finish his voyage to the desired port of London. These he received on December 23 and soon after set up, and on January 3 the Thunderbolt bomb arrived to assist him in coming round. On the 6th he ran out into Cauld Road, and the 10th sailed from thence in company with the Thunderbolt. The 15th he came to Plymouth and ran into Hamoaze, and having taken in some provisions he sailed the 23rd, but the wind shifting he was put back again. He attempted to weigh the next day again, but they could not purchase their anchors; however, the following day he got clear, and the 27th, at night, anchored in the Downs. The next morning, having taken in a pilot, he went over the flats and so up the river of Thames, and the 30th anchored in Galleon's Reach, where (to conclude the command of the Blast bomb), having put out her guns, shells, and stores, on February 2 he laid her up in Ham Creek; and though the Peace of Ryswick had been concluded ever since September 20 before, yet he continued

in commission till October 6, 1698, for want of money
to pay him off. This was the end of a very fatiguing
command and a very dangerous voyage, especially
in the passage from Newfoundland home, wherein
they suffered everything but drowning or starving.
It was the very worst season of the year, long dark
nights and short hazy days, storms of wind, sickness
and death, short allowance of provisions and short
of hands, loss of masts and nothing tolerable to
supply their place. In the meantime, confined to a
small uncomfortable vessel, always under water, and,
besides her leaks, so deep in the water that every
sea she shipped threatened to send her to the bottom.
These circumstances, considered with the fatigue of
mind as well as body consequent thereupon, especially
in the commander, unable thereby to eat, drink, or
sleep to refreshment, demonstrates the seafaring life
of all others to be the most hazardous and fatiguing,
and therefore of all others the least desirable.

Captain Martin's safe arrival after so dangerous
a voyage demonstrated both his good conduct and
good seamanship, and gave him great encouragement to hope for a better command. Adversity in
this case makes many friends, and he would no
doubt immediately have had a postship, if the peace
had not made it necessary to lessen our naval force.
This circumstance of the public affairs fell out unlucky
for all our sea commanders that did not come within
the number limited to half-pay, but it was particularly
so to Captain Martin, who, being by the command of
the Blast bomb only a master and commander, was
in the middle state between the captains and lieutenants, and by that means not entitled to half-pay
as either. This, indeed, was made an argument
with his friends to get him a post ship with the Lord
Orford, who then presided at the Admiralty, and Mr.
Martin, having been sometime his lieutenant at sea,

and the only one that had not taken post, his Lordship had so much regard to promote his own officers,
that he resolved he should not be the only exception.
For this purpose he was actually sworn in, and a
commission ordered to be made out to give him
post. But here, by a remarkable instance of ill-
fortune, it so happened that the commission not
being signed by a sufficient number of hands that
day, the next morning the Earl of Orford was dis-
placed and Sir George Rooke succeeded ; and when
he came expecting to receive his commission, he
found himself disappointed both of that and his
friend at once.[1] He was quite thunderstruck at this
news, and remained like one without hope, for now
he had no prospect but to remain in the same inter-
mediate state, neither captain nor lieutenant without
half-pay, and therefore must submit to be again a
lieutenant to provide a maintenance for himself and
family, which to a man of his spirit was little better
than starving. Indeed, he resented this misfortune
so much, that he resolved to quit the Navy service ;
but here his friends interposed, especially Captain
Leake, who dissuaded him from that resolution by
the prospect of another war, and the expectation
himself had of a ship in the meantime, and that the
same friend that kept him in commission as a captain
would procure Captain Martin to be first lieutenant
of the same ship, in which station he might continue
as long as Captain Leake had a ship, or till he met
with the preferment he wanted. This friendly advice
took place, and Captain Leake being soon after

[1] 'This was done at the earnest solicitation of Captain Wright,
commonly called since, Commissioner Wright, who wrote a letter
to Sir George in favour of Salmon Morrice, he having, as he said,
married his only child ; thereupon Sir George thought proper to
order the name of Stephen Martin to be altered to Salmon
Morrice, and by that unlucky accident he lost taking post till the
next war.'—S. M. L.

appointed commander of the Kent, a third-rate of seventy guns, Captain Martin received a commission May 11, 1699, to be first lieutenant, a station that would not have been tolerable under any other. This ship was fitted out at Deptford, and on May 26 fell down to the Hope, and having taken in their guns and provisions they sailed for the Downs on July 26, but met with such bad weather they did not arrive there till four days afterwards. On August 2 they sailed from the Downs a cruising in the Channel and the Soundings, and the 20th coming in with the land they found themselves before Cork. Having watered, they sailed the 28th, and anchored in the Downs on September 1. Here they received orders to go to Portsmouth, and sailing immediately arrived there on the 8th. Two days after Rear-Admiral Hopsonn [1] came and hoisted his flag on board, but struck it on the 11th. They continued at Spithead till February 1, 1699, when they sailed for Chatham, arrived there on the 22nd, and were immediately paid off.

After being paid off as first lieutenant of the Kent, Captain Martin continued above a year out of commission, but being now upon half-pay as a lieutenant, and in continual expectation that a war would soon break out with France, when he might expect a postship, he bore his fortune very patiently. During this time he had a son born, whom he named Stephen, born January 26, 1700, but died March 21 following. Captain Leake had another ship, and Captain Martin might have been first lieutenant, but

---

[1] **Thomas** Hopsonn was born in 1649, a native of Bonchurch, in the **Isle of** Wight. He served with distinction in the wars with Holland, and commanded the Bonaventure at the battle of Beachy Head. At Vigo, on board the Torbay as vice-admiral, he broke the boom, for which service he received knighthood. Sir Thomas Hopsonn passed the last years of his life at Weybridge, where **he** died in 1717

as she was ordered to sea, and he did not think it advisable to be out of the way, he declined it. But soon after, viz. March 10, 1700, he had a commission for first lieutenant of the Namur, a second-rate, at Chatham, one that was not in a condition to go to sea, commanded by Captain John Munden, a person he was well acquainted with, and who, being a senior officer, every day expected a flag, and accordingly was made rear-admiral of the blue, and left the command of the ship on April 13. He was succeeded in the command by Captain Pickard, an old officer, but Captain Martin was not on board during his time, having leave to be at London, which continued till the ship was paid off on July 11, 1701.

As the preparations for war were now actually under consideration, Captain Martin determined to have no more lieutenant's commissions, which he thought would be rather a hindrance to his promotion at this critical juncture when a war was looked upon as unavoidable, and indeed it soon became so, for upon the death of King James at St. Germains on September 16, the French King, as if to insult the British nation and excite them to war, immediately acknowledged the titular Prince of Wales for King of England. Whereupon our ambassador was immediately recalled from the Court, and the French ambassador ordered home. The Parliament and the whole nation justly resented the indignity, and vigorous preparations were immediately begun to prosecute the war, that a declaration might be followed by some notable action. For this end great expedition was used to get a large fleet and a strong body of forces ready against the spring; but in the meantime the real design, which was against Cadiz, was kept so secret that it equally alarmed France, Spain, and Portugal. This expedition was to be commanded by the Lord High Admiral (the Earl of Pembroke) in person, on board the Britannia, and he was to have (as usual) three captains under him, of whom he appointed Captain Leake the first. Mr. Martin had the offer to be first lieutenant, but he was so angry at fortune for the disappointments he had already suffered, that he swore he would sooner leave the service than go any more a lieutenant. Indeed, it was not without reason he rejected it, seeing a war would soon make room for his promotion, and hoped the preparation then in hand would afford an opportunity, and he had the best claim to it, having already had a command. But here was another instance of ill-fortune, for another Martin who accepted it—this lieutenant's commission—by that means got a postship before him, the Lord High Admiral not going to sea. This enraged him the more, and he wrote a sharp letter to his brother Leake (who, indeed, was remarkably backward to serve his friends), acquainted him there was another bomb ship that would give post, and desired him to speak for it, or else he must think of providing for himself and family some other way, and he would sooner go into the service of the enemy, where he would be sure to have more justice done him. Captain Leake thereupon went to the Lord High Admiral and acquainted him with his brother's request. To whom his lordship replied, ' I did not know, Captain Leake, you had a brother to provide for ; if I had, he should have had the ship given to the other Martin.' Hereupon he was immediately promoted to the command of the Mortar bomb, a fifth-rate, at Deptford, by commission dated March 6, 1701–2, from whence he dated his rank in the Navy as a captain, which, with a small share of good fortune, had happened seven years before. Two days after King William died, but this did not put a stop to the longed-for expedition, for Queen Anne, upon her accession to the throne, immediately declared her resolution to pursue the measures begun by her predecessor, and agreeable thereto proclaimed war against France and Spain on May 4, 1702.

We must now enter upon Captain Martin's proceedings with his ship, the Mortar bomb, at Deptford, where being rigged and the stores taken in, on March 29 he sailed to Galleons ; and having taken on board four months' provisions and his guns, being sixteen in number, he hove aboard the hulk and took in his mortars. Whilst he lay at Woolwich he had a son born April 5, to his great satisfaction, being very desirous of another in the stead of that which he had lost, and named this also Stephen, as his mother desired, who said she would have a Stephen. On May 1 he sailed to the Nore, the 28th anchored in the Downs, and the next day sailed in company with Sir George Rooke and about forty sail, and two days after arrived at Spithead. On June 3 Prince George passed over from Portsmouth to the Isle of Wight to review the land forces intended to accompany the fleet, upon which occasion his Highness was saluted by all the ships at Spithead. The 18th two pressed men on board Captain Martin's ship endeavoured to swim from the ship in the night ; but soon after they were in the water, despairing of success, they cried out, and one was taken up, but the other was drowned. On July 1 the whole fleet sailed under command of Sir George Rooke, with the land forces under the command of the Duke of Ormonde,[1] consisting of

[1] James Butler, second Duke of Ormonde, was a grandson of the Royalist Lord-Lieutenant of Ireland, who died in 1688. The second duke was born in 1665 and was a military officer. He served as lieutenant-general in Flanders in 1693, and commanded

about 12,000 men, English and Dutch. On July 7 they anchored in Torbay, but weighed from thence the 14th, but were put back again, and sailed again the 29th. In this time Captain Martin heeled and scrubbed his ship. On August 12 they anchored off St. Sebastian's Point,[1] near Cadiz, N.E. ½ E., about two leagues distance. The next day, in the evening, they weighed and ran in for the Bay of Bulls, and falling little wind and the flood coming sooner than they expected, it being dark, they imagined themselves further off than they really were; for they had no sooner anchored in eight fathom, but they had several shot fired at them from St. Sebastian's tower. About two hours after, the wind came off shore, and they now berthed in thirteen fathoms, a mile and a half from the town. The next day they now berthed further into the bay, in eleven fathoms of water, St. Sebastian's Point S. by E. ½ E., two miles; St. Catharine's tower E. by N., three miles distant,[2] the French men-of-war and galleys having retired within the Puntales.[3] The same day there was a council, and pursuant to their resolutions the next day the force began to land, having several third and fourth-rates anchored along shore to protect their landing, which was about a mile and a half to the northward of St. Catharine's tower and castle, from whence they continued to fire upon them

the forces intended for Spain in 1702. He was Lord-Lieutenant of Ireland 1703-1707 and 1710-1713, commander-in-chief of the forces and Lord Warden of the Cinque Ports 1712-1714; but in 1715 he was attainted. The duke died in 1745, aged 80.

[1] Cadiz is at the end of a long narrow spit, the east side of which forms one side of the bay. The castle of San Sebastian is outside, on the west side of the town.

[2] Santa Catalina is the point at the northern side of the bay; so the fleet anchored on the north side of the entrance, a little outside.

[3] Puntales is a point on the spit, south of Cadiz, and within the bay, facing the narrowest part of the channel.

from eight in the morning to eight at night; a great number of barcolongos passing and repassing in the meantime between Cadiz and Port St. Mary's,[1] which it was thought conveyed the most valuable effects from the latter to the former, whilst the council of war of sea and land generals could come to no resolution how to proceed. The 16th the forces entered the town of Rota[2] without any opposition, and it having been resolved to bombard the city of Cadiz, Captain Martin with his bomb ship, two other English bombs and two Dutch, were ordered to bombard St. Catharine's fort till the armies approached, and then to forbear. Sir Stafford Fairborne,[3] with six sail, being appointed to protect the bombs in the meantime from the enemy's galleys, which were ready to come out upon them; but seeing the ships anchor by them, the galleys immediately ran up to the Puntales. Here the bombs fired some shells to try their distance, but finding themselves too far off, the next morning early they ran in nearer, and about six o'clock began to bombard, throwing now and then a shell. At night one of the English bombs, called the Firedrake, having received damage in the head of her foremast, hove off; the rest continued to bombard till three in the morning, at which time they left off, our forces appearing before the place. In the afternoon they had possession of the fort, and going on to Port St. Mary, found the enemy had deserted it. The 23rd, in the morning, the signal was made for twenty-two sail of men-of-war, with the bombs, to go into Cadiz bay, to cannonade and bombard the town, but the

---

[1] Santa Maria is a port on the north side of the bay, east of the point of Santa Catalina.

[2] Also on the north side.

[3] Sir Stafford Fairborne was afterwards vice-admiral at the siege of Barcelona in 1705.

E

wind veering, it was put off till the next day. They
then went in and anchored in five fathoms of water,
St. Catharine's fort bearing north, two miles distant,
being right against Cadiz town, just without random
shot, the ships anchoring in a line before the town ;
but nothing was done, the council of war having
altered their resolution of bombarding the town.
The 29th Captain Martin had orders to weigh and
go up to Matagorda Castle, and endeavour to throw
some shells into it. About six he weighed, and two
hours after brought to and fired seven shells, one
falling close under the walls. At ten he anchored,
having orders to desist firing any more till further
orders, and at low water had the misfortune to find
himself aground. Whether the enemy suspected it
or not, is uncertain ; but it is very probable they did,
for just at that time three galleys came out upon
him, and he, endeavouring to weigh, found himself
fast ; and the frigate which was to attend him being
gone from her station, and the rest of the ships too
far off, or not able to help him as he was situated,
he was in danger of being taken in sight of the fleet.
He had nothing but resolution to bring him off, and
fight it out till the tide floated him again, or till the
fleet could relieve him, who must soon perceive the
danger he was in when they saw him engaged.
The galleys, who already looked upon him as taken,
came furiously upon him, and he was as well prepared to receive them. For if they had resolved to
take him, he had resolved not to be taken ; for he
declared to the ship's company that when he could
defend the ship no longer, he would blow her up,
every man shifting for himself ; for they were so
near the shore he did not doubt but they might
escape by swimming. But this was only if matters
came to extremity, which might not happen, for he
encouraged the ship's company to defend themselves

bravely, and consider the enemy were Spaniards ;
and asked them if they would be taken by Spaniards
and in sight of their own fleet? that the tide would
soon set them afloat, and the fleet send them assistance if they did not lose their honour in the meantime.   Thus animated they applied themselves to
their defence, for the seamen are rarely wanting
to behave bravely when excited by a brave commander.   All their sixteen guns they brought to
bear upon the galleys, and the bombardiers prepared
the mortars, and began by throwing shells at a
distance ; and when they came nearer, throwing up
mortars full of shot into the air, which, falling upon
the heads of the rowers and others in the galleys, did
considerable damage.   One fortunate shell fell close
to the prow of one galley and blew up just as it fell
in the water, whereby it was believed she received
considerable damage, for immediately they backed
astern and returned into the harbour ; the two others
plied him close, but one, endeavouring to come under
his stern, touched the ground, and in getting off received some damage.   The other was well plied with
cannon shot, and partridge, as she endeavoured to
board them, and suffered very much.   One of her
yards fell down, and they put off in great confusion,
perceiving assistance coming from the fleet, for fear
they themselves, now disabled, might be surprised
before they got back into the harbour.   At this
retreat, the ship's company, according to the custom
of the English sailors when they perceive they have
any advantage of the enemy, raised a great shout
and pelted them with shot all the way they went.
In the meantime, this battle having been observed
from the fleet, two frigates were detached to Captain
Martin's assistance ; but by the time they got near
him, the enemy being retired, they were of no other
service than by their countenance to prevent a

second attack of the like nature, which, however, could not well have happened, for presently after he got off ; and at six in the evening he weighed, and soon after anchored near the admiral, according to his orders.

The 30th the land forces entrenched in spite of the enemy, who plied them very warmly from the ships and the Matagorda. At night Captain Martin was ordered to command the guard afloat with the boats (the six junior captains taking it by turns), and to scour the bay and alarm the enemy as much as possible, which accordingly he did all night long, but with very great hazard, being attacked twice by the enemy's boats, and pelted with shot from the shore where the alarms were taken ; in which actions he had several men wounded but none killed ; at daybreak they returned to their ships. The seven following days a fruitless attack was carried on by our forces ashore against the Matagorda, but with very little success, the enemy having effectually prevented any assistance they might receive from the fleet, by sinking five or six great ships in the best of the channel, whilst in the meantime the ships and galleys in the harbour very much galled and hindered the besiegers in their trenches. It is true our frigates forced the enemy's ships and galleys from their first station above the castle, but that only removed them to a place of more security, where our ships could not disturb them, but where they could equally annoy our forces, and entirely command that narrow neck of land leading to the Matagorda, whereon our forces must carry on the attack. So that having in vain attempted this strong fort for nine days, with considerable loss and no hopes of success, it was resolved to draw off the forces. Accordingly, on September 7, Captain Martin received orders from Sir George Rooke to take under his command the boats of the fleet, and transport the forces over the river from before the Matagorda. Accordingly the next morning by eight, he began to transport them, and in little more than an hour had put them all over the river, both horse and foot, and, contrary to their expectation, without any attack from the enemy. But after they were landed and marched away, and the boats were going down the river, they received a volley of musket-shot from a party of the enemy who lay hid among the bushes, whereby several were wounded, and one shot passing close by Captain Martin killed the man at the after oar next to him dead upon the spot. They immediately stood to their arms and fired a volley at the bushes from whence the enemy had fired, and Captain Martin making up briskly towards the place as if he intended to land, several parties of horse and foot appeared, and giving a general discharge of their arms, made off, whereby some were wounded but none killed. But from the boats they had a fair mark at the enemy as they ran away, and the satisfaction to see several of them drop. It was not their business to pursue this unequal fight any further than was necessary, wherefore, as the transportation boats had all passed down in safety during the skirmish, Captain Martin, with the guard, made the best of his way down the river, himself keeping in the rear, every other man in the boat standing to their arms, by which means they were enabled to make a running fight with advantage; for the Spaniards knew they durst not land, and therefore did not fail to give them several discharges by the way. But our men were generally so ready to answer them immediately at the place from whence they fired, that the boats' crews received little or no damage, for they fired at too great a distance or with too much confusion to do

much harm, and the boats got in safety on board
of their respective ships. The following day Captain
Martin watered his ship. The 13th, in the morning,
the army marched from Port St. Mary and blew up
St. Catharine's fort; whereupon Captain Martin received orders with the other bombs to weigh and
stand in to the shore to protect the rear of the army
in their march; and, if they saw the enemy's horse,
to endeavour to attack them, to fire a shell or two
amongst them. At noon he fired several shot at
some Spaniards that were going along shore, and
at seven at night anchored near Rota in six fathoms
of water. The three following days the soldiers
were embarked, and they burnt all the Spanish
boats, barcolongos, &c., that they had found there.
This was the conclusion of the Cadiz expedition,
which had so much alarmed the enemy and raised
the expectation of the British nation. The power
we had there was sufficient to have done much
greater things than the taking of Cadiz. But this,
like all other expeditions composed of sea and
land forces under distinct commanders, however
well concerted at home, never prove successful from
a constant disagreement between them. Thus all
the time was spent in councils of war, to concert
measures that should have been resolved before
they came thither; and then, as if they thought they
must do something, but by no means take the place,
they pursued measures whereby it was impossible
to take it, having given the enemy all the time they
could with which to recover their first surprise,
strengthen themselves, and secure the most valuable
effects of Port St. Mary's, which they carried over
for some days, and in sight of the fleet; and it
seems as if, from the time of their arrival, they had
no thought of taking the place. The ill success of
this expedition, so expensive and dishonourable to

the nation, was imputed by some to Sir George
Rooke, and by others to the Duke of Ormonde ; but
without examining into the dispute, it is undoubtedly
true they were both to blame, in not agreeing to
promote the honour and interest of their country,
which ought to have buried all private animosities
or punctilios of their profession and command. It
is not so manifest wherein Sir George Rooke was
blamable, otherwise than not concurring with the
duke in any measure that might best promote the
public service ; but the blame of the army is so
apparent that every one must be sensible of it.
They did not appear by any one step that was taken
to promote the service they were upon, or discharge
themselves like soldiers. They entered the Spanish
town without opposition, and lived there without discipline ; and did nothing like soldiers, but
plunder, to the disgrace of the confederate arms,
and even breach of faith with the nation they were
sent to protect. Then, like a rabble, they endeavoured to do all the mischief they could by their
rapine, and then ran madly upon the attack of the
Matagorda, which their officers at the same time
knew was impracticable to be taken : such a scene
of disorder, folly, and rashness never perhaps
having centred in one expedition. Whereas, had
any tolerable measures been concerted beforehand,
and immediately put in execution, the place must
have presently been taken or yielded. Or, which
was obvious to all that know the place, had they
landed upon the neck of land which leads to the
town, and thereby cut off communication with the
main, they had commanded the harbour, and the
town would soon have been obliged to surrender ; [1]
and even as it was, things would have appeared

[1] This was the way Cadiz was taken by the Earl of Essex and
Sir Francis Vere in 1596.

much more in our favour if the Spaniards had not
been irritated by the ill treatment at Port St. Mary's,
whereby we left things in Spain upon a worse footing than they were before we had been at the
expense of sending so powerful a fleet and army
thither.

The attempt upon Cadiz being thus brought
to an untimely end, on September 18 the fleet
weighed from the Bay of Bulls in order to proceed
to England, with shame and confusion to the principal officers, but soon falling calm they anchored
again. The next day they sailed, and the 23rd were
off Cape St. Vincent; the 27th was hazy, squally
weather, and Captain Martin had the misfortune to
lose one of his men, who fell overboard and was
drowned as he was taking in the foretopmast
staysail. On October 6 a frigate came into the
fleet with an account that the Spanish plate fleet,
with the French men-of-war, their convoy, was
put into Vigo; whereupon it was resolved at a
council of war to proceed thither, and two frigates
were detached before for more certain intelligence.
They returned the 9th, confirming the former
account, and that the enemy's ships lay up the river
in the harbour of Redondalla. The 11th the fleet
entered the harbour of Vigo, and though the town
of Vigo fired upon them as they passed by, the
fleet went on without regarding it. At noon they
anchored within two gun's shot of the French, who
were very busy in booming up the harbour's
mouth, which was about a musket shot over. The
boom was made very strong, and besides a stone
fort, was flanked on either side with a strong battery
of twenty cannon; likewise a seventy-gun ship at each
end of the boom, and five ships of sixty and seventy
guns moored with their broadsides to defend it. In
the harbour were fifteen French men-of-war, three

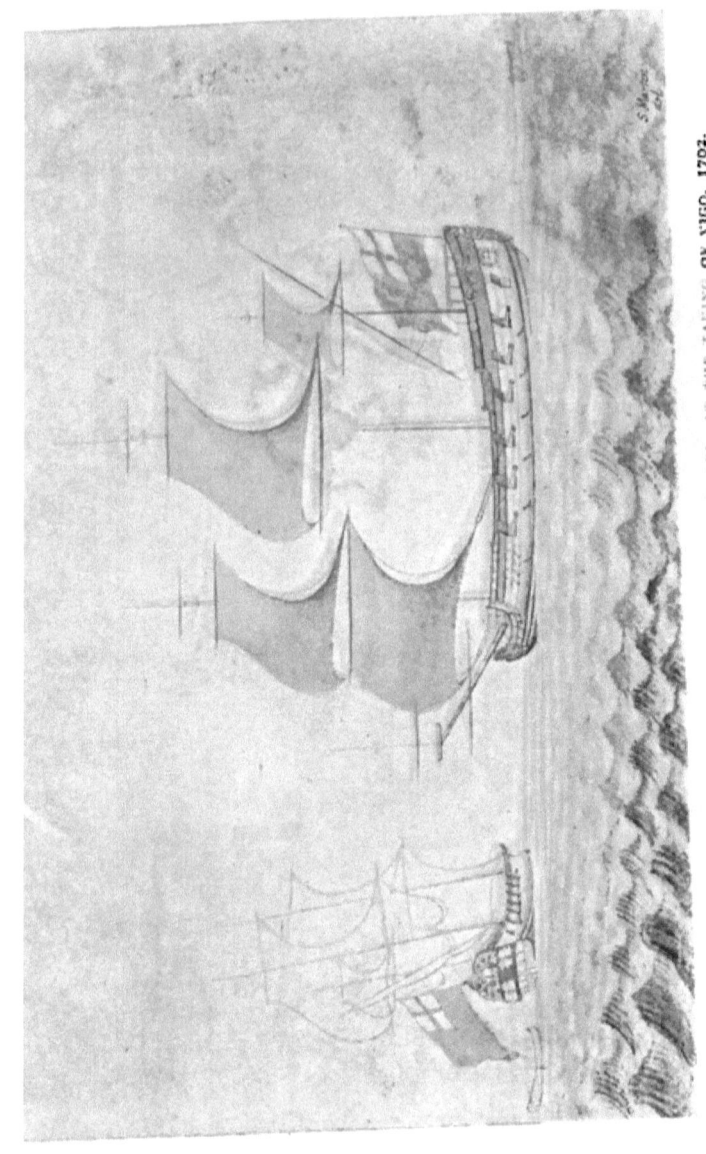

THE MORTAR BOMB, CAPTAIN STEPHEN MARTIN COMMANDER, AT THE TAKING OF VIGO, 1702.

Spanish, with thirteen galleons. As soon as the fleet entered the harbour, Captain Martin and the rest of the bombs and fireships were ordered above the men-of-war, next the enemy, to be ready for bombarding and burning. The next day, being the 12th, they had hazy weather with rain. Early in the morning all the boats of the fleet were employed in landing the soldiers, to the number of 5,000, in order to attack the fort on the starboard side, and the Barfleur to batter it by sea. And the Association to do the like on the larboard side ; a line of twenty-four sail was appointed to attack the boom and force the harbour, Vice-Admiral Hopsonn leading the van, with five sail abreast ; then a Dutch admiral and five sail, and then Sir Stafford Fairborne in the rear with five sail more, the bombs and fireships following close in the rear ; and in this manner they made the attack. Admiral Hopsonn, with the first five, broke the boom, notwithstanding the fire from the battery and ships that guarded it, but his foretopmast was shot away. He was no sooner entered than he was boarded by a fireship which burnt his foresail, but put herself off again with the way she had in coming on board, and soon after blew up ; and being a merchant ship laden with snuff, that, in some measure, extinguished the flames, but almost blinded and suffocated those that were near. While this was doing, the rest of the ships, having got through as fast as they could, were all of a cluster ; and Captain Martin with his ship being amongst the thickest, was so near the fireship that blew up, that the snuff drove into the sides of his ship, and made the planks of a snuff colour, discolouring everything on board. This created such a consternation, that the first lieutenant, purser, and 100 men of Vice-Admiral Hopsonn's ship, jumped overboard, the greater part of whom were drowned. In short, in

less than an hour's time they were masters of the
forts and harbour. The French, as they quitted
their ships, either set them on fire or blew them up;
so that for some time there was nothing to be heard
or seen but cannonading, burning, men and guns
flying in the air, and altogether the most lively
scene of horror and confusion that can be imagined.
This confusion, in some measure, lasted all night,
so that by the next morning all the ships, French
and Spaniards, were destroyed or taken; viz. of the
French ten men-of-war were taken, the remaining
five with two frigates and some smaller vessels were
burnt. Of the Spaniards nine galleons were taken,
the rest destroyed; and this victory was obtained
with the loss of not above 200 men; but the enemy
lost a great number, for besides what were killed in
the fight and defence of their ships, the shores of
the harbour were strewn with their bodies, blown up
and drowned, and no small number were found on
shore at a distance from the harbour, and some a
considerable way up the country, whither they were
come by the force of the gunpowder when the ships
blew up.

The two following days they were very busy
examining the prizes and putting men on board,
also in fitting five sail of French men-of-war—viz.
three of seventy and two of fifty, to carry with them to
England. In the meantime the Spaniards, to do
all the mischief they could, got in companies upon
the tops of the hills that surrounded the harbour,
and now and then, as they had opportunity, fired a
volley of small shot upon the boats or the smaller ships
that lay within their reach, which was always accompanied with abusive language—as English dogs,
rogues, heretics, cuckolds, and the like, and some
of them seemed to come for no other purpose but to
rail. Captain Martin, where he lay in the harbour,

had a good deal of it from a neighbouring hill,
the seamen making sport of it, to call names with
them ; but this being sometimes attended with a
shot, and sometimes a volley of small arms, that
spoilt the joke, he pointed his guns to the place
and kept men always upon the watch, to answer
them sometimes with a round shot and sometimes
a volley of partridge. And one evening, when
there seemed to be a greater company than usual,
discharged them so effectually that they were
heard to call upon their saints, which not only
shortened the discourse at that time, but prevented
those dialogues for the future. The 15th they had
squally, rainy weather, and blew so hard that he
drove with all his anchors ahead ; and the Berwick
came athwart his hawse, carrying away his larboard
cathead and ensign staff.[1]

And in the afternoon Sir George Rooke gave
him a commission for the Lowestoft, a fifth-rate
frigate of thirty-two guns and 160 men ; and he removed on board her the same day in Vigo harbour.
The first thing Captain Martin did when he entered
upon his command of the Lowestoft was to get some
water on board, there being none when he came.
The 16th Sir Clowdïsley Shovell, with about twenty
sail, joined the fleet from England, and the 19th, in
the morning, the forces being embarked, the admiral
sailed from Vigo, leaving Sir Clowdisley Shovell to
complete what was to be done, and follow him to
England. The 20th the Dutch set on fire two
French men-of-war and one galleon, having first
plundered them.

[1] ' As there were now some vacant commands, Captain Martin
wrote to Sir George Rooke, desiring to be removed to a better
ship ; and when he was solicited for another, he bethought himself, and said No, he must not put off Martin any longer, since
he had put him by a little hardly before.'--S. M. L.

In the meantime Captain Martin was employed by the admiral's order in getting off a prize called the Dartmouth, but afterwards the Vigo, which the French had run ashore; which he performed, and afterwards put her in a condition for the sea. The 23rd he had another job of the same kind, to get off a salt prize, which was so near the shore that she ebbed dry. Here he expected to meet with a stout resistance, because the day before some of our people, who had attempted it, were driven off by a party of 300 or 400 horse. Captain Martin, therefore, prepared for an opposition by taking with him, besides his own boats, several French prize boats, well manned and armed, and went on board at midnight and stayed till next morning trying to get her off, but could not, there being not water enough; he therefore left her, designing to try again next day. Accordingly the next day he made a second attempt, going on board about midnight as before. He got another anchor out right astern and hove out into two long boats about twelve tons of salt, which, with the tides lifting her a foot more, got her off about three in the morning, and he brought her to the admiral; but this was not performed without a small skirmish with a party of horse, wherein some of the seamen were wounded, and some of the enemy killed. By this time the admiral, being ready to sail, ordered four French men-of-war and a galleon to be set on fire, and all the other boats and vessels of the enemy which were not worth carrying to England.

The next day, being October 25, they weighed, but being little wind they anchored again a little below the fort. They weighed again in the evening, though they were obliged to anchor at midnight, the admiral being determined to put to sea with any wind, by reason of the shortness of their provisions. The next morning they put to sea, having hazy, squally weather. In the afternoon Captain Martin split his foresail, but soon got up another. It continued to blow hard all night, and the next day he lost sight of the admiral and most part of the fleet, and lay a try under a mizen balanced. In the afternoon he joined twelve sail of the fleet; the following day, seeing nine sail to leeward, he made the usual signal to the ships he was with, and bore away to leeward to them, and it proved to be Sir Clowdisley. In the afternoon he made another squadron, which he likewise joined, being Rear-Admiral Graydon [1] and his division, and the following morning he joined Sir Stafford Fairborne [2] and three sail more to leeward; thus, by his vigilance, he united the scattered fleet, but had so worked his own ship that she made four foot of water a watch. The two following days it continued squally weather, several ships splitting and losing their topsails and courses, and Captain Martin split his mainsail; some had courses bent for topsails and topsails for

[1] John Graydon was commander of the Saudadoes in 1688, and of the Defiance at Beachy Head. He was with Rooke at Cadiz and Vigo, and then went out as commodore to the West Indies. Falling in with the squadron of Du Casse, after the action with Benbow, he avoided an action and let it escape. For this he was dismissed the service. He died in 1726.

[2] Stafford Fairborne was eldest son of Sir Palmes Fairborne, who was Governor of Tangiers when he was killed by the Moors in 1680. Stafford was at the battle of Beachy Head, and served on shore at the siege of Cork. In 1693 he commanded the Monk, and was at the disaster of the Smyrna fleet, serving under Sir George Rooke. In 1696 he went out as commodore to Newfoundland. He was in the Downs during the great storm on board the Association. She broke from her anchors, but he brought her safely into Gottenburg. In 1705 he was second in command in the Mediterranean, under Sir C. Shovell. He afterwards assisted the Dutch under Auverquerque, in the siege of Ostend. In 1707 he was on Prince George's council. Sir Stafford survived until 1742.

courses. On November 1 the weather was more moderate, but they lost company with Sir Stafford and Admiral Graydon, whereupon the Lowestoft was ordered to fall astern and to leeward to take account of who and what number of ships there were, which accordingly he did, and gave an account next morning. He was then ordered to windward to speak to the galleon and learn what condition she was in ; he came up with her at midnight, and upon examination next morning found her in a very good condition as to her hull, but had split all her sails in the last bad weather.

The 4th and 5th they had fair weather. The 6th they scudded away under a foresail all night, and at two the next morning it blew a mere fret of wind, when they lay a try under a reefed mizen. The 8th they had hazy weather, blowing hard, with hail, rain, thunder and lightning. The signal was made on board Sir Clowdisley for the Lowestoft to make sail ahead and sound. Accordingly, he did so, and had sixty-five fathoms, and in the afternoon sixty. At night, going ahead, again he split his foresail and fell astern, and could not get up with the admiral again that night. The next day blowing hard he split his spritsail, and bent another foresail and made sail, but lost Sir Clowdisley. At four in the afternoon he made the land of England, the Start bearing N.E. distance four leagues, and at night he joined Rear-Admiral Graydon. The next day, being November 10, he saw the Isle of Wight, and, crowding all the sail he could, joined Sir Clowdisley at noon ; and about ten at night they anchored at St. Helens. The following day they ran in to Spithead, and two days after Captain Martin received orders to go into Portsmouth harbour to be refitted for Channel service. This was the happy conclusion of a long campaign.

Not only had it afforded **Captain** Martin everything
desirable, and was the more pleasing as it immediately followed a series of disappointments and
misfortunes which had almost made him desperate.
This may serve as a lesson to those whose high
spirits, by their own rashness, disappoint their
fortune, as well as those of more dejected minds
who, not meeting with that success or reward they
are conscious they deserve, meanly despair and lose
all by giving up all for lost. Thus Captain Martin,
being as he thought abandoned by fortune, had all
restored to him by this one campaign. He had,
indeed, been sufficiently mortified by not taking post
as a captain so soon by some years as he might
have done, and being reduced to a half-pay lieutenant
after having been a commander ; but this last sun-
shine of fortune had dissipated that gloominess
which had oppressed his mind, as if it had never
been. He had been, indeed, completely fortunate.
He set out with a command that gave him post, and
in the prosecution of the voyage encountered no
dangers but what added to his reputation. In the
attempt upon Cadiz he acquitted himself with com-
mendable bravery, and gained honour from an
expedition in itself not honourable. In the victory
at Vigo he showed an equal spirit, and added to that
reputation he gained at Cadiz ; and this honour was
not an empty name, for, besides plunder, he received
1,000*l.* for his share as a captain at Vigo, so that it
was essentially the best campaign he ever made
abroad, and served to augment his domestic satisfaction when he returned home. While this trans-
action passed in Europe, his friend, Captain Leake,
had been no less successful in America, for, being
appointed commodore of a squadron to Newfoundland, he had destroyed the French settlements at
that place, and taken and destroyed a great number of

their shipping. Thus returning home with honour, he arrived at Portsmouth the day before Captain Martin. We may imagine it was a joyful meeting between the two brothers-in-law, who had so much affection for each other, especially when comparing the circumstances of their respective voyages, it appeared how much they had both contributed in their respective stations to the honour of their country and to their own reputation and advantage, wherein they could not but sympathise with each other ; but Captain Martin had the particular benefit arising from it, that Commodore Leake's success, as it was a sure earnest of a flag, so consequently it was a benefit to him who was sure to participate in his good fortune. Soon after Commodore Leake was made rear-admiral of the blue, and on December 22 he hoisted his flag at Portsmouth.

In the meantime, the Lowestoft having been docked and put into a condition for Channel service, on January 12 Captain Martin sailed out of the harbour to Spithead. He had orders to take the Rochester prize under his command, and cruise off Guernsey and Jersey, and between Cape de la Hague and the island of Bœuf, to hinder the trade from western France to Dunkirk, and other eastern ports. In prosecution of these orders, he sailed the next day from Spithead, and the 16th anchored at Guernsey, but not without great danger in the race of Alderney, first of oversetting, the Lowestoft being very crank ; and next by ignorance of the pilot, who ran them upon a rock under water that did them some damage. At Guernsey he expected to have found the Sheerness, for whom he had orders, but she not being there, he applied himself to the governor of the place for sealed rendezvous (according to his orders) where to meet with her, but found none ; only he was informed by the governor, that she sailed the day before for

England, as he believed, for provisions, but to what
port he knew not. Captain Martin continued at
Guernsey till the 22nd, during which time they had
very bad weather ; he then left that place with the
Lowestoft and the Rochester's prize to cruise about
the island, leaving the orders enclosed with the
governor for the captain of the Sheerness, in case
he should arrive before his return, which he intended
to do in four or five days. The 22nd and 23rd he
had hazy, blowing weather, with rain, during which
time nothing material happened. The 24th he discovered a sail coming about the island of Sark, bound
through the race of Alderney, which he chased,
came up with, and took. She was a Flushing privateer of ten guns, and had been taken by a French
privateer of twenty-four guns and 200 men the day
before, off the Lizard, and when Captain Martin
took her, had a lieutenant, nineteen Frenchmen,
and three Hamburghers on board. At night he got
out of the race, it blowing very hard, and brought
to under a mainsail. The next morning early he
was about half seas over, but was not able to fetch
the island of Guernsey, and his prize being very
leaky, and being willing to know if the Sheerness
was at Spithead, he stood for St. Helens, and at
night arrived there, it blowing hard. The next day
he had orders to come to Spithead, upon the occasion we shall mention afterwards, and the 29th was
discharged from his command of the Lowestoft.
Commodore Leake, we observed before, being appointed rear-admiral of the blue squadron, hoisted
his flag at Portsmouth December 22, whilst Captain Martin was at that place refitting his ship
the Lowestoft for a cruise in the Channel. It is
the custom for an admiral upon his first promotion
to make choice of a captain to command his ship
for the time being where he hoists his flag. The

F

advantage of this to any captain, besides the reputation of it, is only something better pay than (if he is a
junior captain) he might otherwise have, the pay
of a captain to a rear-admiral being as captain of a
third-rate ; of a vice-admiral as captain of a second-
rate ; and of an admiral as captain of a first-rate ;
though the admiral should hoist his flag on board a
smaller ship.   Nevertheless, there are very few
captains that care to have a flag on board, for besides being then but second in the ship, subject to
the command and humour of the admiral, and
worse accommodated than they would otherwise be,
it is a very troublesome office, the whole management of a squadron, if in a fleet, or if a commander-
in-chief, of the whole fleet resting upon the captain
to the flag, who is to see all his orders carried into
execution.   Besides, it is out of the way of all advantages by prizes, which private captains may
hope for in cruising ships, whereby alone they can
hope to make their fortunes.   For this reason Rear-
Admiral Leake made Captain Martin the offer with
the liberty to accept or refuse without any regard to
him, who, he might be sure, would always be his
friend ; and this choice he made not because he was
his brother-in-law, but because he knew him to be a
brave, experienced officer, for he had been twelve
years an officer, though a young captain, and one
who, he was sure, would always have his honour at
heart as much as his own, a circumstance that must
give a general officer great satisfaction, and very
much contribute to crown all his actions with a
glorious success ; the best designs being frequently
rendered abortive by the infidelity or carelessness of
those who are to carry them into execution.   Captain
Martin, though he could neither make a new friend,
nor lose an old one by taking his free choice upon
this occasion, and was sensible that he might lose

great opportunities to improve his fortune by a
cruising ship and a good station, which his brother's
interest would always secure him, yet could not
resist the inclination he found in himself to be with
him, especially as it was easily to be discerned that
Admiral Leake was desirous to have Captain Martin
with him. Wherefore, before he went out upon his
cruise, it was agreed upon, and thus united in love
and interest, Captain Martin, giving over all thought
of pursuing any other scheme, resolved to follow
the fortune of Rear-Admiral Leake, which he invariably pursued ever after. In consequence of this
union between the two brothers, Rear-Admiral
Leake, by his letter to the Admiralty of January 5,
signified, that he had made choice of Captain Stephen
Martin, then commander of the Lowestoft, his
brother-in-law, to be his captain, and the Royal
William, a first-rate ship in that harbour, to go to sea
in, desiring that Captain Martin might be discharged
from the Lowestoft and have a commission to command the Royal William.[1] A commission was accordingly sent down to Portsmouth, where Captain
Martin found it upon his return from his cruise,
January 29. From this time Captain Martin became the inseparable companion of Admiral Leake's
fortune, unless in some few instances, where matters
of conveniency required their separation, and truly
acquitted himself as a faithful and brave captain in
most of those glorious transactions of the fleet under
the command of Admiral Leake wherein, as it was
his duty to carry all his orders into execution, he
may be said to have acted the second part. But
these being related at large in the life of Sir John
Leake, it will be needless to make recapitulation ;
I shall, therefore, particularise such only as relate

---

[1] A first-rate of 100 guns and 760 men.

F 2

more immediately to the personal conduct and bravery of Captain Martin.

On January 30, 1702–3, Captain Martin entered upon his command of the Royal William, a first-rate in Portsmouth harbour, as captain to Rear-Admiral Leake, who hoisted the blue flag at the mizen topmast head. The 6th being the Queen's birthday, was solemnised as usual by firing guns. The 12th, a court-martial was held on board, at which Captain Martin assisted, and the purser of the Chatham was dismissed his employment; and two days after another court-martial was held, and the 24th another. On March 4 Rear-Admiral Leake received a commission, appointing him vice-admiral of the blue, which flag he hoisted the same day ; two days after he removed his flag on board the St. George,[1] a second-rate, intending to go to sea in her ; but thinking this ship still too large, if he should be suddenly ordered to sea, the 19th he wrote to the Admiralty to acquaint them that he had made choice of the Somerset[2] to go to sea in, desiring Captain Martin might be removed to that ship. On April 12 the admiral received orders by express to go to sea in haste with six sail, and cruise for eight days in quest of a squadron of the enemy. Upon this emergency he hoisted his flag on board the Grafton,[3] a seventy-gun ship at Spithead, then ready for sea, and sailed the 15th, leaving orders with Captain Martin to continue in command of the St. George till he was succeeded by Captain Jennings. Vice-Admiral Leake, having finished his cruise, returned the 24th, and on May 1 Captain Martin received his commission for the Somerset, and hoisted the flag on board that

---

[1] A second-rate, ninety guns and 700 men.
[2] A third-rate, eighty guns and 520 men.
[3] A third-rate, seventy guns and 440 men

ship. On June 5, Vice-Admiral Leake received orders to follow Sir George Rooke, who sailed that morning, but was supposed to have sailed a day or two before. They endeavoured to sail immediately, but falling little wind could only get out to St. Helens, and the Somerset not being a very good sailer, the admiral thought it more advisable to order her back to Spithead, which he did, and striking his flag went privately in the Northumberland [1] for greater expedition, and sailed the next morning. The same day Captain Martin returned with the Somerset to Spithead, but sailed three days after in the squadron under the command of Admiral Churchill,[2] in order to join the fleet. They looked into Torbay, but not finding the fleet there, stood for Plymouth, where they anchored the day following. The next day (being the 12th) they sailed again in quest of the fleet, but Admiral Churchill receiving orders to return to Spithead, altered their motions, and the following day they left Plymouth with the homeward-bound East Indiamen. The 15th, Captain Martin received a verbal order to take the Borneo, East Indiaman, in tow, which he did accordingly, and two days afterwards arrived with her in safety at Spithead. On May 31, Sir Stafford Fairborne, vice-admiral of the red, hoisted his flag on board the Somerset, and Captain Martin sent Admiral Leake's things ashore, he having hoisted his flag on board the Prince George, a second-rate, where he designed to

---

[1] A third-rate, seventy guns and 440 men.

[2] George Churchill, born in 1652, was a younger brother of the Duke of Marlborough. He did good service at the battle of La Hogue. On the accession of the Queen he became principal member of Prince George's Council at the Admiralty for several years. After the death of Prince George he retired, to live in a house in Windsor Park, where he had the finest aviary ever seen in Britain. He died in 1710 unmarried.

continue.   The 21st, Vice-Admiral Leake (with the
fleet) arrived at Spithead on board the Prince
George, and two days after Captain Martin entered upon his command of that ship.   Why Vice-
Admiral Leake chose this ship and so long continued
in her is not easily accounted for, seeing she was by
no means a good man-of-war, for she carried her
guns very ill, and was very tender, both very ill
qualities ; her good qualities were only such as are
common with all tender ships, to be easy in a sea,
and keep her wind well, the first of use only at an
anchor, and the latter of little use in fleets, especially
with leewardly Dutch men-of-war.   The only reason
I can conjecture for giving this preference to the
Prince George, when there were several better
second-rates in the fleet, was for her name's sake,
out of respect and compliment to His Royal Highness the Lord High Admiral, for whom he justly
bore the greatest veneration.

On July 1, 1703, Sir Clowdisley Shovell sailed
with the fleet for the Mediterranean, but all the
ships not being ready, Vice-Admiral Leake[1] was
left behind to hasten them, and follow him to
Lisbon.   The ships were then very sickly, and
what with the scarcity of seamen at that time, and
the numbers they were obliged to send to the
hospitals, it was with great difficulty they prose-
cuted the voyage, though they took on board their
full complement of mariners.   But as dispatch was
necessary, they sailed from St. Helens on the 10th
with five sail, and in eleven days joined the grand
fleet before they got to Lisbon, for they did not
arrive there till two days after.   The fleet then consisted of sixty-nine sail, English and Dutch, and the
King of Portugal took a view of them with great

[1] At this time Admiral Leake was knighted.

satisfaction. Sailing from Lisbon on August 9, they were forced into Tangier Road, but leaving that place they got through the Straits that night. The fleet being in want of water they stretched for Cape Hony, in Barbary, but the Moors would not let them water. Thus their want of it increasing, and abundance of men dying through the extreme heat, it was resolved to go to Altea, in Spain, which they did, and anchored in Altea Bay on August 3. Here they made a descent with 2,500 marines, and watered the fleet ; and the Spaniards, seeing no injury offered to them, readily brought fresh provisions, for which they received ready money. Thus refreshed they sailed on September 3, and arrived at Leghorn on the 19th. Whilst they lay here, there was a storm which forced many from their anchors, and did considerable damage ; the Dorsetshire drove directly into the hawse of the Prince George, though she received but little damage. On the 28th they celebrated the proclamation of the Archduke Charles III., as King of Spain, by firing each ship twenty-one guns.

They were kept at Leghorn by contrary winds, till October 2, when they sailed for England. The 12th, being off Minorca, there arose a sudden storm of wind, with lightning, rain, and prodigious claps of thunder, which did great damage to the ships in their masts, sails, and rigging. The fleet lay by all night, during which time a store pink lost her mainmast and sprung a leak, and coming close to leeward of the Prince George, Captain Martin took her in tow, and two days after, when the weather abated, having stopped her leaks, he fitted a mast for her with yards, sails, and rigging, and enabled her to pursue her voyage home. The 22nd they were off Altea, and watered the ships ; and then, making the best of their way homewards,

November 15 made the land of England, and soon
after came to an anchor in the Downs, having buried
upwards of sixty men in four months, and the
rest in such a languishing condition, that though
their complement was 700 men, they had scarce
enough in health to manage the ship ; and, to
complete the disasters of this unprofitable voyage,
they were no sooner arrived at home, and, as they
thought, in a port of safety, but the most violent
storm came upon them ever known in this kingdom,
in the night between the 26th and 27th. It was
indeed very memorable and very fatal, more
especially in the Downs, where none rode fast but
the Prince George, and that too almost by a miracle ;
Captain Martin, considering the time of year, and
foreseeing a storm, had taken all the means to secure
the ship that human prudence could suggest, which,
under Providence, was the preservation of his own
and all the lives in the ship. He had made a snug
ship, and veered out three long services to two
cables and two-thirds, which enabled him not only
to ride out the storm himself, but to do what was
hardly ever known upon a like occasion, which was
to ride another ship, and that a seventy-gun ship too,
viz., the Restoration, Captain Emes, who drove so
near the Prince George that they were forced to
brace their yards to prevent their coming on board
them ; half an hour the Restoration rode by them
with her anchor at their hawser, which brought
home their best bower, and brought their small
bower ahead. Captain Martin endeavoured all that
in him lay to cut her away, but in vain ; and whether
the Restoration's cable broke, or she slipt, by what
means Providence only knows, but their anchor disappeared, and they drove away, and they knew no
more of the Restoration till next morning, when
they saw her with twelve sail, ashore upon the sands.

Amongst these, besides the Restoration, were two other seventy-gun ships, the Stirling Castle and Northumberland, and the Mary, of sixty guns, Admiral Beaumont, who were all to pieces by ten o'clock, and all the men perished except one from the Mary, and about eighty from the Stirling Castle. It was a melancholy prospect, to see between 2,000 and 3,000 men perish in this manner before their eyes, without any possibility of helping them. But the next day, as soon as the storm was abated, so that they could attempt anything, they sent boats to their assistance, and with great difficulty saved those aforementioned who had got upon the masts, which remained above water, there having been many more, whom they perceived to drop into the water as their strength failed them. As soon as this dismal catastrophe was ended,[1] and Vice-Admiral Leake had acquainted the Admiralty of the circumstances of this misfortune, having leave to go to London, he struck his flag on December 10,

---

[1] The ships lost in the great storm were the Northumberland, Restoration, Stirling Castle, and Resolution—third-rates—the two former with all hands. In the Stirling Castle seventy men and nine officers were saved, and in the Resolution all hands were saved. The Mary, Newcastle, Reserve, York, and Vigo—fourth-rates—were lost; with the Mary all hands were lost except the captain, who was on shore. In the Newcastle only twenty-four men were saved; in the Reserve all hands lost except three officers who were on shore. The crews of the York and Vigo were saved. A mortar bomb and the Eagle advice boat were also lost, but crews saved. This memorable storm of November 27, 1703, did equal damage on shore. The leads on the roofs of the London churches were rolled up like scrolls. London Bridge was choked by a mass of barges and small craft torn from their moorings. Queen Anne and her husband, startled from their bed at St. James's, saw rows of ancient trees being torn up by the roots in the park. Whole families were crushed under their own roofs, including the Bishop of Bath and Wells, with his wife. The loss to the navy amounted to thirteen men-of-war totally destroyed, and 1,519 seamen drowned.

directing Captain Martin to sail with the Prince
George to Spithead. Accordingly he weighed from
the Downs on the 12th, and arrived there on the
16th. Nothing remarkable happened whilst he lay
here, unless it be the arrival of the King of Spain
in the Peregrine from Holland, who was saluted
with twenty-one guns by all the ships. This was
on the 26th, and eight days after the Prince George
went into the harbour, and Captain Martin had
leave to go to London, to taste the balm of social
life after the fatigues and dangers of the late campaign. During this time there had happened some
alterations in his family, by the death of his second
daughter Mary, who died February 15, and the
birth of another daughter, born November 13,
1703, who was named Christian.

The Prince George having suffered very much
in the late storm and the preceding campaign, her
reparation took up more time than was expected;
so that Vice-Admiral Leake, who had received
orders to follow Sir George Rooke with the rest
of the ships and the land forces to Lisbon, was
obliged to strike his flag on board that ship in the
harbour, and hoisted it on board the Newark[1] to
prosecute his orders, directing Captain Martin to
follow as soon as the Prince George was ready.
Two days after Vice-Admiral Leake sailed. On
March 6, Captain Martin sailed out of the harbour
to Spithead, where the next day an unlucky accident happened. Five of the carpenter's crew going
down into the well just after pumping were taken
up for dead, one of whom was quite suffocated, and
the other four, though they came to themselves,
were very sore and much convulsed. The 31st,
having taken in his provisions and marines, he ran

---

[1] A third-rate of eighty guns and 500 men.

out to St. Helen's, and the next day sailed with
four sail of men-of-war and thirty sail of merchant
ships, and on the 21st arrived at Lisbon, where
Captain Martin found Vice-Admiral Leake, who
came and hoisted his flag on board him the next
morning.

On April 27, 1704, the whole fleet sailed from
Lisbon, and on May 10 they anchored in Altea
Bay, and having watered sailed for Barcelona, and
arrived there on the 17th. The town was bombarded and the marines landed, but to no purpose ;
wherefore they re-embarked the forces and left that
place. They bore away for the Isles of Hyères, but
met with such hard gales of wind that the fleet was
dispersed and received considerable damage. Soon
after they had advice of the French fleet, and on
the 27th got sight of them ; whereupon the whole
fleet chased, but the enemy sailed so much better
that they soon lost sight of them. They then
watered at Altea, and on June 14 passed the
Straits, and two days after were joined by Sir
Clowdisley Shovell with twenty-three sail. On July 7
they came to Cape Malaga and watered with some
opposition, and the admirals having determined to
attack Gibraltar (the attempt upon Cadiz being
judged impracticable without more land forces), on
the 20th they put over from the Barbary shore.
The following day the marines were landed on the
neck of land to the northward of the town to cut off
their communication with the country, and the day
after the town was cannonaded and bombarded.
The boats of the fleet made an attack at the South
Mole head, upon which the enemy sprung a mine and
blew 100 of the sailors into the air, whereof forty were
killed and the rest wounded ; notwithstanding which,
they took the platform and a redoubt ; whereupon the governor, having but a small garrison,

surrendered.   After this the fleet watered on the
coast of Barbary, and having completed this necessary work, and standing over for the Spanish shore,
on August 9, about eight in the morning, they discovered the French fleet.

It is not necessary to give a particular account
of the battle,[1] especially as I have already done it in
the life of Sir John Leake; it is material only to
relate the circumstances wherein Captain Martin
was immediately concerned.   The fleets were pretty
near of equal force, but the confederates were foul,
weakly manned, and wanted ammunition, by which
circumstances they were rendered greatly inferior.
Notwithstanding these disadvantages the confederates pursued, and the enemy fled before them two
days, and having entirely lost sight of them, the
admiral thought it not advisable to follow them
further, but soon after, standing in towards the
shore, they discovered the French, who had run till
they were tired, or till they had got them a stomach
to a battle; they seemed, however, not quite resolved, so the confederate fleet bore after them in a
line all night, and the next morning being Sunday,

[1] The English admirals were Sir George Rooke, Sir Clowdisley
Shovell, Sir John Leake, Rear-Admirals Dilkes, Byng, and
Wishart, the Dutch Callenburgh and Wassenaer. Half the marines
left at Gibraltar—900 men—were taken on board the fleet again,
the rest being left in garrison under the command of the Prince
of Hesse-Darmstadt.   The French fleet was discovered off Cape
Malaga, and on Sunday, August 13, they were found to consist of
fifty ships of the line, and twenty-four galleys, besides frigates.
The English force consisted of fifty-one line-of-battle ships, but
indifferently manned and short of their complements. The Comte
de Toulouse was in command of the French fleet, with the Marquis
de Villette leading the van. The allied van was under Shovell and
Leake; Rooke, Byng, and Dilkes were in the centre, and the
Dutch formed the rear. The battle began by Leake bearing
down on the vice-admiral of the enemy, the Marquis de Villette.
They were engaged at half gunshot for an hour and a half.

August 13, they joined battle, Vice-Admiral Leake, in the Prince George, with his squadron, leading the van of the confederate fleet, and began the battle. It was hot work and hot weather, and they had a long summer's day before them. Vice-Admiral Leake and Captain Martin both agreed in opinion to engage the French van close aboard, that every shot might do execution, knowing they were short of ammunition for a long fight; but the vice-admiral of the enemy's van as much avoided it, by sometimes making sail and then shortening, so that the Prince George could get no nearer the French admiral than half-gun shot. About half-past ten the battle began, and the Prince George engaged the French vice-admiral very smartly for an hour and a half, constantly edging down upon him to get close, which he absolutely avoided; and, in short, having enough, forged ahead, the rest of the van following, so that about half an hour past two the French van bore out of the line much disabled, and did not stop till they had got a mile to leeward. Vice-Admiral Leake was desirous to improve this advantage and cut off their van from the rest of the fleet, but being obliged first to have the approbation of Sir Clowdisley, who commanded the whole van, he despatched Captain Martin to him for that purpose. But Sir Clowdisley, out of diffidence, not concurring with the sentiments of Vice-Admiral Leake, the confederates lost an advantage, and the van remained spectators only of the battle in the centre and rear, which lasted till night put an end to it. In this engagement the Prince George was very much torn in her masts and rigging, so that they could not trim the sails, had fifteen men killed, and fifty-seven wounded. They had likewise eight of their guns dismounted, and but three rounds of shot for their upper and quarter deck guns, and none for the

middle and lower tier, though he left off firing some
hours before the centre and rear ; and some of
Vice-Admiral Leake's division had been without
some time before, and had fired with powder only
to amuse the enemy.   Amongst the slain a young
gentleman, a volunteer in the Prince George, had
his head shot off by a cannon ball while he was
receiving orders from Captain Martin, who was
covered with his blood and brains.   Captain Martin
had another escape no less singular : as he was
taking orders from the admiral, upon the poop, to
go to Sir Clowdisley, a shot passed between the
admiral and him, and equally surprised both, not
immediately perceiving whether himself or his
friend were hurt ; and though they both escaped
the shot, yet Captain Martin received several
wounds from the splinters, one of which stuck in
his eyebrow and made him think at first he had
lost his eye, as indeed it threatened.   And as it is
remarkable that Admiral Leake never received but
one hurt, and that a very inconsiderable one by a
splinter, so it is not less remarkable that Captain
Martin never was in any engagement but he received several, so various are seamen's fortunes.

There's another remarkable instance likewise of
an escape in this battle which I can't help mention-
ing.   Captain Martin had a steward whose name
was Daniel Milker, by birth a German, a very faithful, honest servant, by trade a tailor.   This man,
having no proper business on deck, was ordered
below with the chaplain and doctor ; nevertheless,
just before the battle began, he would come upon
the quarterdeck to attend his master, which, when
Captain Martin perceived, he called to him, ' Go
down below, Daniel,' said he, ' you have no business
to be shot.'   ' Sir,' says he, ' do you think I will
stay below while my master is on deck ?   Do you

think I will leave my master? No, sir, I'm a German, I scorn it, live or die, what pleases God.' So he continued upon deck by his master; but he had not been long there before a cannon-ball took him full upon the breast and down he fell, and though an eighteen-pound shot, had only knocked him backwards and taken away his breath. His master, thinking him shot, ordered him to be taken away, but he, discovering his breath a little, got upon his knees: 'Oh Lord, sir,' says he, 'oh Lord, here's the shot that hit me, but I believe I a'nt killed,' at the same time pointing to the shot that lay between his legs. 'Zounds!' cries the captain, 'get up and fight, ye dog, if you are proof against a cannon ball nothing will hurt you.' 'Oh Lord, sir,' says Daniel, 'I have a great pain at my stomach, if you please I'll go down,' and taking up the shot he carried it along with him. Whether every shot (as King William used to say) has its commission, and this its *ne plus ultra*, we cannot determine; but if fate had no hand in it, it will be difficult for chance to determine so exactly; and I believe it is the first example in history that a man has repulsed a cannon-ball with his bare breast, and much less without hurt, for he received only a small bruise. After this Daniel was content to remain below all the rest of the battle, and being a conscientious fellow he religiously observed that day as a thanksgiving for his deliverance, and preserved the shot as a memorial of it. I knew him thirty years afterwards, when he kept a slop shop in Chatham and was in very good circumstances, he then observed that day in the same manner and continued it till his death.

But to return to the battle, or rather the circumstances and proceedings of the fleet after the battle. In the night after the battle the wind shifted, whereby the enemy had the weather gage, and it was in their option to renew the fight; but they declined it, keeping at two leagues distance, looking at the confederates, who all that time were rummaging for shot. But the enemy had been so roughly handled the day before that they had no stomach for a second course, wherefore they stole away in the night, and by help of their galleys were four or five leagues to windward the next morning, and at length got quite off. The confederates followed them, not desirous to renew the fight, but to maintain their honour; but had the enemy been hardy enough to stand another brush, the confederates, to do all that was possible, had resolved to board and fight it out hand to hand; but hearing the enemy were gone to Toulon, they stood for Gibraltar, where they arrived on the 20th, having acquired sufficient honour to fight the French fleet and secure the important conquest of Gibraltar.[1]

Upon the arrival of the fleet at Gibraltar, it was resolved to leave Sir John Leake with a squadron abroad for the winter guard, and to proceed with the rest to England. The Prince George, having received considerable damage in the engagement, not being in a condition for winter service, but under

[1] 'Sir George Rooke, in his account of the battle, says he never observed the true English spirit so apparent and prevalent in our seamen as on this occasion. Sir Clowdisley Shovell says the engagement was very sharp, and he thought the like between the fleet never had been in his time. The French, though their van was forced to give way, behaved remarkably well. For this was the most equal, and consequently the hardest struggle for mastery that had happened between an English and a French fleet. Till this time the French had never ventured a battle but with great odds on their side. Many of the English ships had no more shot and were unable to continue the fight, but this was fortunately unknown to the French. The result of the battle was that Gibraltar was saved, the French retreated to Toulon, and the English remained masters of the sea.'—*Life of Sir John Leake*, 91.

a necessity to be refitted, she was one of those appointed to go home, for which purpose Sir John Leake removed his flag, on August 24, on board the Nottingham,[1] and the next day Captain Martin sailed with the fleet for England. They all kept company till the 31st, when Sir John Leake, with his squadron, parted for Lisbon. The rest pursued their course homeward, some of them in a very bad condition, especially as to men ; the Prince George, what with wounded and sick, of whom above one hundred were down with fluxes and fevers, and the marines left at Gibraltar, which were a part of their complement, she had not three hundred sound men aboard. But having the good fortune to meet with a favourable passage, they arrived in safety at St. Helens on September 24, and four days after the Prince George went into Portsmouth harbour, where she continued till March 8 following. This was an agreeable recess to Captain Martin after the late fatiguing campaign, part of which he had leave to be at London with his family. But as soon as the Prince George came out of the dock he returned to Portsmouth, that he might not be wanting to the public service ; for it is to be remarked, and not improperly here, that he was punctual to an extreme in complying with his duty, and would have his family with him at Portsmouth, when others would have been with their families at home ; and even when he was at Portsmouth confined himself to his ship in a manner that no other captain did. On March 8 the Prince George ran out to Spithead, and on April 3 following to St. Helen's, in order to proceed with three other men-of-war. On the 7th they left St. Helen's to prosecute their voyage, but were forced into Torbay. They weighed from thence

---

[1] A fourth-rate, sixty guns and 365 men.

on the 14th, but the next day were obliged to put
back again, and on the 19th received an express to
stop there till further orders, whereupon, on the 28th,
they made sail for Spithead, and anchored there the
next day, where they remained till May 23, and
then sailed in company with the fleet under the
command of Sir Clowdisley Shovell. They arrived
at Lisbon on June 9, 1705, and on the 13th Vice-
Admiral Leake came on board the Prince George
and hoisted his flag. Three days after the King of
Spain [1] and the Prince of Brazil came off to see the
fleet, and were saluted by each ship with fifteen guns,
and repeated four times. On the 22nd the fleet
sailed from Lisbon to cruise off Cape Spartel till
the Lord Peterborough joined them, which he did
three days after, with the King on board. On the
30th the fleet watered at Altea under the protection
of the marines, and the wind blowing hard at east
detained them in that bay till August 5. They then
sailed for Barcelona, and arrived there on the 11th.
As they designed to attack that place, the forces were
immediately landed, and with very little loss, notwithstanding the sea ran very high. On the 15th, King
Charles landed, under a discharge of the cannon of the
fleet and the general acclamation of the people on
shore. Soon after, by the advice of the Prince of Hesse,
the Castle of Montjuich was assaulted and taken,
but with the loss of the Prince, who was killed in the
attack. After this the siege of the city was carried
on by the assistance of the fleet, which not only
furnished cannon and ammunition, but gunners and
seamen to manage them on the batteries, every ship
furnishing their quota. The proportion from the
Prince George was a lieutenant with thirty seamen,
besides gunners, carpenters, with three cannon ; and

---

[1] Archduke Charles, proclaimed by the allies, and received by
the Catalonians as Charles III.

the boats were constantly employed in carrying ashore ammunition, provisions, stores, and other materials for the use of the land forces. In short, a breach being made on the 23rd, the viceroy capitulated, and the capitulation was signed on the 28th. That day and the following it blew so hard that several of the transports were driven ashore and lost, and a twenty-oared boat, belonging to the Prince George, which had been sent ashore with shells and shot to the camp, was unfortunately lost, and a lieutenant and twelve men drowned. On October 3 the garrison were preparing to march out of the town, pursuant to the capitulations, having a prisoner of state with them ; and as they were passing through the gate towards the Mole, the prisoner, seeing some of the friends of King Charles, called out, ' *Viva Carlos tercero!* ' upon which the French officer who had charge of him immediately drew a pistol and shot him dead upon the spot. Those he had spoke to, seeing this, immediately shot at and killed the French officer, being exasperated at this insolence ; and remembering the tyrannical government of the French and Velasco, the viceroy, at the same time they shot the sentinel at the gate, seized the gate, and, driving the guard out upon the mole, called to arms, proclaiming that Velasco, the viceroy, before he left the town, intended to plunder it and cut all their throats. The alarm bell was rung, and in a quarter of an hour the whole city was in arms, the shops shut, and the streets blocked up to prevent the motions of the horse, every man standing upon his defence.

Captain Martin was ashore at that time, and in a shop in the city, when the tumult happened, so that he was necessarily involved in the tumult, and found himself engaged for King Charles in a manner he never intended, though he was one of his party.

The garrison endeavoured to get to the rendezvous, but were shot from the windows and doors of the houses, and in less than an hour and a half the inhabitants which had got together had made above 1,000 of the enemy prisoners, horse and foot, and, being joined by a regiment of dragoons of the garrison which came over to them entire, they drove Velasco and the rest of his broken army into two of the great bastions, where they were obliged to call in our forces at the breach for their protection. Whilst this disorder happened in the town, a spout broke in the harbour, attended with a whirlwind, which overset several settees, both laden and at anchor, turning them bottom upwards, whereby many were drowned, and those on board were obliged to catch hold of anything near to prevent their being carried up into the air, to the great amazement of the beholders. In the evening Velasco was brought off privately, not daring to stay on shore all night.

Two days after there was a violent storm, attended with extraordinary thunder and lightning and much rain. The thunder and lightning did considerable damage amongst the shipping; on board the Prince George many men were struck senseless for some time, both on the quarter-deck, between decks, and in the hold. It blew so hard that Captain Martin veered away to three cables on his best bower, and several ships drove foul of one another. Some of the Dutch transports were drove ashore and lost, with numbers of boats. The city of Barcelona having been thus reduced to the obedience of King Charles the Third, and the garrison supplied with all necessaries from the fleet, Sir Clowdisley Shovell sailed with the fleet for England, the 12th inst., leaving Sir John Leake in the Prince George, with a squadron under his command designed for the winter service abroad. Two days after Sir John left Barcelona with his squadron for Lisbon ; in their passage took a French settee laden with broad cloth and serge, and forced another ashore and burnt her, and on November 24 anchored at Altea, where he stayed three days to water the ships, under the protection of the marines. They had the misfortune to meet with contrary winds, which occasioned a most tedious passage, and rendered much more so than it would otherways have been by the Dutch men-of-war, the English being obliged to bear down to leeward every day to keep them company, which they did till they were in danger of starving, being reduced to two pounds of bread per man a week. Wherefore, as the contrary winds still continued, on December 8 they left the Dutch.

The 20th they had hard gales which split their sails and obliged them to lay by under a mizen, and the same weather continued all the next day, when they shipped a great sea in the Prince George, which staved a nine-oared boat all to pieces in the tackles, though hoisted close under the upper tier of guns, and a plank in the ten-oared boat on the booms. The day after it blew a storm, wherein the Leopard [1] man-of-war lost her mainmast close to the deck, and the head of her mizen. On the 27th they reached Gibraltar, having been ten weeks and five days from Barcelona. Here they hoped to have been supplied with provisions, but could get only a small quantity of pork, a little bread, and a little butter ; and, being reduced to two pounds of bread per man a week, and half allowance of all other species, they were obliged to take out of a merchant ship thirty bags of rice to supply the want of bread, and fourteen

---

[1] A fourth-rate, fifty guns and 280 men.

casks of oil, paying for the same. On January 5, the wind coming easterly, they sailed from Gibraltar, and, looking out sharp, the next morning one of the squadron took a French merchant ship of twenty-four guns, from Cadiz, laden with wine, oil, and Spanish wool. The following day they had also the good luck to meet with the so long wished for ships with provisions, which the admiral had wrote to Lisbon to be sent to him from thence ; and, having distributed amongst the squadron what was necessary, the victuallers were ordered to go forward in quest of the Dutch. At length, after a miserable voyage of thirteen weeks and three days, they arrived at Lisbon on January 16, having been reduced in that time to a biscuit per man a day, and sometimes to half a biscuit, and for three weeks no bread at all. Water was also wanting some part of the time, so that many who would have recovered, and did recover their distemper, perished for want ; and it was a most lamentable spectacle to see some, grown delirious, fall down and die in the action of feeding themselves. An instance of so long and miserable a passage was perhaps never known before in those seas. Captain Martin buried fifty men on board the Prince George, besides three times that number in a dangerous condition, for they had been sickly the whole voyage ; so that, reckoning from the time he sailed with the Prince George from England, he had buried upwards of three hundred men.

Upon the arrival of the squadron at Lisbon, the utmost dispatch was used in refitting the ships, more especially as Sir John Leake had received orders to proceed as soon as they were ready, and attempt to take or destroy the galleons at Cadiz. As the Prince George was leaky, and under a necessity of being careened before she proceeded upon further service,

Sir John removed his flag to the Ranelagh,[1] and Captain Acton,[2] of the Grafton,[3] being unable by reason of sickness to go to sea, Captain Martin desired to command that ship for the present expedition, for the Grafton being a seventy-gun ship and a prime sailer, and not doubting but they should surprise the galleons in the bay of Cadiz, or come up with them at sea, he would have a fairer opportunity to make his fortune than by continuing captain to the admiral. For this reason his brother very readily agreed to it, and by his order on February 17, 1705-6, appointed Captain Acton, as soon as he was able, to take upon him the command of the Prince George, whereby, in the meantime, he had the command of a second-rate instead of a third-rate.

That the design upon the galleons at Cadiz might be carried on with the greater secrecy, and the enemy surprised, the admiral had procured an embargo to stop any intelligence being carried thither by sea ; proper dispositions were likewise made for attempting the galleons if in Cadiz bay or attacking them at sea. Amongst others, the Hampton Court,[4] Captain Charles Wager,[5] and the

[1] A third-rate of eighty guns and 540 men.

[2] Captain Acton was in the Kingston at the taking of Gibraltar. At the battle of Malaga he was obliged to haul out of action owing to all his shot being expended, together with several other ships. Their captains were tried by court-martial for this, but were honourably acquitted.

[3] A third-rate of seventy guns and 440 men.

[4] A third-rate of seventy guns and 440 men.

[5] Afterwards commodore in the West Indies, when he fought four Spanish treasure ships, his own share of prize money being 100,000*l.* This was in 1707. He was knighted, and became a rear-admiral. He was Comptroller of the Navy from 1715 to 1718. From 1733 to 1742 Sir Charles Wager was First Lord of the Admiralty. He died in 1743, aged seventy-nine, and there is a monument to his memory in Westminster Abbey.

Grafton, Captain Martin, being both seventy-gun
ships, and the two prime sailers of the squadron, were
appointed to go ahead of the fleet and stop the
galleons.   These two captains being thus upon
equal terms, resolved to have equal fortune, and
came to the following agreement: 'We, Charles
Wager, commander of his Majesty's ship Hampton
Court, and Captain Stephen Martin, in command of
her Majesty's ship Grafton, do hereby oblige ourselves to go equal shares in all prizes and profits
arising from prizes that shall be taken by us, or
either of us at sea, or in any of the enemy's ports, or
otherwise during the time we shall be upon the
present expedition under the command of Sir John
Leake ; dated on board the Ranelagh, February 26,
1705-6, and witnessed by the admiral.' This agreement served to prevent any disputes that might otherwise happen about the prizes they should take, and in
that respect was a benefit to the public service.   It
seems they promised themselves a great share in the
galleons, as they were the only two clean ships of the
force, and like two swift eagles, were to secure the
best part of the prey before the others could come up
with them.   Thus had they swallowed up half a
dozen galleons in imagination, and were impatient
till they were upon the wings of the wind.   But the
day before this agreement was executed, viz. February 25, they had a disappointment, which gave
them but a bad earnest of success ; for, attempting
to sail, the castles fired upon them and would not
suffer them to pass, by reason the embargo, as they
alleged, was general, not to suffer any ships to pass,
as well ships of war as others.   It was no doubt a
contrivance of the Portuguese to stop them, they
having a great interest in the galleons ; and it was
afterwards known to be so, and that they suffered
two ships to pass out after the embargo was laid to

give intelligence to the enemy at Cadiz of the readiness of our ships, and to hasten their sailing. The admiral was inclined to have pushed out notwithstanding, but, being at that time upon ill terms with the Court of Portugal, and the Dutch not approving it, he was obliged to stay till an express could be sent to court and return with an order to take off the embargo. It was done, indeed, with as much dispatch as well could be, yet prevented their sailing that day, which was the loss of all. Though they expected the galleons might be sailed from Cadiz, they were not yet without hopes of meeting them at sea. Captain Wager and Captain Martin did not doubt being in the thickest of them very soon. The embargo having been taken off in the evening, they sailed the next morning, being fifteen ships of the line English and ten Dutch, with two frigates, four fireships, and a bomb. The Hampton Court, Grafton, and Falcon, pink, being the only clean ships in the squadron, the admiral detached them to stretch ahead into the station he intended to be in. The 28th these advanced ships chased two or three sail, but not coming up with them at night, blowing fresh, they shortened sail not to lose sight of the fleet. Captain Martin was on deck till midnight, and then going down, left particular charge with the lieutenant of the watch to observe the admiral, that they might not lose sight of the fleet, considering that the admiral might get advice of the galleons and tack in the night, which accordingly happened ; and these advanced ships not seeing the signal when the admiral bore away, they all lost company with the fleet. In the morning, by daybreak, Captain Martin looked out, and found the Falcon in company, but could not discover the fleet from the topmast head. We may imagine he was transported with anger, thus to be disappointed by

the negligence of his lieutenant, whom he treated in
a proper manner, and immediately confined him.
It was then hazy, and concluding they had tacked
in the night, he tacked to the northward, steering
N. in order to join them, the wind at E. by N.,
Cape Spartel bearing E. by N., twenty-two leagues,
Cadiz N.E., thirty leagues, Cape St. Mary's N.N.E.,
thirty-three leagues; at night he saw Cape St. Mary's
bearing N. by E. four leagues.   But not seeing the
fleet, the next morning he ordered the Falcon to
steer S.E., he steering S.W. into the offing till two
in the afternoon.   At night the Falcon joined him,
and then he made the best of his way for Cadiz, the
rendezvous being off Cape St. Mary's, to remain
there twenty-four hours, and then to cruise in sight
of Cadiz forty-eight hours, afterwards to proceed to
Gibraltar, the place of rendezvous.   Thus raging
like a tiger that had been robbed of her whelps,
the next day, being the 3rd, in the morning he
discovered ten sail off Cadiz, which he took to be
part of the fleet, the rather because on sight of
him two sail bore down towards him; but as soon as
they could fairly make him, they hauled upon a
wind plying up to the town, which he then saw
plain, and discovered them to be privateers.   All but
the two latter got into the bay, but he followed them
so close, that not being able to get about St. Sebastian's point, they ran ashore, all sails standing, between two ledges of rock, close under the castle.
The biggest of the two was a ship said to be the
King's, of forty-four guns, the other of twenty-six;
he stood after them within five fathoms and a half of
water, and cannonaded them, the ships and the castle
returning upon him; but as they were so situated
it was impossible to come at them.   Having, therefore, done them all the mischief he could, night
coming on, and likely to be dirty weather, he stood

off to sea, and spoke with a Genoese settee, who informed him the galleons were sailed six days before.

The next day, being March 4, he chased two sail, which proved to be the Panther and Tiger, bound to Barcelona, with money and officers, and soon after he chased a sail to leeward, and spoke with her, being a Dutch privateer. He then tacked, and stood to the westward till midnight, and then stood towards Cadiz. On the 6th he spoke with a Leghorn ship from St. Lucca, who informed him the galleons sailed from Cadiz on February 27, and soon after with a ship from England, who gave intelligence of the fleet and forces coming from England. The next day he made sail for Gibraltar, the place of rendezvous. In the evening he chased a settee ashore under Cape Travelegar.[1] The following morning he spoke with a Genoese bound for England from Malaga, and in the evening anchored in Gibraltar Bay. Here he received the first account of Sir John Leake by a ship that left him on March 2 in pursuit of the galleons. Captain Martin, believing it to be too late to follow them, he resolved to proceed to the Strait's mouth, and cruise there till Sir John's return, or till he received further intelligence of him. The following day he watered his ship, and on the 11th sailed, but was forced back, and detained two days, then sailed again. He spoke with several ships but could hear no further account of Sir John Leake, but had intelligence of a runner from Genoa that Count Toulouse sailed on February 23 for Barcelona ; he likewise spoke with another runner, and a man-of-war settee, with a packet from the King of Spain for Lisbon, where they were bound ; and they being under apprehension of a sixty-gun French ship that had

---

[1] Correctly, 'Taraf-al-ghár ;' from ' Taraf,' a mountain or promontory, and 'ghár,' a cave, in Arabic, now called Trafalgar.

chased one of them some days before. Captain
Martin kept them company as long as they desired,
and blowing a strong Levant, he brought to about
five leagues to the westward of Cape Spartel under
a mizen ballanced.

On the 18th he discovered three sail, and soon
after three more ; blowing hard, he set his spritsail
and bore down upon them, and the wind dullering
he set his courses and topsails.   By eight o'clock he
told seven of them, and concluding they were
privateers designed to scour him off the coast, he
resolved to attack them.   In an hour's time he came
up with the nearest, who informed him the ships he
saw were the Pembroke, Leopard, Roebuck, Gar-
land, and two victuallers.   The three following days
he continued his cruise, and sharpened by his late
disappointments let nothing pass him.   He spoke
with a great many ships, but none such as he wanted.
On the 19th, in the morning, discovering two sail,
he made the signal for the Tartar to chase one,
whilst himself followed the other.   Soon after he
saw several more, and about nine o'clock joined
them, being Vice-Admiral Leake and his squadron
returned from pursuing the galleons, which were
gone too far to be overtaken.   Only two or three
stragglers fell into their hands, but of no considerable
value ; one of them, however, being taken by the
Hampton Court, Captain Wager, something alleviated the misfortune of the disappointment to
Captain Martin, who had his share according to the
before mentioned agreement.   The same evening,
the admiral receiving intelligence of a French
merchant ship in Cadiz Bay ready to sail, he detached
Captain Martin, with orders to proceed within eight
or ten leagues S.W. of that harbour, to wait her
coming out, and to continue there whilst the easterly
wind lasted.   Accordingly he made sail, and the

next day was upon his station. It continued to blow
hard that day and the following, which split his
mainsail and obliged him to lay by under a mizen.
On the 26th he chased a French privateer of fourteen guns, who ran into the bay, colours flying ; and
by some Swedish merchant ships he was informed
there were eleven French merchant ships, two of
them from Martinico, and the very two he put on
shore on March 3, which made the disappointment
seem the greater when he understood what rich
ships he had so narrowly missed ; but as he heard
they would sail the first westerly wind, he had yet
another chance, wherefore he stood off to keep un-
discovered. The next morning he was W.S.W.
from Cadiz ten leagues, and being hazy he tacked
and stood to the northward, lest the ships might
haul a more westerly course. On the 8th he tacked
to the southward, and the next morning to the
northward again. In the afternoon he discovered
two sail, which he chased till night ; the next day
he kept standing off and on, as he did the following
day, when he saw two sail standing from Cadiz,
but the wind being southerly they stood into the
shore again, or because they saw him, to prevent
which he brought to with his topsails upon the cap,
and in the afternoon chased another sail into the
shore. The next morning, being April 1, early in
the morning he saw the same ship again, and
chased her till night, putting her into a sandy bay
two leagues to the eastward of Cape Travelegar,
and anchored close to her. But to his great mortification she proved a Genoese from Cadiz bound to
Gibraltar. He continued his cruise the two following
days, and seeing a fleet, he soon after joined them,
being Commodore Price, with the victuallers and
transports from Lisbon, with whom he proceeded to
Gibraltar where they arrived on the 3rd, and found

Sir John Leake with the fleet.   After this he was
ordered upon another short cruise, and the fleet
sailing from Gibraltar he joined them again in Altea
Bay.   In the meantime, the Prince George being
arrived from Lisbon, Captain Martin resumed his
command of that ship on April 23, and the next day
Vice-Admiral Leake removed his flag thither from
the Ranelagh.

By this time King Charles, being blocked up in
Barcelona by the enemy, both by sea and land, was
in great distress, and even in danger of falling into
their hands.   Admiral Leake used all imaginable
endeavour to hasten a speedy and effectual relief,
and having luckily joined the reinforcement of ships
from England, it was resolved to go directly thither,
and when the fleet got within three or four leagues
of the place, that every ship should make the best
of their way and attack the enemy in the bay.   But
Count Toulouse, having intelligence of Sir John
Leake's approach, retired with the French fleet on
the 26th, at night, and the confederate fleet got into
the bay the next morning.   This escape the French
must wholly attribute to their good fortune, for had
the wind continued fair but a few hours longer, the
whole fleet had fallen into the hands of the confederates ; but it was enough to relieve the King of
Spain and the brave Barcelonians from the jaws of
their enemies, at so critical a juncture, even whilst
they expected they would storm the place ; to
prevent which the marines and land forces were
immediately landed, and marched to the breach,
to the inexpressible joy of the inhabitants and the
confusion of the enemy, who now not only de-
spaired of success, but on the 30th of the same
month raised the siege with precipitation, leaving
a well-stored camp to the besieged with all their
cannon, warlike stores, and provisions.   The

heavens contributed at the same time to the
enemy's disgrace, by a total eclipse of the sun,
which the French monarch had vainly assumed for
his device. This was certainly one of the most
glorious, remarkable, and fortunate events that
happened during the war, from whence, as Mr.
Boyer observes, we may date the epoch of the ill-
fortune that generally attended the united forces of
France and Spain. A medal was struck in memory
of it at home, by royal authority, and King Charles
not only made a public rejoicing at Barcelona for
this happy relief at that time, but observed that day
annually as a solemn thanksgiving for his deliverance as long as he lived. The day appointed for
a public rejoicing at Barcelona was May 5, which
was celebrated by the cannon of the city and the
fleet with all other possible demonstrations of joy.
The admirals of the fleet waited upon the King,
who received them with great favour. They were
afterwards nobly entertained at the palace. Upon
this occasion, Captain Martin, as captain to Sir
John Leake, attended with the admirals and received the same honours. He also accompanied
his brother when he received the first audience of
King Charles upon the arrival of the fleet, upon
both which occasions they were attended at the water-
side by the King's coaches, conducted thither by a
person of honour, and received with great ceremony.

On May 18 the fleet sailed from Barcelona with
the transports, and arrived on the 24th at Valencia,
where they disembarked the forces. On June 1
they left Valencia, and three days after, being got
the length of Altea, some Spanish gentlemen came
off and acquainted the admiral with the disposition
of the people of Cartagena to declare for King
Charles, upon which the fleet proceeded thither.
On the 5th two Spanish galleys came over to the

fleet, and on the 12th they arrived before Cartagena, and the place was immediately summoned. They desired time to consider of it; upon which a disposition was made for landing the marines, and for cannonading the city by sea. This produced the desired effect, and they sent off deputies on board the Prince George to make their submission, whereupon four men of war were ordered into the harbour, and 600 marines into the city to secure the place.

On June 18 they weighed from Cartagena, and two days after anchored in Altea Bay, where they watered the ships, and sailing thence on the 24th, two days after arrived before Alicante. The governor was summoned, but returned a resolute answer, and it being found impracticable to attempt the city without some land forces, it was resolved to stay there till forces arrived, which they expected from the Earl of Peterborough. On July 10 the forces arrived, but consisted of no more than 1,300 effective men, and the garrison of Alicante consisted of 2,500 men, whereof between 700 and 1,000 were regular troops, so that the commanding officer of the land forces (Brigadier George) thought the siege impracticable; but as the admiral was very much for the siege, and promised to reinforce him with the marines of the fleet and some seamen, the brigadier agreed to carry on the attack by land, whilst the fleet did the like on the side of the sea. Accordingly 800 marines and as many seamen were landed on the 21st, and 500 more to work on the batteries—gunners, carpenters, and seamen. The trenches were opened on shore, and at the same time the city was cannonaded and bombarded by the fleet with so good effect that several breaches were made towards the sea; on the 28th the land forces advanced to take possession of the suburbs. The admiral took the opportunity to land a party

of seamen, who bravely mounted the breach, and,
taking possession of the city, opened the gates to
the soldiers, the governor, Major-General Mahony,
with the garrison, retiring into the castle ; but as
they were plainly discovered mounting the hill,
many of them were stopped short by the cannon
of the ships. In this manner the famous city of
Alicante was taken by the mettle of our seamen, but
the castle still remained in the enemy's possession,
a place almost impregnable, being situated upon
the top of a very high rock. But what fortification
is so strong as to resist the power of gunpowder,
which, if it cannot be effected by cannon in the
ordinary way, it may be torn up from the foundation
by mining ; or if the foundation cannot be moved,
fire from the bombs shall emulate destruction from
heaven. Thus it was with this castle ; though they
continued to batter it with cannon, and sought to
undermine it, this had little effect, but they could
not evade the force of the bombs, which, as well
from the ships as by cannon from the tops of the
houses, rained perpetual fire upon them and destroyed everything wherein they trusted. And the
garrison, unable to bear the hardships they were
reduced to any longer, obliged Mr. Mahony to
capitulate, and the capitulations were signed on
August 24.

Whilst the fleet lay before Alicante, Captain
Martin had a violent fever, as many others likewise
had, by the excessive heat of the country at this
season of the year. For his better accommodation
he was removed on shore, and received great benefit
from the extraordinary care of a Spanish gentleman,
who had a very pleasant house a little way out of
the town. As he knew Captain Martin was the
admiral's captain and brother-in-law, he very readily
embraced the opportunity of receiving him ; giving

H

him the best accommodation, and provided him a careful Spanish nurse, by which means he was soon enabled to get aboard again. It was a sufficient recompense for this trouble to the Spanish gentleman and his family to be under the protection of the English admiral, though Captain Martin was not wanting in point of gratitude for this hospitable kindness, to requite the benefit in many instances very beneficial to this gentleman.

For the honour of a Spanish saint it must likewise be remembered that near the aforesaid gentleman's house there was a convent dedicated to St. Facie, and the reverend fathers hearing of the patient so near them, and knowing their saint was not able to secure them in this time of danger, desired to put both themselves and their convent under Captain Martin's protection, which was readily granted.

When the danger was over, instead of acknowledging the obligation, they very modestly told him that his recovery from his illness was owing to the intercession of their saint, and they hoped he would bestow something upon their convent. It was, indeed, an uncommon act of charity for a popish saint to preserve an heretic. Captain Martin, considering the service we were upon, desired to gain the good opinion of the Spaniards, and complied with their request, and made them a present, and likewise procured some things to be returned them which had been taken away from the convent, for which, no doubt, they prayed for his conversion.

There was another incident that happened to Captain Martin during this siege which must not be omitted, because it has often been related by the gentleman concerned with him as an extraordinary instance of courage, and shows how far a sense of honour will prevail against the most apparent danger.

It was during the siege of the castle of Alicante, whilst he remained at the Spanish gentleman's house. Having got rid of his fever he used to walk abroad every day, frequently accompanied by some of his acquaintance that came to see him. One day, being in company with Major Wyvill, a brave officer of dragoons then at the siege (since lieut.-colonel of the Horse Guards Blue), they walked on discoursing till they were very near the castle, not in the least thinking of the danger they were exposed to, when on a sudden they were alarmed by a cannon shot that passed very near them. The major very fairly ran for it till he got to a place of security, from whence he kept hallooing out to Captain Martin to follow him : 'Zounds, captain,' said he, 'you'll be shot, run for it !' It seems (as they learnt afterwards) they had been perceived from the castle coming that way ; and being by their glasses known to be officers, Mahony had offered a reward to two gunners if they shot him, so that two pieces being levelled at them, the first shot was soon followed by another, which came so near Captain Martin that it beat the dirt about his ears. The major thought him demolished at first, but seeing him come on, cried the more vehemently : 'Run, captain, run ! Zounds, why don't you run for it ?' He replied with a great oath, he never did, nor never would run ; and, drawing his sword out of a bravado, faced about and flourished it over his head towards the castle, bidding them fire and be damned, for all the cannon in the castle should not make him move one bit faster, and so very gravely walked off, though he had two more shots made at him before he got out of harm's way. And when the major afterwards argued the case with him, he insisted upon it that a man might make a retreat with honour, but it was a disgrace to run away upon any occasion.

H 2

Soon after this Captain Martin returned on board the Prince George, and, upon the surrender of the castle, the admiral sent him to General Mahony to settle that part of the capitulation touching their embarkation. Entering into discourse of the siege, the story of the two officers was told, the general being desirous to know who they were, especially him who, out of bravado, had flourished his sword at them. But when Mr. Mahony understood the person he was talking to was the man, he told Captain Martin that if they had known who he was they would not have put him in so much danger.

The proper dispositions having been made for securing of Cartagena and Alicante, the fleet sailed September 2, consisting of thirty ships of the line, &c. The next morning they anchored at Altea, and having watered, left that bay on the 5th. The 8th, being near Iviça, the admiral sent a summons to the governor of that island, who submitted upon sight of the fleet, and saluted them with all their cannon, which compliment was presently followed by the governor and magistrates, who came on board the Prince George to tender their duties to the admiral on behalf of King Charles ; and proper measures being taken for the security of the place, they sailed the 13th. The next day they arrived at Majorca, and summoned the viceroy of that island, but did not meet with so ready a compliance as at Iviça, for he sent a resolute answer that he would defend the place. But the admiral's arguments were so strong and convincing, that a few shells being thrown, though at too great a distance, the inhabitants rose and obliged him to capitulate. A flag of truce presently came off, hostages were exchanged, and the next day the capitulations were signed. The 20th being King Charles's birthday, the magistrates were sworn to their allegiance ; the guns of the city fired three round, and answered by the cannon of the fleet; a grand entertainment was made at the palace for the officers of the fleet, with other demonstrations of joy suitable to the occasion. After this, the admiral having appointed a garrison of marines for the security of the place, and two ships to carry away the viceroy and disaffected persons, he sailed the 23rd for England, appointing Sir George Byng, with a squadron, to remain abroad for the winter guard. On October 2, they got through the Straits, and two days after, off the Southward Cape. Sir George parted with the fleet for Lisbon, the admiral, with five sail of large ships and seven Dutch proceeding for England. The 9th they had a violent storm which blew away their foresail and main topsail, and broke the yard in the slings, and obliged them to lay to under a mizen; and the fleet were entirely dispersed, so that the Prince George was left alone, and saw no more of them afterwards. During the storm a Spanish gentleman, who was the admiral's linguist, was thrown to leeward by the motion of the ship, and split his skull against the side of the cabin, so that he died soon after. And the ship took in so much water that they were in danger of foundering, her preservation was very much owing to the judgment and vigilance of Captain Martin. At length, after a very dangerous passage, they arrived alone at Spithead October 18, and the 22nd following the admiral struck his flag and went for London, with as much honour as ever any admiral brought home with him to England. In this applause of the public for the glories of the late campaign, if so much is due to the admiral, something is certainly due to Captain Martin, his captain, who acted in a double capacity, as captain of the ship and captain to the admiral; by the first having the charge and management of the ship immediately under him, and by the latter the direction and management of the whole fleet, immediately under the admiral, which fleet was greater than perhaps had ever before been commanded by a vice-flag, and executed by a single captain in the double capacity I have mentioned; for it sometimes consisted of fifty-five sail of the line, besides frigates and smaller vessels, the various services and multiplicity of orders produced thereby requiring great skill and application to conduct without confusion; besides that Captain Martin, being in all councils of war, was concerned in the forming those designs which he had afterwards the care to see carried, and which were carried so happily into execution. The 28th, Captain Martin received orders to go with the Prince George to Chatham. He weighed from St. Helens November 5, with the Grafton, and the Vulture fireship, but not being able to carry it about the Oaze, they were obliged to anchor again, but weighed the next morning with hard, squally weather with rain. In the evening he came up with the West India fleet under convoy of two frigates. The following day he passed through the Downs, and anchored at the Longsand Head. Here they had hard squally weather, and when they weighed in the morning they found both flukes of the best bower anchor gone, with part of the shank buoy and buoy rope. At night he anchored off the Naze, three leagues distance; in the morning plied to windward and anchored below the buoy of the Spits. The next day, being the 10th, he weighed again, and the pilot standing too near the N.E. end of the Whitaker sand, ran the Prince George aground. The pilot was under such confusion at this accident, that he was incapable of acting, and after half an hour spent to no purpose to get her off, it being now high water, he gave over all hopes. It was then that Captain Martin undertook it, wore her with some difficulty, and by making the ship's company at the same instant run all aft, had the good luck to get her off and anchored near the place, and at night hove up into deeper water. At this time Captain Martin had his wife and son on board, and not knowing when they might get off, or whether they might get off at all, he thought it proper to send them out of harm's way, and brought a vessel to that was going up the river and put them on board ; but before they had got a great way off, seeing the Prince George off again, the vessel lay to, and he sent his barge to fetch them on board again. The following day they sailed and anchored at Black-stakes, where, having put out the guns and powder, the Prince George was brought to her moorings three days after, and the 20th following, Captain Martin had an order to remove himself and the whole ship's company into the Britannia, having a commission to command that ship, reputed the finest first-rate in England.

On January 21, 1706-7, Captain Martin entered upon the command of the Britannia, at Chatham, though his commission was dated the 10th. He was appointed captain of this ship because his brother, Sir John Leake, designed to hoist his flag there ; but he, being obliged to go suddenly to sea with a cruising squadron, which required a ship ready for the sea at Portsmouth, and fitter for the purpose, he never hoisted his flag on the Britannia at all, which ship, therefore, went no further than Blackstakes, where she lay about two months, and returned to her moorings on June 26. She continued here till August 8 following, when Captain Martin was discharged from her in order to have command of the Albemarle,[1] a second-rate at

---

[1] A second-rate, ninety guns, 730 men.

Portsmouth, Sir John Leake having made choice of that ship for the next campaign in the Mediterranean; wherefore the captain took the greater part of the ship's company with him from the Britannia. Captain Martin's commission for the Albemarle was dated July 30, 1707, and, on August 19, he was entered as captain of that ship. On September 21 Sir John Leake came on board and hoisted his flag. On October 10 following a court-martial was held on board the Albemarle to try Sir Thomas Hardy. The court consisted of Vice-Admiral Leake, as president, and seven captains, Captain Martin being one, who acquitted Sir Thomas; but the merchants who had made the complaint against him raised a clamour, as if the court had been partial in acquitting him, so that their proceedings were reconsidered by the Lord High Admiral and six flags, who approved the sentence of the court. But all this not satisfying the merchants, the affair was resumed by the House of Commons, but soon dropped, there appearing no reasonable grounds of complaint. Three days after the trial Sir John Leake struck his flag and went for London; but returned and hoisted it again on the 28th, being ordered to cruise with some ships in the soundings for the protection of the homeward-bound trade. This requiring despatch, he struck his flag in the Albemarle, in Portsmouth harbour, and hoisted it on board the Nassau,[1] at Spithead; but before he sailed, Sir John Norris being appointed to relieve him in that command, he removed his flag back to the Albemarle, but on the 12th following struck it again and went for London. Shortly after this, there being a promotion of admirals, by the unfortunate loss of Sir Clowdisley Shovell, Sir John Leake was advanced to be

---

[1] A third-rate of seventy guns, 440 men.

admiral of the white, and this was soon followed
by another commission appointing him admiral and
commander-in-chief of her Majesty's fleet. By
this command he was entitled to have two captains
in the ship where he hoisted the Union flag, the
first of the two, by way of eminence, being called
first captain, as being first not only of the admiral's
two captains, but before all other captains, as well
for the honour of the chief flag as because he acts
as his vice, or deputy, carrying all orders into
execution for the government of the whole fleet.
Therefore this first captain has the rank and pay of
a rear-admiral, and sits in councils of war with
admirals when no other captains are admitted. The
admiral is in no way confined or limited in his
choice of a first captain, and in consideration (I
presume) that the duty of the first captain best
qualifies him for a flag, and having the rank of a
flag, it would be a dishonour to descend afterwards
to a private command, such first captain is frequently
promoted to a flag in preference to senior captains,
without being thought an injury to them. The
admiral, too, is always looked upon under an
obligation and in honour obliged to promote his
first captain to a flag after a reasonable time of
service. This is certainly a great privilege, and a
favourable opportunity the admiral has to promote
one whom he is desirous to serve. And this was
the opportunity Admiral Leake had now to serve
his brother-in-law, Captain Martin. There was no
other he could be so desirous to serve as him, not
only by reason of the affinity and friendship they
bore each other, but because he had been his captain
in the nature of a first captain in the management
of a very large fleet, and the admiral knew him to
be thoroughly acquainted with the duty of that
office, having so lately experienced it by the happy

conduct of the late campaign. Under these circumstances Captain Martin likewise expected to be first
captain, and thought he need not ask for it, or that
it were better not to ask. But at length he thought
it necessary not only to ask, but to press the matter
to Sir John, for the following reasons: first, he
knew how much influence Admiral Churchill had
over his brother, and heard that by his means Sir
Thomas Hardy intended to apply for it ; second,
he knew Sir Thomas was not qualified for the
office, and was a person disagreeable to his brother ;
and, third, he could not bear to be supplanted by
so worthless a competitor, who, in case he succeeded,
must command him ; lastly, if he did not press the
matter upon his brother, who was of a pliable
temper and fearful to be thought partial to his
friends, he might be the more induced to do an act
disagreeable both to himself and him, in which case
his brother might possibly wish him to press the
matter upon him that he might use that as an
argument to refuse others. For these reasons he
determined to do so, and accordingly did so by
letter, which was dated from Portsmouth, December
23, 1707. In this he acquainted him that he was
under some concern for what was likely to happen
in the affair of first captain ; 'that, as he had had
the honour to be his captain ever since he had been
a flag, with all fatigues, wherein there had been as
much business as was likely to be at any time for
the future, especially in the last campaign, when
there was fifty sail under his charge, and much
business attending it, and he had acquitted himself
to his satisfaction, there was no reason, he believed,
he should be wanting for the future ; that he had, in
concurrence with the opinion of other flags, admitted
him to sit at councils of war; it had put him before
upon the very foot of a first captain, and wanted

only the title, whereas there being a first, he could not be admitted to that honour, which must lower him both in the eyes of the English and Dutch to see one put between them, that had been so long and closely united, and look like a disgrace and putting backwards. Besides that, it must be grievous to him to take orders from a second that had been used to take them from the first, and, indeed, look too much like a separation. That if it was objected there were many older officers, how many were postponed in making flags, much more for first captain, which is not a matter of right but of favour only. That amongst his seniors there were very few he would think fitly qualified, and if there were two or three he could think so, yet there were other reasons, he believed, why he would not choose them ; and, if he would not have any in the list after Wager, there was hopes left he would have none over him, seeing that this had been done by other flags and could be no prejudice to any older officer who looked for a flag, which he did not, but might indeed entitle him to what he might otherwise miss, which was half-pay as first captain in time of peace. That the reason why he had so few making application to him (as he had been told by several) was because they naturally supposed it would fall to his lot ; so that if the Council did not impose one upon him, which he was sure would not be very agreeable to him, and which, if he objected to, would hardly be done, by naming him, it would be a means to prevent any other that he might like worse. Concluding thus, sir, I did not speak so much for myself the other night, not having sufficiently weighed this matter. But considering the relation I have been in, and am to you, I must still desire to be the first and nearest to you. Begging you to put a favourable construction upon it, for as I have no other friend but yourself to whom I owe my all, I would lose any advantage and submit to any inconvenience rather than put you to any difficulties upon my account ; being with great truth, &c.'

Though this letter contained such reasons it was impossible to answer, yet it was without effect. As Captain Martin suggested, so it proved ; for the Council, or some of them, being influenced by Sir Thomas Hardy's friends, pressed the matter so close that Sir John could not get off, and imposed Sir Thomas upon him for first captain ; and this was chiefly owing to Admiral Churchill, to whom Sir John thought he owed so much, that he must deny him nothing.   It was, indeed, an unfriendly action to impose a captain upon him when he ought to have chosen, and they were conscious of his desire, both by inclination and in justice, to serve his brother. But when, besides this, Sir Thomas was disagreeable to him and most unqualified for that post, it was intolerable, as must evidently appear, by giving a short sketch of the man : he had been raised by Admiral Churchill from being captain's clerk to be a captain, at which time he was so wholly ignorant he did not know one rope from another.   What little experience he got after he was a captain served only to make his ignorance more conspicuous, and though by birth a Guernsey man, he never was a seaman. To these disqualifications were added the most unhappy disposition, wholly composed of pride and ill-nature, which he showed in his outward behaviour, and by a malicious grin ever upon his countenance ; and it was impossible to live a day with him without observing many ill-natured actions, ever being full of flaring taunts not to be endured by men of spirit. Add to all this he was a coward, having no sense of honour, though he had received the honour of knighthood, and at the same time receiving a present

of 1,000*l.*, not for his good behaviour, but for being
the messenger of our success at Vigo. He had
indeed suffered some inconvenience and dishonour
by the merchants at the late trial, and it seems this
was to make him amends for it ; a very unpopular
act, and a very bad reason for putting him upon Sir
John, who was condemned by some for submitting
to it when he might so justly have refused an ob-
noxious person to serve his brother. But we must,
in justice to Sir John, remember at the same time
that all his friends were in the interest of Sir Thomas,
and he must have disobliged all to serve Captain
Martin, which was indeed to disserve him. Wherefore, as soon as Captain Martin learnt how the
matter stood, he gave up all pretensions to it, being
ready to relinquish any advantages (as he said in his
letter) rather than put his brother under any difficulty upon his account. But there was a much
greater difficulty yet remained. It was an easy
matter for Captain Martin to give up his pretensions
to first captain in favour of another, as affairs were
circumstanced, but it was not so easy to submit to
be second captain. The reasons alleged in his letter
are sufficiently strong, but yet made much stronger
when we consider whom this submission must be
made to, to the very man who had supplanted him
contrary to reason and justice ; to a man of such a
temper and inferior qualifications, from whom he
must receive orders, and with whom it was impossible to be on tolerable terms. This was indeed a
difficulty not easily overcome by one of Captain
Martin's spirit, and, indeed, he hardly overcame it ;
but having that extreme friendship and gratitude to
Sir John, he made good his words to him (in his
letter) submitting to the greatest inconvenience
rather than put his brother to any ; whereby, instead
of receiving a favour, he laid an obligation, and Sir

John was very sensible of it. This was the result of the business of first captain, which, though it seemed a proper conclusion, yet time showed to be otherwise; for by postponing Captain Martin's preferment to be first captain he lost a flag, which, by this means, had been effectually secured to him.

By this time the Albemarle was in readiness for the sea, having been very much forwarded by the application of Captain Martin, now second captain, who, as such, is properly captain of the ship, the first captain attending to what relates to the economy of the fleet, and removable with the admiral, whilst the charge and command of the ship remained with the other, who is commonly called second captain (though he is not called so in his commission) only because there is a first, so-called in his commission, which implies the other to be second. On January 18 Sir John Leake hoisted the white flag at the maintop masthead as admiral of the white, and two days after the Union flag, as admiral and commander-in-chief of the fleet for that expedition, upon which occasion he was saluted by the garrison and all the shipping. But though everything seemed now ready, the main thing was yet wanting, which all the vigilance of the officers could not supply, and that was seamen. This deficiency was so great as could not be made up by landmen and marines, for the ship's company was already made up of them. The scarcity of seamen was chiefly owing to the pernicious and unjust practice of turning the men over from ship to ship, without paying them their wages, which was next to serving for nothing; and the marines were no better off, so that when some of them were ordered on board the admiral's ship they mutinied in general for their pay, and would not stir till they were satisfied. When they had overcome these difficulties, and were in all respects ready to put to sea, they were perplexed by contrary winds, which, with the clog of merchant ships, made it impossible to stir. Many times they attempted to sail, but were hindered by the one or the other. At last, on February 6, they sailed from Portsmouth, and by the 10th were got four leagues to the west-ward of Plymouth, when they were forced to bear away for Torbay. On the 21st they sailed from Torbay ; the next day were off Plymouth, and were joined by the trade from thence, but the wind com-ing southerly they were obliged to stand to sea, and were forced back again to St. Helens, the 25th. No sooner were they arrived here than they were advised that the French were at sea and had a design to force Portsmouth harbour, whereupon the proper dispositions were made for securing it, and the fleet was formed in a line at anchor to prevent its being surprised by the enemy. But it being soon known that the enemy were gone for Scotland, their fears for Portsmouth were dispelled, and on March 3, Sir John sailed with the fleet, but not far, for he was put back again the next day, than which nothing could be more vexatious. At length, after these repeated disappointments, the wind favouring, they sailed on March 8 from St. Helens with the squadron, nine sail of transports, and 400 merchant ships. The next morning a ship was despatched to Plymouth to bring out the outward-bound trade from thence, and in the afternoon they joined the fleet. During all this time the admiral had not seen his first captain, Sir Thomas Hardy, since he hoisted his flag. This might have proved very inconvenient to him, by reason of the multiplicity of business which attended the direction of so great a number of ships, besides the business whilst he continued at Spithead and Portsmouth, if he had not had his brother-in-law, Captain Martin, for second captain, who, having acted in that double capacity so long, made the matter easy to him. Sir Thomas took so much time at London to equip himself for the voyage, as if he intended to avoid the troublesome part of his duty, presuming too much upon the interest by which he was made first captain. But apprehending the fleet was actually gone the last time they put back, he made a greater mistake by embarking on board a man-of-war at Plymouth, in order to follow the admiral to Lisbon. By this means he arrived there before him, so the first news the admiral heard of his first captain was on March 27, when he arrived at Lisbon. Sir John only told him his absence would have been very inconvenient if he had not had Captain Martin with him.

On the 27th the fleet sailed from Lisbon with 102 sail of ships of war and transports, and on May 4 got the length of Gibraltar. The next morning they passed the Straits' mouth. On the 12th, being about fourteen leagues from Barcelona, they surprised a fleet of corn vessels, being settees and tartans laden with wheat, oats, and barley, bound to Peniscola, for the use of the enemy's army, of which seventy-five were taken, eight only getting off. This, besides the straits it put the enemy to, afforded great relief to Barcelona, they being in extreme want of corn at that time. Three days after this success, the fleet arrived at Barcelona. The officers of the fleet were received with all imaginable marks of honour and esteem by his Catholic Majesty, and the acclamation of the people, continually repeating, ' *Viva la reyna Anna.*'

From Barcelona the fleet sailed on May 19 in order to transport the Queen of Spain and some troops from Italy thither.[1] The noblemen to whom

---

[1] Elizabeth Christina, daughter of the Duke of Brunswick, wife of the Archduke Charles, called by the allies Charles III. of Spain.

the king committed the charge of his bride were,
Prince Lichtenstein, Count Propesca, and some
others, who embarked on board the Albemarle.
On the 29th they arrived at Vado,[1] in Italy, and
were saluted by the castle of Savona. From hence
the admiral dispatched his first captain to the
queen to Milan to know her pleasure in relation to
the embarkation, and hasten her to the seaside. In
the meantime the forces were embarked with the
dispatch the occasion required, which was very
much owing to the diligence and application of
Captain Martin, who, it must be observed, by
reason of the frequent absence of Sir Thomas
Hardy, and his inapplication and disqualification,
frequently performed the whole and always some
part of the duty of first captain. The queen being
now come almost to the seaside, the admiral removed his flag on the 27th on board the Cornwall,[2]
and sent Captain Martin in the Albemarle with
four other men-of-war to Genoa, to attend her
Majesty's coming. Accordingly he anchored with
the Albemarle near the Mole of Genoa, and took
on board her Majesty's equipage. On June 30, in
the evening, the queen arrived at San Pietro
Darena,[3] near Genoa, but would not go into that
city because they refused to acknowledge her as
Queen of Spain. The next day Captain Martin
new berthed the Albemarle nearer to the place
where her Majesty lodged, and received her bag-
gage on board ; and the following morning she
herself designed to have embarked, but blowing
a fresh sea breeze, she was prevented. However,
about six in the evening, it proving calm, and the
sea much down, her Majesty came on board the

[1] A small port in the western Riviera, west of Savona.
[2] A third-rate of eighty guns and 500 men.
[3] About a mile west of Genoa.

I

Albemarle, upon which occasion they fired twenty-five guns, and every other ship twenty-one. Immediately they weighed anchor, and the next day, at noon, joined the fleet at Vado. The admiral presently rehoisted his flag on board the Albemarle, and gave orders for sailing, but a strong wind prevented them that day. The next morning the whole fleet sailed, consisting of about ninety-six sail, men-of-war and transports, and in ten days arrived at Malero. The same evening the queen landed under a triple discharge of the cannon of the fleet, and on the 21st both their Majesties made their public entry into Barcelona, which was attended with great rejoicings both in the city and fleet. There was a grand entertainment at the palace for the officers of the fleet, and a ball at night, where Captain Martin had the honour to dance with one of the great ladies of the court, being the only officer of the fleet then present, either English or Dutch, that could dance. Her Majesty was likewise pleased to return her thanks to the admiral, Sir Thomas, and Captain Martin, for their care of her person during the time she was on board the Albemarle, and as a grateful acknowledgment of it was pleased to present each of them with a diamond ring. That to the admiral being valued at 300*l.*, that to Sir Thomas at 200*l.*, and that to Captain Martin at 100*l.* ; though none of them of the value they were intended for, but the presents of princes are to be esteemed more for the honour than for the advantage they bring with them.

On July 25 the fleet sailed from Barcelona towards the island of Sardinia, to endeavour to reduce that place to the obedience of King Charles, and arrived before Cagliari, the metropolis of that island, on August 1. Immediately the viceroy and magistrates of Cagliari were summoned to surrender

the island and city. They desired time to consider
it, which was denied them, and the city was bombarded all night. The next morning the marines
of the fleet and some few other forces in the fleet
were landed with 900 seamen ; but the bombard-
ment put the inhabitants into such a consternation that before the forces had reached the town,
they submitted to capitulate upon such terms as
the admiral thought fit to grant, and part of the
garrison listed themselves in the service of King
Charles. His Majesty likewise, by this conquest,
received a supply of 2,000 horses designed for the
enemy, and 3,000 sacks of corn. In the meantime
the new viceroy entered upon his administration,
and on the 8th made a grand entertainment for the
officers of the fleet.

On August 18 the fleet sailed from Sardinia in
order to proceed to Civita Vecchia, to put in execution her Majesty's orders for demanding satisfaction of the Pope, and upon refusal to put his
country under military execution ; but a letter from
King Charles proposing an attempt upon the island
of Minorca put a stop to it ; a council of war resolving that was the most effectual service they
could proceed upon. Accordingly they proceeded
directly thither, and on the 25th arrived before
Mahon.[1] On September 3 the forces and marines
were landed, upon which the town of Mahon submitted, but the strong castle of St. Phillip's held
out. Soon after Major-General Stanhope arrived,
and the trenches were opened ; and it being impossible the castle could hold out long, the admiral
left a squadron to attend that service, and sailed
with the rest on the 8th instant. They touched
at Majorca, and received the compliments of the
viceroy, and having watered, sailed on the 17th.

[1] Port Mahon.

The next day, off Ivica, they received advice of the surrender of St. Phillip's Castle and the whole island of Minorca. On the 26th they passed by Gibraltar, and pursuing their voyage for England, arrived at Spithead on October 19. Three days after, the admiral struck his flag and went for London, leaving orders with Captain Martin to go with the Albemarle to Chatham. He attempted accordingly to sail on the 30th, but was put back, but the next day he sailed with the Stirling Castle and Cambridge. On November 5 he got to Black-stakes, and on the 16th to the moorings at Gillingham. The next day he assisted at a court-martial, held by Admiral Baker on board the Stirling Castle, and continuing at moorings till December 27 ; he then removed himself and company to the Royal Sovereign,[1] at Chatham, having a commission to command that first-rate, reputed the best man-of-war in England.

Soon after Captain Martin came to Chatham he had leave to go to London, and continued with his family a great part of the winter, but in the spring he made frequent trips to Chatham to attend the refitting of the Royal Sovereign, and the beginning of February attended his brother thither, who, being again appointed admiral of the fleet, hoisted his flag on board the Royal Sovereign on February 7, 1708–9. On March 6, Captain Martin sailed to Blackstakes, and from thence, on April 4, to the Nore. Here he entertained two young Muscovite noblemen on board, who came to see the fleet, and particularly the Royal Sovereign, after which they went away in the Mary yacht for Holland. Everything was now ready for a voyage (as they thought) to the Baltic, under the command of Sir John

---

[1] A first-rate of 100 guns and 780 men.

Leake ; but that design being laid aside, and Sir
John appointed to cruise with a squadron in the
Channel, Captain Martin received orders to turn
over part of his ship's company into the Russell, a
third-rate of eighty guns, and to return into the
harbour ; pursuant whereto, on May 14, he turned
over 300 men into the Russell, dispatched them
by his own tender, and on the 23rd sailed with
the Royal Sovereign to Blackstakes.   On June 10
he sent away the admiral's equipage, and the next
day discharged himself and the rest of the ship's
company from the Royal Sovereign to the Russell,
then at the Nore, and went himself on board that
ship the day following.   On the 18th, Captain Martin
sailed with the Russell from the Nore.   On the 20th
he anchored off the North Foreland.   On the 22nd
he weighed and plied in for the Downs, blowing
hard, but just as he was clear of the Gulf Stream
he met Sir John coming out of the Downs in the
Newark, and saluted him with twenty-one guns.
Soon after Sir John came on board and hoisted his
flag, and they were obliged to anchor.   The next
day they sailed with only six sail and a yacht, and
anchored off Ostend, sending two ships and the
yacht, to look into Dunkirk.   The following days
they had hard blowing weather, wherein two of the
squadron and the yacht were driven out to sea, but
joined them on the 29th ; but the Lyme yacht
having received much damage, was sent back
to England.   The following day they weighed and
cruised off the Scaw with very untoward weather.
On July 12 they took two cornships, one of twenty-
four guns the other of eighteen, and retook a collier
pink ; and the next day another cornship was taken.
They continued to cruise off the Scaw till the 24th,
when the Lord Dursley arrived upon the station to
relieve the admiral ; whereupon they made sail for

England, and on the 27th anchored in Dover Road with four sail. Here they took in some beer and water and sailed for Plymouth, and arrived there on August 6.   On the 16th they sailed from Plymouth to cruise in the Soundings for the homeward-bound trade with eleven sail. On the 22nd, being in latitude 49, they chased four sail from morning to night, but being little wind they got from them, and the admiral finding the Russell a very heavy sailer, shifted his flag on board the Kent[1] the day following   The same day a St. Malo privateer of eighteen guns was taken. On the 25th they met with the Turkey and Lisbon trade with their convoy, and having seen them as far as the Lizard returned. They then cruised between the latitude of 46 and 47 for the enemy's trade, and on September 8 took a French ship from Martinique of sixteen guns. Thence they proceeded to their former station to cruise as long as their provisions would last, and the Russell and Berwick, being foul and sailing heavy, were ordered to Plymouth to clean.   Pursuant to this order Captain Martin left the squadron on the 12th, and three days after arrived at Plymouth, running in directly to Hamoaze.

All possible expedition being used to clean and refit the Russell for the sea, on October 6 she was again in Plymouth Sound ; and on the 10th Captain Martin sailed in company with the Newark,[2] Captain Vincent, and four sail more to cruise in the Soundings. On October 19 they chased some ships, which soon after joined them, and proved to be the Lord Dursley with five sail. Two days after a small prize was taken, and on the 24th another from Martinique.   On November 2 they saw a fleet and chased ; the Russell, being nearest, was soon in

[1] A third-rate of seventy guns and 440 men.
[2] A third-rate of eighty guns and 500 men.

the thickest of them, but they proved the Barbadoes fleet, consisting of thirty-eight sail. These the Lord Dursley ordered Captain Martin to take under his convoy to the Downs, and one of them being a much heavier sailer than the rest, he took her in tow. On the 5th he parted from the Lord Dursley with his convoy, and the Weymouth and St. Albans, who were to accompany him on his way to Plymouth. The next day, coming off the Eddystone, he ordered the Weymouth to stand in and make the signal, and for the two prizes to come out, who stood ahead immediately; but finding the wind scanted upon her, Captain Martin stood in and made the signal himself, viz., an English ensign at the fore-topmast head and three guns fired; and then tacked to the northward, repeating the signal; and then to the southward, under his topsails only for that night. Next morning the Weymouth stood in, and joined him in the afternoon, with an account that the prizes could not get out but at Grimsby Sound, which would be late; and, having a lee tide under foot, durst not bring to, so thought proper to join him before night. The next morning (the 8th) at daybreak he saw nine sail ahead, standing as he did; whereupon he made sail and showed his colours. They answered with Dutch. Then he chased, ordering the Weymouth and St. Albans to do the same, being satisfied they were French; six sail immediately kept the wind, the other three bearing away. Nevertheless the St. Albans took two and the Russell one, and retook the Endeavour transport, laden with junk, from Plymouth to Bristol, which had been taken the day before by five privateers, from thirty to twelve guns. One of the prizes was laden with salt, the other five being the privateers before mentioned. Captain Martin pursued, but finding it to no purpose, gave over the chase. The following day he sent the St. Albans into Plymouth with the prizes, a Barbadoes ship called the Plymouth Merchant, with an express from Lord Dursley, and then made sail ahead with the Russell and Weymouth after two privateers, but not coming up with them by eleven o'clock, he returned to his convoy. In the evening it began to blow hard and continued so all the next day, in which time they ran fifty-six leagues, and on the 9th, at night, he anchored with his convoy in the Downs. The next day the merchant ships sailed for the river, and the following day Captain Martin put some French prisoners on shore.[1] Being directed, he continued in the Downs till further orders; and some few days after he put Sir John Leake's equipage on board a tender for London. Captain Martin continued in the Downs till December 15, when he weighed and turned out of the Downs with twenty-four sail of merchant ships under his convoy, and two days after anchored with them at Spithead. Here he continued till January 17, when he ran out to St. Helen's, but was remanded back to Spithead the same day. On the 29th following he ran out again in company with the Lancaster (Commodore Rupert), the Nonsuch, and fourteen sail of merchant ships, most of them East Indiamen. The next day they sailed from St. Helen's and stretched it to the northward; but two of the Indiamen having received damage, one of them by going ashore, and the other by losing her foremast and bowsprit, put back to Spithead. The day after they got the length of the Start, and blowing hard, and not being able to fetch Plymouth, they bore up for Torbay and anchored there. On February 3 they received an express,

[1] On December 9, 1709, his sister-in-law, Lady Leake, died at Mile End, in the fifty-third year of her age, and was buried at Stepney.

with an account that the Kent had been chased into Plymouth by a French squadron ; whereupon the captains had a consultation, and, considering the wind was westerly, the Indiamen uneasy, and that two East Indiamen and one West Indiaman of their convoy were behind, it was resolved to return to Spithead ; but if the wind came to the eastward before they got thither, to proceed. Accordingly they weighed from Torbay, and kept on with a fine easy gale to the eastward ; but, falling little wind, they anchored, Peverel Point bearing N. by W. four leagues, but weighed again upon the flood. The next morning they kept plying up to Dunnose, and in the afternoon were joined by the Dragon, Severn, and Aldborough, with thirty-three sail of merchant ships. They then bore up again for Plymouth, and the next day arrived there ; but, turning in, the Russell had the misfortune to strike upon the Tinker or Swiftsure rock at dead low water, but got no damage, though she lay near an hour upon it.

On February 27, 1709-10, Captain Martin sailed from Plymouth with four sail, as convoy to sixty sail of merchant ships, from thence to Spithead ; by the way he hauled in shore, for the Topsham trade, and being joined by them, made sail, and the next day arrived at Spithead. Here he continued till April 1, when he went into harbour to have the Russell cleaned and repaired, and having put out the guns, stores, &c., the 19th hauled into the dock, when they discovered some of the false keel gone, and there not being water enough to get her on blocks in the dock, they got her out of the dock again, and were obliged to careen her. On May 5, he sailed out of the harbour, and continued there till June 10, being then ordered to St. Helen's to relieve the Torbay as guardship there, and the Hare sloop was put under his command some days after. On July 6, he ran into Spithead, being appointed one of the squadron under Admiral Aylmer, which sailed two days after. On the 12th, the fleet arrived in Portland Road, and struck yards and topmasts, it blowing very hard, which continued for several days. But the 21st they weighed, and the next day anchored in Plymouth Sound. They made no stay here, only till the Lisbon trade got out, with whom they sailed the next day, the fleet consisting of fifty-eight sail of merchant ships under convoy of thirteen men-of-war. On the 27th the Cornwall, with three sail more, parted with the trade for Lisbon, about sixty-eight leagues west of the Lizard, latitude 48° 13', which being their appointed station, the squadron lay by. The next day they made sail, and the following discovered fifteen ships, whereupon the whole fleet chased, and continued to do so with a pressed sail all night ; at eight in the morning the Assurance took one, being a merchant ship with salt for Newfoundland ; about eleven the Kent was well up with his chase, who, observing him to be greatly ahead of the rest, and finding no way to escape, bore down right upon him, and gave him a broadside. The dispute held near an hour, by which time Captain Martin and two other ships coming up, she struck, and proved to be the Superbe,[1] a French man-of-war, of sixty guns and 460 men, who was convoy of fifteen sail for Martinique, to see them out of the Soundings. It was very fortunate to meet with this famous ship of the enemy's at this time, not only because she was the prime sailer of the French fleet, and had taken many prizes, but because, hav-

---

[1] This Superbe, though a king's ship, was lent to the merchants, and was at the time a privateer. There was a curious question about the exchange of her captain.—See Laughton's *Studies in Naval History*, pp. 258-9.

ing been three months off the ground, she was so
foul, which gave our ships an opportunity to come
up with her, which the best of our ships could never
do before, and even now might not have done so, but
through an error of the French captain, who, cutting
her anchors from the bows to favour her escape, it
spoilt her sailing, else she might probably have got
off. She had between forty and fifty men killed
besides wounded ; the Kent had only twelve killed
and thirty wounded, being mostly damaged in her
masts and rigging. The fleet lay by all night to
refit the Kent and the prize ; as they did likewise
the greatest part of the next day, and the prisoners
being distributed to several ships, sixty-four of them
were put on board the Russell. After this they
continued the cruise till August 7, when the admiral
made the signal to bear away, which was done accordingly, and the next day they arrived in Torbay.
Here they watered and continued till the 14th, when
they sailed, and the 19th anchored at Spithead. On
the 21st, the Russell was ordered into the harbour,
and some few days after went into the dock.

On September 2, the Russell being cleaned and
in a condition for the sea, Captain Martin sailed out
of the harbour and anchored at Spithead, and being
short of his complement of men, received ninety-five
from the Royal Sovereign. On the 17th he ran out
to St. Helen's, and on the 20th weighed from thence
in company with the Newark and Torbay, but soon
after meeting with the Sunderland and four East
Indiamen ships, which they were going in quest of,
they all returned to Spithead. On the 29th following, Captain Martin sailed in company with the
Newark, Torbay, and Sunderland, as convoy to the
four East India ships and homeward-bound trade to
the Downs, where they anchored in the afternoon,
and found orders to see the East Indiamen as far as

the gun fleet. Whereupon they weighed the next
morning, proceeding with them. They were obliged
to anchor that night in Margate Road, but the next
day, having seen them to the buoy of the Gunfleet,
they returned to the Downs. Here Captain Martin
continued till the 14th, when, having received orders
to go for Plymouth, he sailed with the Norfolk and
Torbay, and two days after arrived at that port.
Soon after his arrival at Plymouth, he received
orders to proceed with his own ship, the Norfolk,
and Torbay directly for Lisbon, and being arrived
there to receive on board the Russell and the other
two ships a considerable sum of money, and bring
the same to England for her Majesty's service.
Hereupon he made the signal to unmoor the same
day, being October 20, and soon after sailed with
the Russell, Norfolk, and Torbay. In their passage
they met with hard blowing weather, wherein the
Torbay lost her topmast, and three days after another ; so that Captain Martin was obliged to spare
him a topmast. Nevertheless, on the 30th they
saw the Burlings, and the next day anchored
in Lisbon river. Here each ship took on board a
considerable sum of money, but not without great
hazard in getting it off, the same being death by
the laws of Portugal. Nevertheless, a prodigious
quantity is continually brought from thence, which
is done by the priests for advantage, and is the only
safe way of doing it, that method being known and
winked at by the government. But when our men-
of-war are employed upon such service, they do it
in the evening with a party of seamen well armed,
and bring it off in their own boats. There is, indeed,
a guard boat afloat to examine all that pass, which
hailed Captain Martin, and ordered him to bring to,
a man standing with a match ready to fire a swivel
gun if they refused, and they threatened to do so,

even when they knew it was an English man-of-war
boat ; but when he told them, if they fired, he would
return a volley into them, rowing up close to them
with their arms presented, they suffered him to pass.
The money being safe on board, he sailed from
Lisbon November 11, and after a passage of twelve
days arrived at Spithead. On the 28th, Sir John
Jennings, admiral of the white, hoisted his flag on
board Captain Martin's ship, and continued there
till December 8, when the Russell went into the
harbour. But not being in the dock, on the 14th
the flag was hoisted again for that day on board
the Russell, to hold a court-martial to try Captain
Drake, whereat Captain Martin assisted. A few
days after, the Russell went into the dock, and being
refitted returned to Spithead on January 14. Soon
after he received orders to proceed, in company with
the Norfolk, to see the outward-bound East India
ships safe out of the channel, and look out for the
homeward-bound. On the 27th they sailed from
Spithead, and the next day, having seen the trade
safe into Plymouth, made sail with five East India
and three Virginia ships. On the 29th, at noon, they
had hazy weather and much rain, with a great sea
from the S.W., which made the Russell pitch very
much, being N. by E. fourteen leagues distant from
the Lizard. About three in the afternoon the wind
shifted at once from the S.E. to the S.W., blowing
very hard both ways, with a confused sea, enough
to devour a ship, whilst other ships were at the
same time becalmed. Captain Martin hauled out
his mizen and braced to his head sails, the fleet
having done the same, at which time he saw one of
the East India ships without a foremast. Soon
after, word was brought him the bowsprit was sprung,
whereupon he gave directions for carrying the fore
runners and tackles to the catheads, and lowering

the foreyards, &c., in order to secure the masts ; but in less than three minutes' time the bowsprit broke short off, just without the gammoning, and canted fore and aft on the deck, bringing with it the foremast in the waist, and the mainmast falling at the same time with its head on the starboard fifth rail, injuring the mizenmast, which also fell soon after upon the starboard quarter, beating down the ensign staff and poop lanterns. This accident likewise destroyed all her boats and lost their sheet anchor. Captain Martin fired all the guns he could to give notice of his distress, but the weather came on so thick and hazy he could not have any assistance In this accident, however, he had the good fortune to lose but one man, which was the gunner, but several others had their limbs broke and were much bruised. The storm still increased to a very great degree, attended with a prodigious sea, and the ship wanting a proper balance by the loss of her masts, rolled gunnel in, with so quick and violent a motion that made it impossible to stand the deck, or to continue long swinging by the hands, the legs being now useless, for she rolled as if she would have taken a round turn and gone over and over, whereby several of the quarter-deck guns went overboard, three other guns went down the hold, many broke loose and threatened to drive out the sides of the ship, and with great difficulty were secured ; and to hasten the misfortune, having seen an enemy the day before and expecting to have been attacked, the shot were in the garlands, and the cartridge shot cases broke loose, and driving from side to side carried destruction all over the ship. The half ports were likewise broke away, whereby the sea had a free passage in the ship.

In this scene of confusion and distress the men, without hope, got into holes and corners, thinking

only how to secure themselves from being beaten to
pieces by the violent motion of the ship ; so that,
out of 580 men, very few were to be seen upon
deck. Even the lieutenants discouraged the seamen by their example, instead of encouraging them
(though they were esteemed good officers, and
proved afterwards brave captains). But what was
wanting in others Captain Martin made up by his
courage, activity, and presence of mind, which he
never more eminently distinguished than upon this
memorable occasion. He continued upon deck all
night, animating the men, who, seeing their captain
undismayed, were encouraged to keep the deck and
perform his orders. Thus, attended by a few brave
fellows, he performed all that was possible for their
preservation in the present exigency. With infinite
difficulty and labour they made a shift to cut away
the masts, which threatened to beat out the ship's
sides, except the mizenmast and topmast, which
kept fast to the ship by the rigging, and they could
by no means cut away. In the meantime the guns,
which had broken loose and threatened destruction,
were with great hazard secured, as well as others
which, with the ports, were continually working
loose by the prodigious rolling of the ship, so that
no sooner was one secured than another called for
their assistance ; and, had it been neglected, would
soon have sent them to the bottom. This was their
constant employment a dismal, long, dark, winter's
night, yet short of their fears, for none expected to
see the light of another day ; and, indeed, though
they used the means for their preservation, yet,
quite spent with fatigue, they were careless of the
event. At length the day appeared, but without
alleviating their misfortunes, for the same dark,
blowing weather continued. Nevertheless the men,
inspired by the conduct of their captain, appeared

more cheerful and ready to do their duty, and the lieutenants, ashamed of their behaviour the night past, assumed their posts, but with a dejection which showed they had no hopes, fears arising from want of judgment to apply the necessary means in time of danger, and not a cowardly fear. The skulkers which the night had covered were now driven out of their holes, and, conscious of their faults, appeared the more ready to perform their duty. The first thing to be done was to clear the deck, when they missed three of their upper deck guns, several others being dismounted, and discovered that both their spare topmasts were broke asunder; but there was a necessity, as the weather continued bad, to do something, and therefore the captain set up a top-gallant mast and sail for a mizen, to keep the ship to, and got a hawser fast to the mizenmast and topmast, and carried it forward to her weather bow to keep the ship up to the wind. They saw three sail, but none came near them. The next day it continued hazy weather, blowing hard, attended with much snow and sleet. However, they got up a pair of sheers, in order to raise a foremast, which was made of two pieces of their spare topmast, and, finding an opportunity to get on board their mizen-mast, &c., which was fast to the bow, in the after-noon they saw several ships and made the signal of distress; but none came to their assistance. The following day, being February 1, they had moderate weather, but with a great swell. They saw two sail, one of them without a foremast, which Captain Martin judged to be one of their late company. He got up the mizenmast for a foremast, and a foretop-sail yard with a topsail reefed for a foresail. In the afternoon a French privateer of twenty-four guns came near them, within gunshot, and showed Dutch colours; but upon their showing British colours made off, telling him they would send two French men-of-war to his assistance; whereupon Captain Martin fired several shots at him, which did him some damage before he could get clear. This threat of the privateer put them under some apprehensions that if they escaped the danger of the sea they should fall into the hands of the enemy, not doubting but the privateer would be as good as his word and give intelligence of the condition they were in to some French men-of-war, who might easily take them; 'For what defence,' said they, 'can we make?' This was said even by some of the officers, who, perhaps, had rather have been relieved by an enemy than left to the mercy of the sea. When this came to Captain Martin's ears it made him very angry. 'What,' says he, 'are not we able to defend ourselves? We are still a man-of-war, I hope, and not afraid of any one or two ships. Are we not an eighty-gun ship? If we have no sails to manage we have no masts to lose, and the more men to stand to the guns; and let them board us if they durst, the Russell shall never be taken whilst I live or she'll swim.' The following day the bad weather returned, hazy and blowing very hard, with much rain, the sea running so deep and hollow that it made the ship roll gunnel in with an extraordinary quick motion, and not having sail enough to keep her to, Captain Martin ordered to bear up W. by S., the wind at S.E., resolving to continue her so till better weather.

About eleven they passed by a small English runner that lay by under her bare poles; soon after the Russell's foresail flew all to pieces, and immediately they got a mizen topsail bent to a yard, which was hoisted by two tackle foils a small height upon the back part of the foreshrouds, which answered and kept the ship scudding until they bent a spritsail for

K

a foresail. The 3rd was hazy, blowing hard, but being not quite so much sea as the day before, set their mizen, hauled up their foresail, and brought to, with some butts veered away by a hawser from the weather-bow to keep her head to the wind. Notwithstanding all these endeavours, the sea and wind rising caused the ship to roll gunnel in again, which obliged him once more to cut loose and scud away W.S.W. for the ease of the ship, and cut off at the lower reefs two of their topsails for two courses. About twelve at night the wind came at S., he then wore with his head to the eastward, lying E. by S. under a foresail and a mizen. The next day, February 4, and the seventh day of their misery, it pleased God to send moderate weather, whereupon the captain ordered a pair of sheers to be raised for setting up a mainmast, which was made out of two pieces of spare topmast, and they got it up, as also a mizenmast made, with the mizenyard and a suitable foremast. They saw several sail of privateers that came and viewed them, but upon firing some shot at them they made off. The 5th they saw three sail, and spoke with one of them, an English brigantine, who informed Captain Martin that he saw four French privateers that parted four days before from two French men-of-war of sixty guns each off the Southward Cape.[1] That day they bent a mainsail and got up a main topmast, so that they had now as complete jurymasts as they could make themselves ; and it is remarkable, the ship, at best a heavy sailer, went very near as well with these as with her proper mast. In the afternoon the wind came to the S. by E., which obliged him to bring to under a mainsail, but some hours after, the wind coming to the S.W., he made sail again. All night they had a great sea with much wind, and the next day at noon

[1] Cape St. Vincent.

they sounded, and had fifty-five fathoms ; at four they
saw the Wolf Rock between Scilly and the Lizard.
Steering away E. by S. all night, it blowing
extremely hard, with much rain and a great sea,
they ran with their small courses between eight and
nine knots, and split their main topsail, which they
unbent and mended. On the 7th it blew very hard
at W.N.W., with a great sea. They heard several
guns fired, which Captain Martin judged to be a
signal for some fleet to bring to ; and now being to
the eastward of the Start, he resolved to put for
Spithead. But by the violent motion of the ship
the fore-topmast came by the board at midnight,
wherefore he bore up for Plymouth, it blowing hard
at S.E. The greatest part of the following day
they had moderate gales, when he got up another
fore-topmast, and the wind coming to the S.W. he
bore up again for Spithead, being in no condition to
beat the sea with a contrary wind. Soon after he
spoke with an English ship from Gibraltar, called
the James, who informed him he had been attacked
the day before by a French privateer of twenty-
eight guns and boarded, but they were obliged to
put off again, and that he believed they gave over
on seeing Captain Martin in the offing, so that,
although he was disabled and incapable of helping
himself, he had the good fortune to relieve another.
On the 9th it was hazy weather, blowing hard, with
a great sea and much rain. At one in the morning
they wore the ship to the westward, at which time
they lost the fore-topmast. They sounded, and had
twenty-two fathoms of water, whereupon Captain
Martin, believing they were near the shore, at
three he wore again to the eastward, the wind
being then at S W. by S. At daybreak he saw
four sail to windward, one of which he made to

be the Lancaster,[1] who had lost her foremast and bowsprit, the rest merchant ships who had lost most of their masts. At noon, though it was extremely thick weather, he resolved to haul in for the land, and as he expected, saw Dunnose, which, if he had not done in half an hour's time, it would have been impossible to have done that night. About four he anchored at St. Helen's, and the next day (still hazy, blowing weather) he turned in to Spithead. Three days after the Darley, East Indiaman, came in, which was the ship they saw lose her foremast and bowsprit just before they lost their own masts. On the 14th, Captain Martin brought the Russell to her moorings in Portsmouth harbour, and on the 21st following, himself and the officers were discharged for the purpose hereafter mentioned. This was the happy conclusion of the most dangerous and fatiguing expedition, for the time, that Captain Martin had ever experienced. There was not one of the ship's company that expected to survive the first night of the storm, and even afterwards, considering the circumstances they were in, the season of the year, and how they lay exposed to the enemy, had but small hopes. There was such a general panic in the ship that might have brought upon them the misfortunes they feared, had they not been supported and encouraged by their captain, whose presence of mind never failed him in time of danger, and which, under God, was their preservation. This I have heard his lieutenants (when they were captains) own, and at the same time confess their surprise to see him not the least moved whilst they were in the utmost confusion and despair. The inferior officers and common seamen were no less affected by his brave conduct, and declared under his command they would fear nothing. I myself

[1] A third-rate of eighty guns and 500 men.

was a witness to an instance of this kind many years after, when some of his ship's crew, meeting him by accident, expressed their love and admiration of that action with the greatest transport, and even tears in their eyes, so ready are the sailors, though accounted rude and brutish, to acknowledge a benefit, and so much do they admire and love a brave officer.

As soon as Captain Martin arrived at Spithead he received a commission appointing him first captain to Sir John Leake, as admiral of the fleet, which was dated January 26, 1710, the day before he sailed from Spithead with the Indiamen, and had it arrived one day sooner, had saved him all the anxiety and danger of that voyage. But it never could come more seasonably than now, to dispel the gloom that hung upon his mind, and made him forget the fatigues and dangers of the late cruise. As this set him quite at liberty, so, having discharged himself and officers (the 21st) into the Cumberland,[1] where the admiral intended to hoist his flag, he set out to London to take a short calm after the late storm, and taste the pleasures of social life, the very opposite to that which he had so lately experienced.

Captain Martin had now arrived to the first command as a captain, which gave him both the rank and pay of a rear-admiral; for which reason persons from that office are usually preferred to a flag in preference to senior captains, which was the case of Sir Thomas Hardy, who, being appointed rear-admiral of the blue, made room for Captain Martin to succeed him. I have said so much of this office before, when Captain Martin was supplanted by Sir Thomas Hardy, that it will be needless to mention anything further in this place, only to observe that giving Sir Thomas the pre-

[1] A third-rate of eighty guns and 570 men.

ference that time was the occasion that Captain Martin never had a flag—a consequence, could it have been foreseen, neither Sir John nor his brother would have relinquished. This shows the necessity of persevering in what we think right, never to defer a good action, and to serve our friend when it is in our power, for an opportunity once slipped can never be recovered.

Though Sir John Leake had appointed his first captain and chosen the Cumberland, a third-rate of eighty guns, to go to sea in, it was only, as usual, to prepare matters against the spring, when the ships should be ready for the sea, for it was not for any particular service he was appointed, but to command at home, either in the Channel or Soundings, as there might be occasion ; so that Captain Martin had an agreeable recess for some months to blot out the memory of the late disaster. The ships intended to form this home squadron were appointed to rendezvous in the Downs, for which place the admiral and Captain Martin set out on May 9, and the next day the flag was hoisted on board the Warspite,[1] the Cumberland not being yet arrived in the Downs. On the 11th, the Cumberland and four other ships joined him, and two days after the flag was removed on board the Cumberland, the admiral's proper ship. On the 15th, upon advice of fifteen sail of privateers fitting out at Dunkirk, Sir Thomas Hardy, rear-admiral of the blue, was dispatched with nine sail to watch their motions ; and soon after, the admiral having received orders to cruise between Brest and the Lizard, to prevent the enemy's ships getting to sea from that port, he sailed himself on the 22nd, with fourteen sail, and five days after arrived at Plymouth, but left that place

---

[1] A third-rate of seventy guns and 400 men.

the next day, upon advice that the enemy, who had sailed from Brest, were put back. They were now twenty-two sail. The next day, being off Ushant, several ships were sent to look into Brest, and took a boat, which informed them that Mon. du Guay was sailed twenty days; and going close into the harbour mouth with boats, they saw plainly there were no ships there; wherefore, at a council of war, it was agreed to be more for the public service to cruise off the Lizard for the protection of the trade till further orders. On June 9 they received orders to look again into Brest, which was done, and the former account confirmed. Nevertheless, orders came a third time to send some ships to look into that harbour, which, in compliance with his orders, the admiral caused to be done, but to the same purpose as before. At the same time a small privateer was brought into the fleet. On the 26th the admiral received further orders to proceed to Belle Isle, St. Martin's Road, and the road of Rochefort, in quest of the Brest squadron; but a council of war considering the state of water and provisions in the fleet, it was resolved they could not undertake that service without exposing the fleet to great extremity; and the admiral, having appointed Sir Edward Whitaker,[1] with five sail, to cruise in the Soundings twenty days for the protection of the trade, made sail for Plymouth, and arrived there on the 28th. He stayed no longer at Plymouth than to give the necessary directions before he left that place; and on July 9 Sir John and Captain Martin set out together by land for London, which finished their campaign this year.

---

[1] Captain Whitaker commanded the Dorsetshire at the taking of Gibraltar, and led a party of men on shore, for which service he was knighted. He succeeded Sir John Leake in the Mediterranean command.

As Captain **Martin's** business now depended wholly upon the **motions** of the admiral, he had no further employment till Sir John resumed his command as admiral the next spring ; and, indeed, the negotiations for peace seemed to afford **little** prospect of any further operations at sea ; but the Congress at Utrecht proving ineffectual, the campaign was opened by land, and preparations made to do the same by sea. This, however, was all grimace, for the Duke of Ormonde shortly after withdrew the English forces, and declared a cessation of arms with France, the French king having previous thereto agreed to several articles, one of which was the giving up immediately into our possession the town of Dunkirk. For this purpose it was necessary to have a squadron of men-of-war, which her Majesty was pleased to put under the command of Sir John Leake, to be accompanied by a body of land forces under General Hill. The admiral's commission on April 3, 1712, in like manner was Captain Martin's as first captain ; and the Bedford, a third-rate of sixty guns, was appointed for the admiral's ship. The fleet was ordered to rendezvous in the Downs, for which place the admiral and his captain set out on June 27, and the next day hoisted the flag on board the Bedford, there being twenty sail of men-of-war, **besides** transports for 2,000 men. On July 6, the troops being embarked, the fleet sailed, and the next day, about one in the afternoon, arrived in Flemish Road within two leagues of Dunkirk, as near as the pilots could take charge of the ships ; then the transports and yachts were sent in upon the appointed signals, the soldiers landed, and the place delivered up. The next morning the fleet got in, having no pilots before. Upon this occasion, the French colours being struck, the Union flag was hoisted in three several places of the town, and the same salute was made to the admiral, as usual, from her Majesty's fortifications, which was returned first by the admiral's ship and then by the whole fleet. Of this proceeding an express was immediately sent to England. The next morning Sir John and Captain Martin went ashore to view the town, and on the 10th the yacht and transports were despatched for England. After this nothing passed but balls and entertainments between the late French governor and the present English one ; Sir John likewise made a grand entertainment on board the Bedford for the governors and principal officers, both English and French ; but the air did not agree with English constitutions, for abundance of men fell sick of a fever, thence called the Dunkirk fever, which they afterwards carried with them to England. On the 15th the admiral received orders to return to England, whereupon he sailed the next morning from Flemish Road ; but the wind being contrary, they did not arrive in the Downs till the 20th. By this time the Dunkirk fever had spread so much that the Bedford alone had 150 men sick of that distemper, and it became so general that few escaped, though the admiral and Captain Martin had the fortune to do so.[1] The admiral continued in the Downs some time to execute some orders, and on the 30th he received her Majesty's leave to come to London ; whereupon, having appointed Sir Edward Whitaker to take upon him the command of the ship in the Downs with proper instructions, the next day he struck his flag, and with Captain Martin set out by land for London.

After this Sir John had another commission for

[1] 'October 11, 1712, Captain Martin was chosen an Elder Brother of the Trinity House.'— S. M. L.

admiral of the fleet, dated March 17, 1712-13, and Captain Martin a commission as first captain ; but though it is probable he hoisted the flag upon this occasion, and they both continued in commission till August 25, it is certain he did not go to sea, for the peace was concluded fourteen days afterwards, though not proclaimed till May 5 following, which put an end to a long and glorious war and to the naval transactions of Sir John Leake and Captain Martin.

The peace thus concluded and the admiral's flag struck, Captain Martin entered upon half-pay as first captain on August 26, 1713, in expectation to have a flag very soon, as Sir Thomas Hardy, his predecessor, had ; but the misfortune of the Queen's death, which happened on August 1, 1714, not only put an end to this hope, but divested him of what he then had.   Soon after his Majesty's accession to the throne there was a thorough change in the face of public affairs, and Sir John Leake being divested of all his employment in the navy, Captain Martin was necessarily involved with him, and on October 28 was struck off the half-pay list as first captain, and entered according to his seniority.   As to Sir John, he had a pension of 600*l.* a year granted him, which, by the persuasion of Captain Martin, he accepted of for the reasons I have mentioned in Sir John's life.[1]

---

[1] 'George I. arrived at Greenwich on September 18, 1713, and was crowned on October 20.   His supporters made the abuse and detraction of Queen Anne a test of allegiance to the new order of things.   Sir John Leake had too much honour and gratitude to traduce the memory of the good queen, and his enemies drew arguments of disaffection from his reserve.   He desired to serve the new king, but he scorned to do it upon dishonourable terms. On November 5 he was divested of all his employments.   He was granted a pension of 600*l.* a year, which was so small as to be below what he was actually entitled to.   He was persuaded not

As Captain Martin had long ago devoted himself to Sir John, and determined to follow his fortune, so now he very cheerfully attended him in his retirement, and he would have been very unhappy without it. Their friendship was mutual, and the two families seemed already united in one. Sir John would often say, 'Captain, you suffer upon my account, and I am afraid will suffer more ; if you don't offer your service to the Admiralty Board, you may lose your pretensions to a flag hereafter.' But though he was sensible this might be the case, he generously refused his advice, having too much honour and gratitude to quit him when he stood most in need of him. Sir John was fully sensible of this, and freely said he found his company now of more value than ever ; as a friend in adversity is more valuable than a friend in prosperity, for he had had many of the latter, but now he had him only left, and therefore it would touch him very nearly to part with him. Captain Martin replied they had lived long together, and often looked death in the face together ; that he had always been ready to die with him, and nothing but death should separate them. 'Well, captain,' says Sir John (for that was his usual way of speaking), 'you shall not be a loser if I can help it' ; and he was as good as his word. Notwithstanding this, Sir John had a son, an only child, a captain in the navy ; but instead of a blessing, his greatest misfortune, one abandoned to all extravagances, so that there remained no prospect of his amendment or even of his life, now near spent with debauchery. Wherefore his father considering

to refuse it, because his enemies might use such a course of action as an argument that he was disaffected. Sir John Leake divided his time between his country seat at Bedington, in Surrey, and a small house he had built for himself at Greenwich, with a view over the river.'—*Life of Sir John Leake.*

Captain Martin as a brother, he made his will as shall afterwards be particularly mentioned.

As Captain Martin had laid aside all thoughts of going any more to sea, in July 1719 he bought the house he then rented in Mile End town. This is a mistake that more men run into, and more especially the gentlemen of the sea, who, having been used to an active life, fall into building and gardening, as what offers itself more readily to employ them, besides the satisfaction of having a house of their own. This was unfortunately a very old house, and gave room to lay out a great deal of money, so that what cost at first but 890*l.*, was improved by workmen's bills to 1,187*l.* 18*s.*, which was afterwards sold in 1763 for 350*l.*

In the meantime, except the uneasiness his son gave him, Sir John passed his time in great tranquillity, with the society of Captain Martin and his family. The management of his fortune he left wholly to Captain Martin, except a small part of his estate which lay near him at Bedington, and his household affairs were managed by Mrs. Martin and her daughters. Thus he continued without any visible defect in his constitution till August 1719, when he had a kind of apoplectic fit.[1] On March 2 following, his son, Captain Richard Leake, died at Mile End, in the thirty-eighth year of his age, and was buried at Stepney. These two shocks, no doubt, contributed to his death, which happened at Greenwich a few months after. The immediate cause was a mortification in his back ; there was none but myself[2] with him when it was first perceived.

[1] 'On January 27, 1719-20, Mrs. Martin, Captain Martin's stepmother, died in the Park, Southwark ; by whose death some houses in the Park where she lived, which were purchased by his father, came to him. What she had besides she left to one that lived with her many years.'—S. M. L.

[2] The author, Stephen Martin Leake.

Captain Martin and the rest of his family were at Tunbridge, but they immediately came to him. It was a very affecting sight to see that brave gentleman suffer what was judged proper upon that desperate occasion, and imagining that he could bear it with so much resolution. But the exquisiteness of the pain gave him a fever and convulsions, which carried him off, Captain Martin and myself receiving his last breath. His will, which was dated February 18, 1717, showed the great esteem he had for Captain Martin and his family, for he had done everything for him but disinheriting his own son. To Captain Martin's eldest daughter, Hannah, he left a house at Mile End of 25*l.* a year, and an annuity of 100*l.* To his second daughter, Elizabeth, a house at Mile End of 16*l.* a year, and an annuity of 60*l.* ; and the rest of his estate to Captain Martin and two other executors, in trust for his son and his issue. But as there was no possibility of his having issue by his wife then living, his father had tied him up in the strictest manner from making away with anything. The household furniture, the great diamond ring, gold cup, and sword he was to have the use of, giving security to leave the same at his death,[1] so careful was Sir John that all should come entire to Captain Martin or his heirs if his son died without issue ; in which case he left to his aforementioned niece,[2] Hannah, a further annuity of 150*l.*, and his house and furniture at Greenwich for life ; and to Elizabeth, a further annuity of 40*l.* ; two other small annuities of 20*l.* and 13*l.* ; 816*l.* in legacies ; and to his son's wife, Martha, the use of the house he then lived in at Mile End for her life. All the residue, both real

---

[1] 'The diamond ring given him by Prince George, weighing 23 grs. ; that left to his daughter Hannah weighing 15 grs.'—S. M. L.

[2] His wife's niece.

and personal, came to Captain Martin **as executor** and residuary legatee, to the amount as follows :

Real Estate.

	£	s.	d.
At Bedington, in Surrey, the mansion house and premises, containing about 16 acres, two small farms, and a cottage, of the yearly value of 75*l*., which together were sold some years after to the Lord Viscount Falmouth for	3,500	0	0
Lands at Oxtead, in the same county, sold for	1,330	0	0
Houses at Mile End, 110*l*. per annum, valued at 14 **years'** purchase.	1,540	0	0
The reversion of Greenwich house and goods	250	0	0

Personal Estate.

In bank stock 5,150*l*., then at 129 per cent.	6,643	0	0
In Exchequer annuities 434*l*. per annum, at 25 years' purchase	10,850	0	0
The great diamond ring, 23½ grs., valued at	500	0	0
The gold sword, weighing 16 oz. 2 dwt., and the gold cup and salver, weighing 12 oz. 10 dwt. 6 grs.	105	13	4
Silver dishes and plate, 783 oz., and other plate	362	1	3

	£	s.	d.
Pictures 200*l.*, and household goods about 350*l.*	550	0	0
Cash 115*l.* 10*s.*, pension due, and other debts, about 900*l.*	1,015	10	0
	£26,646	4	7
Deduct legacies, 1,051*l.*, and funeral charges, 400*l.*	1,451	0	0
	£25,195	4	7

But then out of this were annuities payable to the amount of 383*l.*, as before mentioned.

By the funeral article it appears no cost was spared. Captain Martin left it to the undertaker to do it in the handsomest manner. Sir John having laid in state at his house at Greenwich, was buried from thence with great funeral pomp on August 30, at night. The hearse was preceded by all the trophies and the several flags he had borne as an admiral at sea, and followed by sixteen mourning coaches and six, attended with an infinite number of branch lights, proceeding in their solemn manner from Greenwich to the parish church at Stepney, where his remains were deposited in a vault he had built for the family when his wife died. The churches of Greenwich, Stepney, and Bedington were all hung in mourning, and no ceremony omitted that might express Captain Martin's respect to the deceased. But this might have been performed with much greater honour to both, had Captain Martin been as well informed of these matters then as he was afterwards, by having a ceremonial suitable to Sir John's rank, with the attendance of the heralds. He was in the case of most other people upon these occasions, who, being obliged to send presently for an undertaker, are made a property of by them before they have time to consider, else no man would pay for their troops of black guard only to increase the expense. Order and decency attend regular funerals, which are suited by the heralds to every degree, and ensure the honour of having the trophies carried by the king's officers of arms in their proper habits, which then become trophies of honour, and denote as well the right of the deceased to those trophies, as that he died a loyal and faithful subject. On the contrary, such trophies, being carried in a clandestine manner by mean persons, are a disgrace, and insinuate the deceased had no right to have them otherwise borne. No person is qualified to carry a trophy before a deceased who could not have done the same office with reputation to the deceased in his life time. No general would have a scoundrel to be his esquire or armour bearer, nor any gentleman call a porter to bear the honour of his family, wherefore it is not the least privilege to be attended by his Majesty's officers of arms upon these occasions. But I considered all this pomp had better been spared, as Sir John was not then in any public employ, and by his will had directed that no more than 100*l.* should be expended on his funeral.

After the funeral Captain Martin discharged all the debts and legacies, and finding a very distant relation of Sir John's, aged and infirm, who was under necessity, he put her upon the same foot with Mary Roberts, who had an annuity left her of 13*l.* a year, and paid it her as long as she lived. And that I may here finish the account of affairs relating to Sir John, I must observe that Captain Martin (at the instance of his son)[1] soon after took

[1] The author, Stephen Martin Leake.

upon him the name and arms of Leake, by virtue
of his Majesty's warrant under the signet and sign
manual, which was as follows:

'GEORGE R. George, by the grace of God,
King of Great Britain, France, and Ireland, De-
fender of the Faith, to our right trusty and right
well-beloved cousin, Henry, Earl of Berkshire,
deputy to our right trusty and right entirely be-
loved cousin, Thomas, Duke of Norfolk, our Earl
Marshal, and hereditary Marshal of England,
Greeting. Whereas, our trusty and well-beloved
Stephen Martin, of Bedington, in our county of
Surrey, of Mile End, Old Town, in our county of
Middlesex, and of Thorphall, in our county of
Essex, Esquire, hath humbly represented unto us,
that Sir John Leake, Knight, late Rear-Admiral of
Great Britain, Admiral and Commander-in-Chief of
our late Royal Sister, Queen Anne's fleet, and one
of the Commissioners for executing the office of
Lord High Admiral of Great Britain, &c., did some
years before his death make his will, and therein
settle his estate upon the said Stephen Martin, and
his heirs for ever, and did afterwards express his
intention that the said Stephen Martin and such
his heirs should take his surname and arms, to continue a memorial of the said Sir John Leake for
ever. Know ye, therefore, that we of our princely
grace and especial favour, at the humble request of
the said Stephen Martin, and in consideration of
the premises, have given and granted, and do, by
these presents, give and grant unto him, the said
Stephen Martin, and to the heirs and other descendants of his body lawfully begotten, and to
every of them full power, license, and authority, to
assume and take the surname and bear the arms
of the said Sir John Leake, which said arms by
his death became extinct. And our further will

L

and pleasure is, that you, our deputy Earl Marshal, to whom the cognisance of matters of this nature doth properly belong, do require and command that the said arms be duly exemplified and assigned to him, the said Stephen Martin, by the name of Leake, to be borne either singly, or in the first place quarterly with the arms of Martin, according to our will and pleasure herein before expressed, and that you do also direct and require that this our concession and declaration be registered in our College of Arms, to the end that our servants, the king's heralds and pursuivants of arms, and all others upon occasion, may take full notice and knowledge thereof, for which this shall be your warrant.

'Given at our Court of St. James, the 19th day of December, 1721, in the eighth year of our reign.

'By his Majesty's command,

'CARTERET.'

In pursuance of this warrant John Anstis, Esq.,[1] Garter, and Sir John Vanbrugh,[2] the Clarenceux kings of arms, by patent under their hands and seals of office, dated February 19, 1721, exemplified and assigned the said arms and crest in the following words, viz., 'The coat of Leake : *Or upon a saltire engrailed azure, eight annulets argent, in a canton gules, a castle triple towered of the third;* and for his crest, *on a wreath of the colours, a ship carriage and thereon a piece of ordnance, mounted all proper;* to be borne and used either single or in the first place quarterly with these arms, Scilt. *Paly of six or and*

---

[1] This was the elder John Anstis, the learned editor of the 'Black Book' or Register of the Order of the Garter, and of an essay on the Knighthood of the Bath. He was Garter from 1719 to 1730, when he was succeeded by his son, also named John Anstis. The author of this memoir, Stephen Martin Leake, succeeded the younger John Anstis as Garter, in 1754.

[2] The dramatist and architect, builder of Blenheim and Castle Howard. He died in 1726.

azure, on a chief gules three martins of the first, by
the name of Martin.'

This was the only instance that remained to
show the high esteem he had for Sir John Leake as
his brother-in-law, his captain, his benefactor ; and
this he did, as the most public testimony he could
give and the most grateful means whereby he might
convey to posterity this memorial of their friendship.
Having dispatched this affair, we must now look
back to the beginning of this year 1720, which may
truly be called wonderful, for never was there known
in any age an infatuation seizing a whole nation
against reason and plain facts as did the South Sea
scheme, which involved all England.   It was like a
pestilence, few families totally escaping, but those in
the iniquitous secret, whereby the greatest revolution
was made in private property that was possible in
the time, and which, by any other means, a whole
age could hardly have effected.   This immense loss
served to no other end but by the ruin of thousands
of families of worth and honour, to raise a few of the
baser sort ; for of the South Sea directors and their
friends, who were the only gainers, there were
hardly any amongst them but such.

The foundation of the abominable wickedness
was an act to enable the South Sea Company to
increase their capital by purchasing, or taking in by
subscription, the annuities redeemable by Parliament.   On May 19 they made their first proposals
for that end, and to promote their scheme and draw
in the annuitants to subscribe, by management they
presently got the stock up to 500, which made the
annuitants easy.   By May 25 two-thirds was subscribed.   By June 2 the stock was 890 ; but then,
falling to 750, to keep up the credit of their stock
the company lent 400*l.* upon 100 stock, and by

management worked it up to 1,000. Nevertheless, by the end of July it fell to 900. To keep up the stock it was necessary to draw in the rest of the annuitants. Some persons in eminent stations who were deeply concerned with the directors took great pains to promote the subscription, and, to my certain knowledge, used base and villainous means, not only to persuade, but to threaten and command those over whom they had influence, to subscribe, whilst themselves were getting out at any rate. By this means the remaining annuities were subscribed at 800, except some few. To keep up the stock new subscriptions were taken in at 1,000, and promoted by those in the secret with so much success that crowds of subscribers appeared, and not a few of the nobility, who were drawn in with the rest to give a sanction to it, so that presently it bore a premium. But the directors, their friends and associates, who had been served with the former subscriptions, bringing their stock to market, lowered the price, and they had recourse to the former expedient, the latter end of August, of lending 4,000*l.* upon 1,000 stock, a new expedient to enable the subscribers to make their payments upon the subscription without selling stock. Lastly, to pin the basket, on August 30 they resolved to make a dividend of 30 per cent., and afterwards, for twelve years, not to divide less than 50 per cent., to make the stock worth 1,000*l.* After this *ne plus ultra* this enormous monster sank under its own weight and subsided till, by Michaelmas, it diminished to 150, and many that had borrowed on their stock to pay into the subscriptions, not able to redeem, forfeited their pledge and lost all.

Stock-jobbing had been for some time a fashionable vice, like gaming ; both arising from a desire of gain, and a possibility of getting much by a

lucky hit, which we cannot do by the common
course of industry and application to business. This
by degrees had prepared and worked up the minds
of people to the South Sea frenzy. It seemed an
amusement, or rather business, to those who had no
other. Captain Martin did as the rest, with various
success, but, on the whole, I find was a considerable
gainer till the year 1720. When this South Sea
scheme began he had 6,000*l.* or 7,000*l.* in the
public funds, most of it in the South Sea Stock,
which he sold out at 350 ; he thought this a prodigious gain. But the stock continuing to rise, and
even wagers laid it would be 1,000, he came in
again at 700. In short, he thought himself already
so rich, that he set up his coach, and agreed with an
acquaintance for an estate of 140*l.* a year in Essex
at thirty years' purchase, which was indeed a bargain, reckoning the South Sea stock at 1,000, as all
men did. Even the great calculator, Sir Isaac
Newton, bought at 800 (notwithstanding he was
advised to the contrary by a friend who sold at the
same time), for, he said, he had calculated it would
be 1,500, and indeed it might well pass at 1,000,
when a dividend of 50 per cent. was declared for
twelve years to come. It was at this critical juncture that Sir John Leake died, and Captain Martin
became possessed of his fortunes as before mentioned. Very unfortunate was it that Sir John died
just then, for had he lived a month, nay, a fortnight
longer, that unhappy step had been avoided. It is
indeed unaccountable how Captain Martin could
be prevailed upon to subscribe so large a quantity
of annuities at the very last, when the South
Sea affair began to have a very bad aspect, Sir
John having in his life time refused to do it, and
Mrs. Martin given her opinion positively against it.
But he was influenced by some who were set on

purposely to persuade him, and whom he never suspected to have any such design.   However that be, certain it is he subscribed all the annuities Sir John left him, which were taken in as follows :

	£	s.	d.
To the long annuity, 200*l*. per annum.			
In stock 800	6,400	o	o
In bonds or money . . .	800	o	o
	£7,200	o	o
For 9 per Cents., 234*l*. per annum,			
520 capital stock	4,160	o	o
Total 1,320 capital stock at 800 is .	10,560	o	o
In cash.	800	o	o
	£11,360	o	o
5,150*l*. Bank was then worth . .	11,587	10	o
	£22,947	10	o
Now adding the other articles before-mentioned	9,152	14	7
	£32,100	4	7
The estate left by Sir John was then worth	1,451	o	o
	£30,649	4	7

This was the state of Sir John's fortune which came to Captain Martin at the time of subscribing the annuities into the South Sea, when immediately after the enormous monster sank under its own weight, and involved the whole nation in the ruins. As Captain Martin drank deep of this bitter cup, he suffered deeply, and, upon the whole, found himself above 20,000*l*. the loser.

Nevertheless, this great misfortune might have been somewhat alleviated if proper measures had been applied. But, instead of that, by his conduct, he made bad—worse, for having borrowed 4,000*l.* upon 1,000 stock of the company, when it was at 800, and the company, when it fell too far, demanding the money, he inadvisedly paid it (as indeed some others did), which he need not to have done, for it was afterwards determined that as the company, when they lost the money, thought the stock an ample security, they had no further demand upon the borrower. This was a tormenting reflection. Besides all this he had, before Sir John's death, agreed for the purchase of an estate in Essex, at a South Sea price, when the stock was at the height, but did not sell out to pay for it, which, if he had done, would have been no bad bargain, but gave his bond for the money, which was not paid till above two years after, so that what Norton purchased in Chancery in May 1718 for 2,400*l.*, he gave 4,200*l.*, and it cost him near 1,000*l.* to complete it. But his spirit could not stoop to misfortunes, or rather he seemed insensible so long as he could bear it out, putting off the evil day, and not conceiving, perhaps, things so bad as they really were. Indeed, this was the case of most of the unfortunate South Sea adventurers; for seeing so many upstarts rolling in wealth and splendour, as it was, to triumph over the unfortunate whom they had ruined, it made them struggle to maintain their figure, disdaining to truckle to every South Sea scoundrel, whereby they were completely ruined, though the fatal effects did not fully appear till several years after.

On March 23, 1721, Captain Martin's eldest

---

[1] Hannah Martin was born November 16, 1692, and on March 23, 1721, she married Thomas Bennet, Master in Chancery, son of Sir John Bennet, judge of the Marshal's Court. They lived at Boxford, in Suffolk, where Hannah was buried in 1743. She had two daughters, who died unmarried.

daughter, Hannah,[1] was married to Thomas Bennet, Esq., councillor-at-law and clerk of the custodies of lunatics in Chancery, second son of Sir John Bennet, Kt., sergeant-at-law, and judge of the Marshal's Court. To whom, besides her fortune, left her by Sir John, and 500*l.* of her own, her father, notwithstanding his losses, gave her 1,500*l.* On April 1 following died, in the eighteenth year of her age, Christian Martin, his youngest daughter, of a consumption she had laboured under many years, which had stunted her growth, so that she was extremely little, but withal so perfect, both in shape and features, that nothing could be more complete, except a large mole in the middle of her forehead, about an inch long, exactly resembling the rind of bacon, and rising very high above her forehead. What was the occasion of it could no way be accounted for. She was perfectly neat and ingenious, very fond of her brother, and beloved by him as well as her father and mother. Her death was a great affliction to the whole family, and though long expected, yet surprised them, and happened in the night, and so sudden, that she died before any but the servant with her knew of her illness. She was buried in the family vault at Stepney. The unlucky have made an observation that our misfortunes seldom come alone, and so it happened with Captain Martin, as if the poor remains of the South Sea were yet too much, and it was his fate to be ruined. The first of these was the loss of a bond of 120*l.*, by one Purder, a broker, and some others ruined by the South Sea. Next he had a lawsuit with Mrs. Leake, widow of Captain Leake, in relation to some pictures which Sir John had formerly given him by his son, and which she now claimed as hers. The chief cause of this suit was revenge for the disappointment she met with in Sir John's will, by which she

was only left her life in a house, and that upon
terms that displeased her. Accordingly she brought
an action of trover for those pictures in the King's
Bench, which was tried at Guildhall, June 23, 1721,
when, by the consent of both parties, it was ordered
that the matter in difference should be referred to
arbitration, for there could be nothing proved on
either side but Sir John's own words in common
discourse, wherein he sometimes called them the
pictures my son gave me, and, sometimes, my son's
pictures, meaning thereby the same thing. Upon
this reference it was agreed to put an end to all
matters between the parties, and therefore Mrs.
Leake proposed, for a consideration, to give up her
term in the house at Mile End, wherein she then
lived. Whereupon the arbitrator adjudged Captain
Martin to pay to Mrs. Leake the sum of 450*l.*, which
he paid on October 21, and on November 13 Mrs.
Leake executed a deed of assignment of the house,
allowing her to live in it till February 20 following,
which put an end to this dispute, though much to
the disadvantage of Captain Martin, the things in
dispute not being worth half the money, and the
greater part of the pictures being in the possession
of Thomas Bennet, Esq., who married his eldest
daughter Hannah, being part of the goods in the house
at Greenwich, left to her for her life by Sir John.

Another event that happened was the more grievous because it promised, at first, to be fortunate, and
to make some amends for the misfortunes of the preceding. Taking a contrary turn it proved only an
aggravation of them. His son [1] was then a clerk in

---

[1] Stephen Martin Leake, the author of this Memoir, born
April 5, 1702 ; clerk in the Navy Office, 1718 ; of Mile End, in
Middlesex, and Thorpe Hall, Essex. In 1735 he married Anne,
daughter of Fletcher Powell, Esq. In 1727 he had become
Lancaster Herald, and Norroy King of Arms in 1729, when he
resigned his place in the Navy Office. In 1745 he was appointed

the Navy Office at 40*l.* a year, where he had been
ever since September 1718. This office was thought
a proper introduction to business, but not for preferment, therefore it was intended he should remain
there no longer than till something more suitable
offered. There unfortunately happened at this time
the offer of a place in the Treasury which seemed to
promise everything desirable, but in the sequel had
a fatal reverse ; and because this affair was attended
with some extraordinary circumstances, I shall be
more particular in my relation of it. Old Lowndes,[1]

Garter King of Arms. He died on March 23, 1773, and was
buried in the chancel of Thorpe Church. His wife died at
Marshalls, at the age of eighty-eight, in 1802. He had nine
children between 1735 and 1755, his son John continuing the
line. Besides the 'Life of Sir John Leake,' he was the author of
'Nummi Brittanici Historia.'

Garter's son, John, was born in 1739, and was appointed
Chester Herald at the early age of fourteen, in September 1752.
In 1760 he became an ensign in the Essex Militia ; and in 1761
he married Mary, daughter of Peter Calvert, Esq., of Hadham.
He was appointed a clerk in the Treasury in 1763. He went to
Germany on two occasions with his father, who was sent to invest
Prince Ferdinand of Brunswick and the Duke of Mecklenburg-
Strelitz with the Garter. In 1770 John Martin Leake took a
house in Bolton Row, in 1773 he was elected F.S.A., and in 1777
he removed from Bolton Row to Fludyer Street. 1782 chief
clerk in the Treasury. In 1797 he took a house in Harley Street,
and in 1802 he succeeded to Marshalls on his mother's death.
He died in 1836, aged ninety-six, leaving three sons—John and
Stephen, who succeeded each other at Marshalls, and Colonel
William Leake, the antiquary and topographer of Greece and
Asia Minor, who died in 1862 without children.

[1] William Lowndes was born at Winslow in 1652. In 1679 he
became a clerk in the Treasury, and in 1695 he was secretary. In
that year he made his report on the debasement of the silver coins,
and on a scheme of re-coinage. Silver was then the only standard,
and the proposal of Lowndes amounted to a degradation of the
standard 25 per cent. The Government carried a measure for
re-coinage on December 10, 1695, and Lowndes was elected
M.P. for Seaford. He died in 1724. He sat on committees
relating to financial questions for many years, and the term 'Ways
and Means' was originated by him.

the famous ways and means man in the House of
Commons, was then one of the secretaries to the
Treasury, and Mr. Horace Walpole the other. He
had a worthless nephew, a Thomas Lowndes, and
not knowing what to do with him, made him one of
the clerks of the junior or inner room ; but this not
being in any degree equal to his extravagances, he
was soon forced to abscond for debt. Some said he
was mad, as an excuse for his behaviour, because
he sometimes acted like a madman ; but he was not
otherwise mad than by extraordinary acts of folly
and extravagance, which are indeed pretty much
like it. In short, he durst not appear for debt, and
consequently could not attend his duty. There was
no other method found but privately to sell his
place to stop the mouths of his creditors, and his
uncle undertook to procure their lordships' leave
to admit any person he could bring to his terms.
To this end he set his emissaries to work to look
out for a purchaser. One of these was Captain
Whinyates, a broken land officer (afterwards Rich-
mond Herald), a man entirely fit for his purpose ;
and Captain Martin had the misfortune (I don't
know how) to have some slight acquaintance with
him. Whinyates knew Captain Martin had a son
who he wanted to provide for ; he represented it as
a place of 300*l.* or 350*l.* a year, and where a man
might be sure to rise if he did not misbehave himself. That it was a very genteel thing, and one of
the prettiest places for a young gentleman in the
revenue ; and if he had a son capable of it, he said
he would borrow the money to do it. That it was
a mere accident he knew it, and immediately he
thought of him, and desired Lowndes that his friend
might have the refusal, which he promised him,
though he had partly agreed with another person.
That Captain Martin might depend on it, everything

would appear even better than represented, with
many other arguments to excite a desire for it ; and
concluding, that if by his means he procured it, he
should expect a gratuity, which was agreed to.
This was the beginning of October 1721, and pursuant to the previous agreement, on the 14th,
Captain Martin and his son, Thomas Lowndes and
Captain Whinyates, met together.   At this meeting
Lowndes affirmed he had full power to dispose of
his place, confirmed all that Whinyates had said
before, and demanded 800 guineas for the purchase
of it ; and to make Captain Martin more eager, and
the better to deceive him, he affirmed he had been
offered that sum, but at Captain Whinyates' request had given him the preference, and offered to
give him time to assure himself of the nature and
value of the place, for if he did not approve of it,
it would be no inconvenience to him, having another
that would immediately give the money demanded.
Captain Martin did not take all that he said for
truth, but from the frankness of the man, whom he
esteemed a person of some credit, and the pretended
friendship of Whinyates, believed the place to be in
some degree as represented, and though worth but
half the value pretended, would be worth the pur-
chase-money.   And though Lowndes were a rogue,
he thought he durst not attempt a fraud of that
nature ; that if he did, the Lords of the Treasury
would not give him any countenance, and that even
the law could never justify so notorious a cheat.
His son, too, who was present, showed a visible
inclination to have it. He did not much like the
Navy Office, and had very great notions of the
Treasury as the fairest prospect for preferment,
and his father having had some acquaintance with
Horace Walpole abroad, enjoined him to go on.
All these reasons contributed to engage Captain

Martin to make the absolute bargain immediately
without further inquiry, especially when Lowndes
voluntarily proposed that, though an agreement was
signed, Captain Martin should nevertheless have
three days' time to consider it and give his answer;
and if he should in that time disapprove of the said
place (which would be no inconvenience to them),
he could and would then sell it to the other person
who had offered him the sum of 840*l.* for the same.
Upon this declaration notes were interchangeably
signed by both parties, whereby Thomas Lowndes
promised to quit his clerk's place in the Treasury,
and to procure Mr. Stephen Martin, son of Stephen
Martin, Esq., to be admitted youngest clerk in the
inner room, on consideration of which he was to
receive of the said Stephen Martin, senior, 840*l.* on
October 16, 1721. And at the same time Captain
Martin signed a note whereby he promised to pay
to Mr. Thomas Lowndes the sum of 840*l.* so soon
as he had quitted his clerk's place and procured his
son to be admitted as youngest clerk in the junior
room.

That very evening Captain Martin, in his way
home, meeting with Mr. John Hale, his stockbroker,
and telling him what he had done, he seemed
astonished at it ; told him he knew some persons in
the Treasury, and the nature of those clerks' places
very well ; that they had only 50*l.* a year salary, and
doubted whether they had any perquisites ; besides
that, there was no course of succession in the office,
but as they had friends ; that buying and selling of
places and pecuniary bargains of that kind were
always very much discountenanced by the Lords of
the Treasury, and the place being during pleasure,
the enjoyment of it, in case his son was admitted,
would be the less certain. Upon this information
Captain Martin the next morning, and before any

surrender or resignation had been made by Lowndes, gave him notice, from the reasons above, that he did not intend to proceed with his bargain, and that he might sell the place to the person he had intimated would buy it if he did not, and desired they might deliver up their respective notes. Lowndes, in answer, told him he would oblige him to stand to the agreement. Thus the affair rested till November 20, 1721, when Captain Martin was served with the following paper :

'Whitehall, Treasury Chambers. November 20, 1721.

'Present:

'Mr. Chancellor Exchequer, Sir Chas. Turner.

'The two Secretaries do approve of Stephen Martin, junr., being admitted a clerk in the inner room, in the stead of Thomas Lowndes, and my Lords agree that the said Stephen Martin shall have the allowance of 50*l.* as the youngest clerk there.   (A true copy, exad.)

'P. M. F. HEEKER.'

Upon the receipt of this, Captain Martin was the more determined against it, and, being irritated, he went to the Treasury and complained he had been deceived. He waited upon Mr. Horace Walpole, who was one of the Secretaries, who told him he should have justice done him. In the mean time Captain Martin's son was desirous to take the place upon any terms, being fully persuaded it would prove advantageous in the end, and that the consideration of his being imposed upon in the purchase might incline old Lowndes, if not the lords who knew it, to favour and advance him. And at length he prevailed with his father that he might go and accept the place. Accordingly Captain Martin, on November 23, being but the third day after the date of the admission, went with his son to the

Treasury to accept it. In the meantime this affair, having made a great noise, came to their lordships' ears, and, judging their order to have been obtained in a surreptitious manner, and a gross imposition, to make it impossible for Lowndes to perform his agreement, and to discountenance such proceedings, they had been pleased to recall their former order of admission, and instead thereof to order that the said Stephen Martin, junr., should not be admitted upon any pretence whatever. As Mr. Martin was refused admission, the captain refused to pay the money, upon which Lowndes sued him for the money, and, on a hearing in the Exchequer before the Lord Chief Baron Montague, June 14, 1722, obtained a verdict for the same with his full costs, the plaintiff having tampered with the jury, as it was found afterwards; for the foreman, one Martin, a baker of Westminster, meeting Captain Martin's servant in Westminster Hall, asked him about his master, what Martin it was; and when he had told him, he then recollected he had formerly known him. ' Gad,' says he, ' I wish I had known it before the trial; for your master had wrong done him. I was foreman of the jury, and could have directed them which way I pleased; but I knew nothing of your master, and we had been spoke to in favour of the plaintiff.'

Upon this unreasonable verdict, whereby he was likely to lose both money and place, he preferred his petition to the Lords of the Treasury, setting forth his case, and praying them to set aside their last order; but for the same reasons they made that order they rejected his petition, so that he could not have been admitted in case the agreement had been fair. But Lowndes might have had his place again, but refused it, in order to support his claim against Captain Martin.

Though Lowndes had got a verdict at common

law, yet rather than the plaintiff should bring the
case into Chancery, he was solicitous to come to a
composition, and for the encouragement thereto
promised he would take part of the money, and
could undertake to procure the place if, when that
was done, he would agree to pay the remaining part.
This was a reasonable proposal which ought to have
been accepted. But Captain Martin, being exasperated, would listen to no terms, depending upon
the equity of the case, and for that end, on December 20, obtained an injunction for stay of the proceedings at law and the debt. Lowndes having put
in his answer to the plaintiff, Martin's bill denying
the whole equity thereof, on January 5 it came to a
hearing, and the injunction was dissolved, whereby
Captain Martin remained without remedy either at
law or equity. This was certainly a flagrant instance
of injustice, if we consider that the very letter of the
agreement was that Lowndes should procure his son
to be admitted, and there was no time limited to
attend this admission, and he actually did attend the
third day after the date of the order to be admitted,
and not being admitted, it is manifest he did not perform the terms of the agreement. As to the value
of the place and the verbal agreement of three days
to consider of it, this was denied by Whinyates, who
was in the secret, paid for his roguery. But Lowndes
admitted he received notice the day after the agreement that Captain Martin was off his bargain, and
that he mentioned he would give him three days'
time to consider of it ; but that it was in case he had
not then come to an agreement. And he confessed
that he said he had another would give the same
money if he did not, and believed he might have had
it. So that he neither was under a necessity to have
surrendered, having truly notice not to do it ; nor
sustained any loss when he had surrendered, by

Captain Martin's refusal, having another chap. By his own answer he acknowledged he had received intimation by a letter from a friend in the Treasury Office that he might come and accept of his place again if he would deliver up Captain Martin's notes, so that the surrendering was an apparent fraud to support his claim against Captain Martin, and with a view probably to reassume it again afterwards, which, indeed, happened. And notwithstanding the Lords of the Treasury at that time seemed to discourage this infamous fellow and his practices, and he would come into no terms they proposed to put an end to that scandalous affair, he was not only restored to his place, but yet a few years afterwards he received promotion in that office, as if it was to reward him for his villainy and insolence, whereby he has at this time (1740) acquired a handsome fortune with no better character than he had before, the same Chancellor of the Exchequer (Sir Robert Walpole) continuing at that board, whereby the Treasury Board, or Mr. Chancellor rather, are culpable for this fraud ; while the costs of this trial amounted to above 1,200*l.*, besides what Captain Martin suffered by a rogue of an attorney, one Orlando Hamlyn, of Lyons Inn, who drew sums of money from him from time to time to carry on the cause for which he never accounted. For this reason it was many years before Captain Martin could get his bill, and then he never could bring him to settle an account, nor would his executors do it. The reason was obvious, for by collecting the memorandum of sums paid him by Captain Martin's pocket-book they amounted to above 60*l.* more than his full bill untaxed, which was a very extravagant one, and there is reason to believe he played booty in the cause. Upon the whole the loss could not be computed at less than 1,200*l.* It was a hard bargain to

M

pay so much for nothing, but it was a bad throw, and the money was gone. The disappointment only remained, which sat very heavy on both father and son. 'What was past could not be recalled;' was there any hopes left to get into the Treasury? for it now appeared more desirable than ever, and all means were used to find out some person that had an influence with Sir Robert. At length a person was found out, one Manning, said to be Sir Robert Walpole's private secretary, who could do anything for money. Captain Martin would not appear in it himself. The young gentleman and the lawyer met him one evening at Cavsack's, in the city, and after representing the hardships of the case, Manning frankly told them he could do what they wanted for the sum of 500*l.* In vain they urged the justice and reasonableness of the thing, the great sums Captain Martin had already paid, and the smallness of the place, and at length offered him 300*l.* But it had no effect, he said he must have 500*l.* or he would not undertake it. This appeared so unreasonable for a clerk's place of 50*l.* a year, that they broke up and never again attempted anything further, and on April 1, 1723, Lowndes signed a general release, acknowledging satisfaction for the money and costs. There are, perhaps, very few instances of fraud, oppression, and injustice more flagrant, and this may serve to warn us from the like misfortune, and afford some useful reflections. As, first, never to sign to anything without being fully satisfied of the consequences, but when we have done so, to make the best of a bad bargain by performing it, lest by endeavouring to avoid a lesser evil we run into a greater. Second, to be very careful how we buy preferments, lest we lose our money and friend together, remembering how there is neither faith nor honour in such dealings; for great men must support their missions, and none but such will thrive by them; and thirdly never to go to law, but when you can be satisfied to lose the case and afford to pay the costs. The loss of 1,200*l*. was a great hole in a small fortune hardly saved out of the ruins of the year '20, and coming so immediately after it, made the misfortune much more insupportable. If the place had been at length obtained, though upon hard and unreasonable terms, it might have been tolerable, but to pay so much for nothing, and to be obliged, after so public an affair, to sit down in the old place without a possibility of resenting this treatment or retrieving the misfortune, was so great a mortification that could not be borne with any tolerable degree of patience. It extorted this conclusion from Captain Martin, that he was to be unfortunate in his worldly affairs; but I think this was more applicable to the son, who, besides the loss of so much of his father's fortune, most certainly lost the fairest opportunity he ever had to raise himself in the world, for in six months after there happened two vacancies in the Treasury Office, thus everything concurring to aggravate the disappointment, as if he had been the sport of fortune. It had, however, good effect upon the son, that all his ambitious hopes sank, and he had now to bring his mind to his fortune. But it had a bad effect upon his father, making him careless and indifferent as to his affairs, as it frequently happens in such cases, when a man finds all his care and industry in vain, he is too apt to abandon himself to his ill-fortune, giving all over for lost. A man who can submit to such misfortunes with an equal mind, he must have a great stock of virtue and resolution, or be very insensible.

On June 14, 1722, he was sworn into the Commissioners of the Peace for Middlesex and Surrey.

As a consequence of these misfortunes may be

M 2

reckoned the death of **Mrs.** Martin, Captain Martin's
wife.   She was too sensible of the situation of his
affairs, it gave her great uneasiness, and made a
bad constitution much worse.   She had a fit of
illness which everyone thought would have ended
her life, but she recovered to a miracle, yet not
likely to continue long.   The time that was allowed
her she endeavoured to improve in settling Captain
Martin's affairs in the best manner for her darling
son (for her daughter she looked on as provided for
by Sir John's will).   She knew Captain Martin
could not support himself in the figure he then
lived ; she persuaded him to let Bedington, which
he came into with reluctance.   She disposed everything there for that purpose, reserving some things
in hopes **of** better times.   At **the same** time she
removed **from the house** in Mile **End T**own to that
at the Grove, for **she said she would settle** the
family and then leave them, as indeed **it** happened,
though she appeared in better health and spirits
than she had been a great while.   Upon that very
evening of the night (September 14, 1723) she
died suddenly in the middle of the night ; with a
difficulty of breathing she expired in a few minutes,
Captain Martin, her son, and daughter Elizabeth
being present.   She was the sister of Lady Leake,
and best beloved **by** her mother, because she always
showed the most affection and duty for her.   She
was a virtuous and religious woman, of an ingenuous
nature, of good understanding, of a most healthy
disposition ; a good housewife, exercising herself
with great application in all social duties, though
labouring under a tender constitution all her life, and,
in particular, was troubled with an inveterate head-
ache to a degree almost of distraction, sometimes
for eight or ten days together almost ; but at other
times she was very cheerful, having then spirits

beyond her strength. As to her person, she was little, well-shaped, always neat, of a brown complexion, black hair, and much pitted with the small-pox.[1] All her defects were virtues in excess ; she was too religious, too compassionate, and too affectionate to her children and relations. For her religion was something superstitious, and made her think herself and others not good enough. She was affected with the misfortunes of others to her own heart, and too anxious for the welfare of her children ; in particular, she was immoderately fond of her son (it was her only one, and she had seen her sister very unhappy in hers), and it was apparent she loved him best ; and this excess towards him doubled every misfortune that happened to the family. Yet it is to be admired in her conduct towards her children that, notwithstanding her exceeding affection, she always brought them up in a proper manner, never allowing them any liberties when children that might spoil them, careful to instil into their minds virtuous and religious principles. As she was charitable out of principle as well as a compassionate temper, she did much good with the little she disposed of, and that little, as she saved it by frugality, she was careful to apply properly, her charity, as her piety, being pure and unaffected. In short, as in every relation of life she was unblameable, so everyone in the relation they bore to her justly lamented her ; and as things were circumstanced in the family, her loss appeared every day more and more. She was buried in a handsome manner at Stepney, in the family vault, on September 23, aged fifty-seven. Dr. Landon, lecturer of the parish, preaching her funeral sermon, according to her desire, because (as she said) he knew least of her,

[1] 'She was rather too fond of physic, which impaired her health, and made a bad constitution worse.'—S. M. L.

and therefore could not flatter her; for she thought
funeral sermons were very beneficial as seasonable
exhortations to the living; for this reason she made
choice of St. Paul's words when he took leave of the
elders of Ephesus to go to Jerusalem, when he
tells them that he should see their face no more,
viz., Acts xx. 32 : 'And now, brethren, I commend
you to God and to the word of His grace, which is
able to build you up, and to give you an inheritance
among all them which are sanctified.'

In February 1723-24, Captain Martin's daughter
Elizabeth was married to Christopher Wyvill, Esq.,
third son of Sir Marmaduke Wyvill, Bart., of Constable Burton, in the county of York, a man of no
fortune, and had then only a place in the Excise
Office of 80*l.* a year.[1]   She had refused a very
advantageous match in her mother's lifetime (on
account of this gentleman); but now, her father
being very easy about the matter, and she resolved,
it was made a match, and they were to live with the
captain as long as it was agreeable to all parties.
Mrs. Bennet and her husband promoted the match,
and not only persuaded Captain Martin to agree to
the match, but to give her the same portion, additional to what she had, as he had formerly given to
Mrs. Bennet, though his circumstances were now
very different, and he could not possibly raise the
money without selling part of the estate.   This
was sufficient reason for not doing it, but it was
cooked up so nicely, and under a notion the money
might never be paid in his lifetime, it went down;
but it did not pass so easily with the brother (who
always disliked the match).   He knew it must one

---

[1] She died in 1731, leaving a daughter, Elizabeth, who married
her cousin, the Rev. Christopher Wyvill. The daughter succeeded
to the whole of the Wyvill estates by the will of her brother-in-law,
Sir Marmaduke, who died unmarried.

was but a small part of Sir John Leake's estate intended to be his, and that Sir John himself had
given his two sisters a large portion of his fortune,
he thought it very hard his father should make this
additional incumbrance upon the poor remains of
that fortune; and that, too, in favour of a match against
his inclination, and to a person who had nothing to
add to it; but it was the son's fate always to be the
sufferer. If Captain Martin's fortune had been
much larger, there had fallen out so many unlucky
accidents to lessen it, that made it impossible to
support the way of living he was in. This consideration had forced him to a resolution to let Bedington
House before Mrs. Martin's death, and preparations
were made by her for that purpose. The further
charges which attended her death (which, with the
funeral and mourning, amounted to between 300*l.* and
400*l.*) and his daughter's marriage, the ready money
all gone, the estate swallowed up by annuities and
in arrear, besides debts incurred, these made it more
necessary. Several tenants offered, but none agreed
till April 19, 1724, the Lord Viscount Falmouth
agreed for it, for one year, at 110*l.*, and liked it so
well that, in December following, he took a lease for
five years, at the same rent, and was a very good
tenant, and this made a considerable alteration in
his affairs.

And here it may not be improperly asked, why,
in this declining state of his affairs, he did not try
to recover them by getting the command of a ship.
His son, who was in the Navy Office, and knew what
might be done, pressed him to apply for a command.
He told him what was said of him. That he did
not desire to be employed, and had not offered his
service since King George's accession to the crown,
which was insinuating that he was not well affected

to his Majesty. That if he asked for a ship it would take off this reflection, even though he was not commissioned ; and if he was, it would entitle him to something more hereafter. That as to his claim as first captain, to be preferred before his seniors, though in reason it should be so, it was not a matter of right but of favour, as appears by several instances of persons who had been first captains and afterwards private captains ; and as to favour, if his brother Sir John Leake did not promote him to a flag, it was not incumbent upon those that superseded him to do so, who had first captains of their own, besides that Sir John made one first captain a flag, namely, Sir Thomas Hardy ; and hardly any admiral had made two flags, which, if that were the rule, would be to postpone the senior captains. But what was most material, if he per- sisted to maintain this obsolete claim of first captain to be a flag, he would certainly lose his undoubted right when it was his turn by seniority ; for by not having been employed by the present administration, he was looked upon as already post- poned, whereas if they once put him in commission, though but for a day, that would wipe off the blot, and then they could have no pretence to reject him. In short, to support his claim by repeated applica- tion, and thereby show his desire to be employed. This was what everybody agreed was right, and at length, partly convinced, yet acting as by constraint, he did apply to the Earl of Berkeley in January 1722 ; but in high terms he laid before him his pre- tensions, and desired his favour for a flag, or to be a commissioner of the navy or victualling. But he found this was to little purpose. In December 1723 he was prevailed upon to apply again to his lordship upon more reasonable terms, for he was now convinced he must get a ship or he would lose his pretensions to a flag. He, therefore, now only desired to have a guardship, and at the same time made application to the Admiralty Board ; and his lordship thought this request so reasonable that he promised to think of him. He likewise made a friend of Mr. Chetwynd, another of the Lords Commissioners of the Admiralty, who had the greatest influence with Lord Berkeley, and stood a fair chance, but at that time there was no vacancy. In November 1724, upon the death of Admiral Strickland, there were two flags vacant, and Captain Morrice, commander of the Sandwich (a second-rate guardship at Chatham), was to be one. As the Sandwich was to become vacant by that promotion, he thought it was a fair opportunity, and renewed his application to the Earl of Berkeley for that ship ; and his lordship certainly designed it for him, for it was not only reported so at the Admiralty Office, but at Chatham, where I heard it, and expected to hear it confirmed at London. Nevertheless, it was somehow prevented, though by what means I never could certainly know. But this much is certain, that, in order to stop it, the nomination of the two flags was delayed some time till they could bring Lord Berkeley to another mind. It was sus- pected to be done by some vile insinuations of Sir George Byng, excited and impelled by those behind upon the list that had the next expectation, and looked upon his being employed as a sure presage he would anticipate their preferment to flags, there being no possible objection to him had he succeeded to that command. But now, disappointed and with- out hope, he looked upon himself as already post- poned. He did, indeed, make a further application, in August 1727, to the Lord Torrington, upon his succeeding the Earl of Berkeley at the Admiralty Board, but met with so little encouragement that he resolved never to make any further attempt, so that when it came to his turn by right of seniority to be an admiral he would not ask for it.

In the year 1725, upon the revival of **the Order** of the Bath, Mr. Leake, his son,[1] had the honour to be one of the Esquires to the Earl of Essex, deputy Earl Marshal of England. This brought him acquainted with John Anstis, Esq., Garter, principal King of Arms, and was the occasion of his coming into the herald's office. Anstis showed an inclination to dispose of his office, and Mr. Leake and his father were both so desirous of it, that it was resolved to agree for it, if their whole fortune **would** purchase it, **that** place being, no doubt, **one of** the genteelest **of** the value for a private gentleman under **the** crown. **In** short, the price **was** fixed at 4,500*l.*, **and** the son **was** to insure 2,000*l.* upon his life as long as his father lived. But it was soon discovered that Anstis had **no** design to sell his place ; and if he had, the Duke of Norfolk would by no means consent to it. On the contrary, he took pains to fix him, so that after above a twelvemonth's solicitation, he obtained a new grant of that office jointly to himself and his eldest son, and the survivor of them.[2]

The time was not, however, wholly lost, for though the Duke of Norfolk would not admit Mr. Leake in place of Mr. Anstis, he promised him the first vacancy that happened in the office. But this did not satisfy him, he was now desirous to come into the office directly ; and his father approving it, he purchased the place of Lancaster herald for 350 guineas, which was granted to him by patent dated June 1, 1727 ; the charge of this and other expenses amounting in the whole to 460*l.*, of which sum he

---

[1] The Author.
[2] See note at page 146.

had of his father only 400*l.*, and this was the only
money he had had of him from his entry into the
Navy Office in 1718 to the present time, and even
afterwards till his marriage. As Captain Martin
could not raise any money at this time without
borrowing, nor borrow (already owing above 1,000*l.*),
he was obliged to mortgage his estate for 1,500*l.*,
August 3, 1727. It is true he had retrenched a
great deal from his former way of living, had laid
down his coach, kept only one man-servant and one
maid ; and thus he and his son, in the most frugal
manner, without keeping any company, immured
themselves, his daughter Wyvill having been gone
some time from him, her husband not proving
altogether agreeable, and the retrenching scheme
requiring it. Frugality can only save a declining
fortune, but never recover a broken one. It might
have done by a timely application, but now could
only spin out a poor thread, which one unlucky
accident must break. So it happened upon the
expiration of Lord Falmouth's lease, when that
house fell upon his hands, 5 per cent. interest, and
350*l.* a year annuity, and 110*l.* a year empty, would
soon invade and swallow up the principal, and then
where must the annuitants be paid ? There was no
way left but to sell a part to save the whole.
Nothing but the fear of absolute ruin could have
brought Captain Martin to consent to it. It was the
last and only remedy. Upon this occasion he was
very unfit to treat for the selling of it ; and as his
daughter Bennet had the greatest interest in it, he
signed an agreement March 23, 1729, to convey
Bedington House, with the land at Oxtead, which
was all he had in the county of Surrey, to trustees,
to be disposed of in order to buy out the annuities,
viz. 250*l.* a year to Mr. Bennet, and 100*l.* to Mr.
Wyvill, at thirteen years' purchase. Three days after

the signing this agreement he was seized with a paralytic disorder, as he was walking and musing in his parlour, which took away the use of one side, and confined him some time before he was fully recovered of it.   All this while the Lord Falmouth was treating for the estate, but by another person, till June following, the price being agreed upon, the purchaser was known, and on July 8 Captain Martin and all the other parties concerned joined and conveyed the premises to trustees for his lordship and the Lady Falmouth, the same being purchased with trust money of her ladyship's, viz., for Bedington House and ground, with the two farms of 70*l*. a year, together, the sum of 3,500*l*.   For the lands at Oxtead, being 50*l*. a year, 1,330*l*. ; making together 4,830*l*., which was disposed of in this manner—350*l*. a year at thirteen years' purchase, 4,550*l*. ; one quarter's annuity, 87*l*. 10*s*. ; some incidental charges about the house and writings, 72*l*. 10*s*. ; and the remainder, 120*l*., Mr. Bennet put in his pocket for his trouble, which, considering the occasion and who he acted for, that it was for his own benefit, and how good a price he was allowed for the annuities, was thought ungenerous.   Besides this, Captain Martin received about 250*l*. by the sale of goods and pictures of Bedington House.

In the meantime his son succeeded to the place of Norroy King of Arms, by patent, December 17, 1729, upon which occasion he resigned his clerk's place in the Navy Office, as well because he thought it more consistent with, and a discredit to the place of a King of Arms, as because it was disagreeable in itself, both to him and his father, and had especially been so for the last year and a half, when he had been employed at Portsmouth, Chatham, and the Nore, not only in the summer time, but all the hard winter, by which Captain Martin lost his son's

company and was left alone. This had made him
very uneasy, and as he had, ever since his wife's death,
shown a strong inclination to marry, his son was
willing even before this happened to quit the Navy
Office, and confine himself and prevent any designs
of the nature, which, if effected, would have made
father and son very unhappy. Having mentioned
this disposition to marry, I shall observe that there
was a particular person who he was desirous to
marry soon after his wife's death, one Mrs. Eliza
Wilson, a relation of hers, to whose honour I mention it, that though she was in very low circumstances, refused to marry him out of regard to the
family. She married some time afterwards and
died a widow. As there appeared this strong disposition to a second venture, his children having
no right to oppose it, they considered how to improve it by a suitable match, thereby to prevent an
unsuitable one, and this was almost brought about
with a very deserving woman, with a good fortune,
but after having waited upon her several times, and
the thing in a manner agreed upon, he broke it off.
Some time after the parting with his estate in
Surrey, he met with another misfortune which did
not less affect him. I have before mentioned a
diamond ring given to Sir John, by Prince George
of Denmark. It was one single stone, weighing
23 grains and esteemed worth 500*l*. He was extremely fond, not to say vain, of this jewel; he
never pulled it off but when he washed his hands
or went to bed, when he put it in a case in his
pocket. It was on April 7, 1731, he went to a
concert at Stationers' Hall, on Ludgate Hill, with
his ring upon his finger. His son was with him,
they came home in a coach. It was very dark, and
by the way, in Paternoster Row, he pulled it off his
finger, and fumbling to put it into the case, dropped

it, as he supposed, into the coach. He did not miss it till the next day ; going to put it on, he found an empty case. He was astonished, and when the first surprise was over, reflected how it must happen. All possible means were used to recover it, and 100*l.* reward offered for it, but to no purpose. All the information that could be got was from a butcher in Paternoster Row, who saw a kennel raker take up such like a ring out of the kennel next morning, who supposed it was a stone ring, and carried it away. Indeed, it was to be admired it had not been lost long before, considering that he always had it about him, and sometimes came home late in the evening alone, and at one time lost his sword, and at another his watch, beside several rings and other things of value by pickpockets, which used to be very troublesome about Aldgate.

In April 1749 was the first time I had any certain account what became of the ring, when Mr. Meadows, my bookseller, informed me that the son of that butcher told him that the ring was found by his father's apprentice ; that, having concealed it above a twelvemonth, he sold it to a goldsmith in Covent Garden for 80*l.*, and was discovered by this means. Soon after he had sold it he was taken ill and died, and, making his will, bequeathed that 80*l.* to his sister, upon which his master, questioning him how he came by the money, he confessed the whole. But this seems only a story made of the apprentice to cheat his master's roguery, for at the time he saw a kennel-raker take it up ; and why did he not inform the loser or Mr. Meadows, whom he knew, and who had made strict inquiry at the time of him and others, as soon as he discovered what became of it, and take the reward of 100*l.* which was offered for it ?

But he had another, much greater loss, which

followed this, by the death of his daughter Wyvill, who died on May 19 following (1731), which was not only a great misfortune with regard to her, but a remarkable instance of his particular ill-fortune. It was not eleven months since he had sold a considerable part of his estate to pay off his daughter's annuities, and now to the loss of his daughter was added the loss of 1,200*l.*, for so much it would have been clear in his pocket, as it was now in Mr. Bennet's. It was his particular ill-fortune, I say, because no one saw her declining state. Her husband refused to take thirteen years' purchase for it, and some others Mr. Bennet offered it to, when, behold, every circumstance contributed to render one unfortunate and the other fortunate!

This daughter, Eliza Wyvill, was deservedly beloved by all her relations, friends, and acquaintance. She was gentle and agreeable, both in her person and behaviour, inheriting the virtues of her mother, and, like her, of a hearty, generous disposition, free from pride and affectation. If she was blameable, it was for too much affection towards her children and too little regard to herself. He, unhappily, had no passion but for himself, and she experienced that love must be mutual, and otherwise there cannot be a mutual and lasting harmony, and even then there must be a sufficient composure to make life comfortable. She childed very fast, and was careless and indifferent as to herself, and became a sacrifice to disappointed love. He, happy in himself, never knew an uneasy moment. She was buried on May 24 at Thorp, in Essex, in the chancel belonging to her father, her brother attending and, not without tears, performing this last office.[1] Of the several children she bore, one only,

[1] 'Here lies the body of Elizabeth, daughter of Stephen Martin Leake, Esq., first captain of the Navy under Admiral Leake (who

a daughter, remained, who, as it is expressed upon her gravestone, it is hoped will imitate the virtues of her mother.[1]

After this Captain Martin had several paralytic fits at times, and the last, which took away his sight, made him apprehend some danger; but by the application of a perpetual blister for some time that difficulty was removed, and by taking mustard-seed every day he overcame his paralytic disorder so as to have no return of it afterwards as long as he lived; after this he continued in a perfect state of health, with a spirit and activity beyond his years, to which, no doubt, his regular and abstemious way of life contributed not a little. By this means his decay of nature became insensible. In the meantime his whole satisfaction was at home. Upon all occasions he showed an extreme fondness for his son (who, indeed, debarred himself of all diversions to make him easy), and this affection seemed to increase with his years. He would often reflect on some mistakes and condemn himself for not having taken better care of his affairs for his son's sake, and freely owned to him that it was owing to him that there remained what was left, that he had a right to all, and he wished it was much more. He often used to say that he and his son lived together rather like intimate friends or affectionate brothers than father and son, and showed a deference to his son's opinion on all occasions to an extreme, except in one instance, and

made him his heir). She married Christopher Wyvill, Esq., son of Sir Marmaduke Wyvill, Baronet, by whom she had six children, who all died before her, excepting Elizabeth, who, it is hoped, may one day imitate the virtues and possess the good qualities of her mother, who had few equals and no superiors. Obiit May 19, 1731, aged 35.'—S. M. L.

[1] Her daughter Elizabeth married a cousin, the Rev. Christopher Wyvill, but had no children, and died in 1783.

that was setting up his coach again. He had now only one thing he desired to see before he died, and that was to see his son married. It was what his son was not averse to, but he did not think it so convenient to live with his father when married, and that a wife would not choose to do it, and he resolved not to leave him. Besides, he resolved to please himself, and he was very cautious, and therefore it seemed unlikely to happen. But Providence was pleased to give him this satisfaction by bringing into the neighbourhood a young lady to his mind, a phœnix that he could not resist. In short, they were married on January 23, 1734, to the great satisfaction both of father and son. The old gentleman did all he could upon the occasion, and had the happiness to see the fruit of it, a daughter—a good earnest that there might be one day a son. This he but just lived to see, for she was born on November 3, 1735, and he died on January 19 following. On Saturday, the 17th, at night, he was perfectly well, and read till bed time in the Turkish history aloud, and with his usual emotion when he read of a battle, as if he was engaged in it. He would have gone to church the Sunday morning, but was too late. At noon he complained of a sickness at his stomach, and when dinner came upon the table could not bear the smell, had a violent retching to vomit, and a great rumbling of wind in his bowels, yet continued in the room, sometimes sitting and sometimes walking about very nimbly. In the afternoon, finding himself more disordered, he said he would go to bed, undressed himself, took out his gold shoe and knee buckles, and put them in the drawer. 'Here, Stephen,' says he to his son, 'are my buckles, if I should have no more occasion for them,' went to bed, and told the maid he should die. He seemed to be something better for being abed,

N

but in the night was very much out of order ; the next morning was very sensible, and appeared only weak.   A physician was sent for, which he was against, for he was always averse to them (having never had one till his paralytic disorder), and the doctor found him so low that he did not expect him to live, and what things were ordered him he refused to take, out of a prepossession he should die, as he told the servant, though he would not acknowledge so much to his son ; and yet he retained so much of his usual spirits that, when his son incited him to take the medicines with hopes of success, and not be dejected, he replied, with warmth, 'What! do you think I am afraid?' and said he thanked God his death was neither untimely nor unprovided ; for, though he had no visible decay, he had had a sensible, though a gentle one, and had for a considerable time past thought of his end, was now quite easy, and desired to die.   Not long after this he called for his granddaughter and blessed her, and, after a few faint struggles with nature, without sickness or pain, he closed his eyes in his son's arms, and sank into eternal rest without a groan.

He was buried in the family vault at Stepney on January 26, and out of regard to the deceased, as well as the station his son was in, it was thought suitable to bury him according to the strict rules of heraldry, attended by his Majesty's officers of arms. The funeral procession was performed by daylight from his dwelling-house at the Grove at Mile End to the parish church of Stepney in the following manner : first, four conductors with gowns and staves, then six servants on horseback in cloaks ; then Richard Mawson, portcullis pursuivant, on horseback, attended on each side by a servant on foot ; then John Kettel, gent., on the right, bearing a pennon of the arms of Leake and Martin, with

Charles Hay, gent., on the left, bearing a pennon of
Trinity House, both on horseback, and each a servant on foot; then Charles Green, Esq., Lancaster
herald-at-arms, bearing the helm and crest, attended
by two servants on foot; then in like manner
Edward Stibbs, Esq., Chester herald, bearing the
coat of arms; then the hearse, drawn by six horses
adorned with feathers, two dozen of buckram escutcheons, twelve shields and six crests, attended by
twelve pages, and followed by four coaches, with
four horses each, for the mourners and four ministers,
to each coach two pages. When they came to the
churchyard the procession was made on foot in the
following manner, viz., the conductors and servants
as before, then the four ministers, then portcullis
pursuivant, then the two pennons, then Lancaster
and Chester as before, then the body covered with a
velvet pall and eight silk escutcheons, then Mr.
Leake, his only son and heir, as chief mourner,
supported on the right by Thomas Bennet, Esq.,
son-in-law to the deceased, and on the left by
Fletcher Powell, Esq., father-in-law to Mr. Leake.
After them the rest of the mourners, two and two.
Thus they proceeded into the church, and divine
service being ended, from thence in like manner to
the vault in the churchyard on the south side, where
the body was deposited with the remains of his wife,
Sir John Leake, Lady Leake, and others of the
family, and the following inscription was put upon
the tomb:

'Here lyeth the body of Stephen Martin Leake,
Esq., one of the Senior Captains in the Royal Navy,
and sometime First Captain, an Elder Brother of
the Trinity House, and in the Commission of the
Peace for the counties of Middlesex, Essex and
Surrey, who died the 19th day of January 1735-6,
in the 70th year of his age.'

N 2

He married Elizabeth, sister to the Lady Leake,
the wife of Sir John Leake, Knight, Admiral, to
whom he was still more closely united by the strictest
acquaintance, having been his captain and shared
the same common dangers in twenty years' wars, so
that the said Sir John Leake, having survived his
wife and the issue he had by her, made him heir to
his whole estate. And he, in return for so great a
benefit, added the name and arms of Leake to his
own, as the most grateful means whereby he might
transmit to posterity the memorial of their friendship.

To complete this account of Captain Martin, and
give an idea of the whole man, I shall describe his
person and character.

As to his person, he was what is called a little
man, being about five feet four inches high, as
he stood or walked, for by breaking his thigh he
lost two inches (the right leg being so much longer
than the left); which, added to his height, would
have brought him to the middle size. This difference in his legs made him go a little lame, but did
not hinder his walking; only keeping one knee
bent while the other was straight, had a disagreeable
look. He was otherwise clean limbed, was square
set, had a ruddy complexion, light brown hair, sharp
grey eyes, thin lips, and a rising nose, and in his
dress and mien he carried the air of a military man.
Mars and Venus seem to have been in conjunction
at his birth. In his youth he had a thin habit of
body, and when he married was thought to be con-
sumptive, but afterwards grew plumper, and in his
latter days lusty, though not what we may call fat.
He had naturally a tender constitution, and was
troubled with a rupture on both sides the groin,
which, as he grew in years, became very troublesome. Yet, notwithstanding this weakness, he did

not neglect any exercise or fatigue which his
business required ; and any excess he might be
guilty of in the former part of his life he so well
corrected by a regular and temperate course of
living towards the latter part, that he spun out the
thread of life without the usual infirmities incident
to old age better than most strong constitutions
can do. For he had no complaint, and was full of
spirits and active to the very last, and this strength
of spirit enabled him to overcome many difficulties
and fatigues that more robust persons sank under.
From the same cause he was hot and passionate,
but this was but of short continuation, being in his
nature good humoured, compassionate, and for-
giving, and easy to be wrought upon by fair means.
He had an extreme sense of honour and bravery,
and, like the Romans, thought virtue properly represented by a military person, a brave mind being
the epitome of all virtue. He was pleased with a
brave action as a benefit done to himself, and was
ready to take the part of an injured person, whilst
every cowardly, base action offended him ; and he
could not help exclaiming against it and exposing
it without caring whom he offended, which, though
right in itself (for every man should publicly condemn and discountenance what is base and un-
worthy), yet made him many enemies, and was a
main reason why he was not promoted in the navy ;
for if anything went wrong they could not stop his
tongue, he could sooner affront than flatter any man ;
and, considering his temper (easily affronted), it is
to be wondered at that he never had any private
quarrel, which can only be imputed to this, that
being always ready to fight, by that means he
always avoided it. Notwithstanding his warm
temper, no one ever treated his officers under him
more like a gentleman, nor the seamen with more

humanity.   He always allowed them more indulgence than himself, never suffered the men to be ill-treated, nor any advantages to be made of them by others which he scorned to do himself.   If his officers were not good seamen he made them so, for no man was better qualified in his profession, both in theory and practice, as appeared by his conduct upon all emergencies, and his opinion in councils of war, and the management of the fleet under Sir John Leake.

He always kept his own journals, for he said he was accountable for all, and would trust to no man, and was so very strict upon himself in his duty, that when his ship was in port, and other captains would be ashore with their families, he would be aboard with his, by which strictness upon himself he made the duty of others much easier.

Above all, he was particularly remarkable for a happy presence of mind, whether in battle, storm, fire, or other accidents ; upon such occasions he never was confounded, but always ready to apply the best means, with a surprising temper, which temper was the more extraordinary in one where courage bordered upon rashness, for it was a maxim he laid down never to yield.   He took it for granted a prisoner must be insulted and ill-used, which no man of honour could tamely submit to, though it were in the midst of an army, therefore it was more eligible to die fighting, or be drowned, than to be sacrificed to the will and pleasure of an enraged enemy.

As to his capacity he certainly had good natural parts, which, properly improved, might have made a considerable figure in civil life.   He showed upon all occasions a good judgment where passion did not cause him to err, and notwithstanding his natural warmth, was to be convinced and brought over by

cool argument. He always showed an ingenious
nature, as in drawing, which he did neatly, though
not well, and in playing on the flute—both which he
taught himself, and did some notable things in
surgery, upon sudden accidents where a surgeon
was not at hand, purely from observation. Besides
these he danced (much better than could be expected from his misfortune), fenced, and rode a horse
well, and few men shot so well either with a gun
or pistol. He was very neat in his person and dress,
and though he hated fine clothes, was very curious
in everything he wore, as his buckles, his sword,
buttons, rings; everything of that kind must be
remarkably curious; and he did not value to expense, for he was of a generous disposition. Even
old age and some degree of necessity could not
make him covetous. Economy, therefore, was what
he wanted; he never could bring himself to it, if
he could, his affairs would have proved better. But
if he used it in one thing he forgot it in another;
indeed, this is a foible which the brave and generous
mind is most liable to, and can seldom overcome.
As to his principles: he had a great dislike to all
dissenters from the Church of England as being all
Republicans, and thought the Whigs to be all such in
their hearts, and consequently enemies to the constitution; and no less detested Popery, not by hearsay
only, but from what he had seen of their practices in
Popish countries, and consequently was averse to the
Pretender, the hope of Popery in England. He,
therefore, professed himself an honest Tory, was for
preserving the constitution in Church and State, as
by law established, and could not bear to hear the
Queen abused. And though, because he was warm,
some thought him a violent Tory, it was more from
the natural warmth of his temper than of his principles, and because he thought himself bound in honour

(though against his interest) to speak well of Queen Anne, who he seriously believed to be the mother of her country, in opposition to those violent Whigs who, for their own interest, traduced her memory to please the new comers. But when party spirit cooled, he was as moderate as others, though always for the Church of England, and liberty and monarchy, in opposition to fanatical schemes. In short, he was a man of honour, a gallant and an excellent seaman, which character he never forfeited. If he was passionate and amorous (by constitution), he was also brave, generous, good-natured, and compassionate; never affected drinking and abhorred gaming. If he took some liberties in his youth, which were incident to his profession, he rectified all by a temperate old age, and died as men might wish to die.

[EXITUS ACTA PROBANT.]

APPENDIX A.

A List of Ships of the Navy in 1685.

| | Dimensions | | | | | Built | | | Price of the Hull |
	Length	Breadth	Depth	Draught of Water	Tonnage	When	Where	By Whom	
	ft. in.	ft. in.	ft. in.	ft. in.		A.D.			£
FIRST-RATES.									
ROYAL SOVEREIGN . . .	127 0	47 6	19 0	23 0	1,545	1637	Woolwich	Mr. Pett .	29,840
ROYAL CHARLES . . .	136 0	45 4½	18 6	20 8	1,441	1675	Portsmouth	Comr. Deane	21,100
ROYAL JAMES . . .	136 0	45 4½	18 6	20 8	1,441	1675	„	Mr. Pett .	—
ROYAL PRINCE . . .	138 0	44 10	19 0	22 0	1,400	1670	Chatham .	Mr. Pett .	—
LONDON (706 men, 96 guns)	129 0	43 9	18 8	21 0	1,348	1670	Deptford .	Mr. Shish .	—
ST. ANDREW (706 men, 96 guns) .	129 0	43 5	18 8	21 0	1,313	1670	Woolwich .	Chr. Pett .	—
ST. MICHAEL . . .	122 0	40 0	17 5	20 0	1,107	1669	Portsmouth	Comr. Tippetts	15,630
BRITANNIA (754 men, 100 guns) .	146 0	47 0	19 7½	22 0	1,739	1682	Chatham .	Sir Phineas Pett .	—
CHARLES . . .	128 0	42 6	18 6	21 0	1,257	1668	Deptford .	Mr. Shish .	19,470
SECOND-RATES.									
ROYAL KATHERINE (524 men, 84 guns) .	120 0	40 0	17 4	20 8	1,050	1664	Woolwich .	Chr. Pett .	14,800
VICTORY (754 men, 100 guns) .	114 0	42 0	17 6	20 10	1,029	1665	Chatham .	Peter Pett, sen. .	—
HENRY . . .	120 0	38 0	15 9	20 8	1,020	1656	Deptford .	Mr. Callis .	10,307
ST. GEORGE (688 men, 96 guns) .	117 0	38 9	16 6	18 6	900	1622	„	Mr. Burrell .	11,064

APPENDIX A.—SECOND-RATES (*continued*).

	Length		Breadth		Depth		Draught of Water		Tonnage	When	Where	By Whom	Price of the Hull
	ft.	in.	ft.	in.	ft.	in.	ft.	in.		A.D.			£
TRIUMPH (640 men, 90 guns)	117	0	38	0	15	0	18	0	898	1623	Deptford	Mr. Burrell	18,030
UNICORN	110	0	35	8	16	0	17	6	845	1617	„	Mr. Bright	18,100
VANGUARD (640 men, 90 guns)	126	0	45	0	18	1½	20	0	1,357	1679	Portsmouth	Mr. Dan. Furzar	—
WINDSOR CASTLE	142	0	44	0	18	3	20	0	1,462	1679	Woolwich	Th. Shish	—
SANDWICH (640 men, 90 guns)	132	6	44	6	18	3	20	0	1,395	1679	Harwich	Isaac Betts	—
DUCHESS (640 men, 90 guns)	137	0	45	0	18	4	20	6	1,475	1679	Deptford	Th. Shish	—
ALBEMARLE (640 men, 90 guns)	132	0	44	4	18	3	20	6	1,273	1680	Harwich	Isaac Betts	—
DUKE (640 men, 90 guns)	142	6	45	2	18	9	20	6	1,546	1682	Woolwich	Th. Shish	—
OSSORY (640 men, 90 guns)	139	7	44	6¾	18	2	20	0	1,415	1682	Portsmouth	Dan. Furzar	—
NEPTUNE (640 men, 90 guns)	130	0	45	0	18	6	21	0	1,407	1683	Deptford	John Shish	—
CORONATION	—								—	1683	Portsmouth	Isaac Betts	—

THIRD-RATES.

	Length		Breadth		Depth		Draught of Water		Tonnage	When	Where	By Whom	Price of the Hull
ROYAL OAK (456 men, 74 guns)	127	0	40	6	18	3	18	8	1107	1674	Deptford	John Shish	—
EDGAR (432 men, 72 guns)	124	0	39	10	16	0	18	4	998	1668	Bristol	Mr. Bayley	7,912
HARWICH (226 men, 48 guns)	123	8	38	10	15	6	17	0	987	1674	Harwich	Mr. Deane	8,883
SWIFTSURE (408 men, 70 guns)	123	0	38	8	15	6	17	0	978	1673	Harwich	Mr. Deane	8,793

Ship									Tonnage	Year	Place	Builder
CAMBRIDGE (408 men, 70 guns)	121	0	37	0	16	4	17	6	861	1666	Deptford	John Shish
WARSPITE (408 men, 70 guns)	117	6	38	0	15	4	17	9	892	1666	Blackwall	Mr. Johnson
RESOLUTION (408 men, 70 guns)	120	0	37	6	15	9	16	9	885	1667	Harwich	Mr. Deane
MONMOUTH (389 men, 66 guns)	119	0	36	0	15	6	18	0	880	1666	Chatham	Phi. Pett
RUPERT (389 men, 66 guns)	119	0	36	3	15	6	17	1	813	1665	Harwich	Mr. Deane
DEFIANCE (378 men, 64 guns)	117	0	37	3	15	3	16	6	902	1675	Chatham	Phi. Pett
MARY	116	0	34	8	14	6	17	6	795	1649	Woolwich	Chr. Pett
MONTAGU	117	0	35	2	15	0	17	9	809	1654	Portsmouth	Mr. Tippetts
HENRIETTA	116	0	35	7	14	4	17	6	763	„	Horslydown	Mr. Bright
DREADNOUGHT (346 men, 62 guns)	116	8	34	6	14	2	17	0	735	„	Blackwall	Mr. Johnson
PLYMOUTH (332 men, 60 guns)	116	8	34	8	14	6	17	6	752	„	Wapping	Capt. Taylor
YORK (332 men, 60 guns)	116	0	34	6	14	2	17	6	734	„	Blackwall	Mr. Johnson
LION	112	0	35	0	15	6	17	0	727	1640	Chatham	Capt. Taylor
DUNKIRK (332 men, 60 guns)	112	0	32	6	14	0	16	6	704	1651	Woolwich	Mr. Burrell
MONK (332 men, 60 guns)	107	0	35	0	14	0	17	6	696	1659	Portsmouth	Mr. Tippetts
LENNOX (446 men, 70 guns)	131	0	39	8	17	0	18	0	1032	1678	Deptford	Mr. Jo. Shish
RESTORATION (446 men, 70 guns)	123	6	39	8	17	0	18	0	1032	1678	Harwich	Mr. Isaac Betts
HAMPTON COURT (446 men, 70 guns)	131	0	39	10	17	0	18	6	1105	1678	Deptford	Mr. Jo. Shish
CAPTAIN (446 men, 70 guns)	138	0	39	0	17	2	18	0	1,164	1678	Woolwich	Mr. Th. Shish
ANNE	128	0	40	0	17	0	18	0	1,089	1678	Chatham	Mr. Phi. Pett
HOPE	124	5	40	0	16	9	18	6	1,058	1679	Deptford	Mr. Castle
ESSEX (446 men, 70 guns)	124	0	40	3	16	6	18	0	1,068	1679	Blackwall	Mr. Johnson
KENT (446 men, 70 guns)	124	0	40	2	16	10	18	0	1,064	1679	„	„

APPENDIX A.—THIRD-RATES (*continued*).

	Length		Breadth		Depth		Draught of Water		Tonnage	When	Where	By Whom	Price of the Hull
	ft.	in.	ft.	in.	ft.	in.	ft.	in.		A.D.			£
GRAFTON (446 men, 70 guns)	138	0	40	2	17	2	18	0	1,174	1679	Woolwich	Mr. Th. Shish	—
EAGLE (446 men, 70 guns)	120	0	40	9	17	0	18	0	1,047	1679	Portsmouth	Mr. Dan. Furzar	14,723
BERWICK (446 men, 70 guns)	128	0	40	0	17	0	17	0	1,089	1679	Chatham	Mr. Phi. Pett	—
NORTHUMBERLAND (446 men, 70 guns)	131	0	40	3	16	10½	—		1,128	1679	Bristol	Frn. Bayley	—
STIRLING CASTLE (446 men, 70 guns)	131	0	40	0	17	3	18	0	1,114	1679	Deptford	Jo. Shish	—
BREDA (446 men, 70 guns)	124	6	39	10	16	9	18	0	1,055	1679	Harwich	Isaac Betts	—
EXPEDITION (446 men, 70 guns)	120	0	40	9	17	0	18	0	1,059	1679	Portsmouth	Dan. Furzar	15,145
BURFORD (446 men, 70 guns)	137	6	40	1	17	3	18	0	1,174	1679	Woolwich	Mr. Th. Shish	—
ELIZABETH (436 men, 74 guns)	124	6	41	0	16	10	18	0	1,108	1679	Deptford	Capt. Castle	—
PENDENNIS (226 men, 48 guns)	128	6	40	0	17	0	17	0	1,039	1679	Chatham	Mr. Phi. Pett	—
EXETER (346 men, 60 guns)	123	0	40	2	16	7	17	10	1,070	1680	Blackwall	Sir Hy. Johnson	—
SUFFOLK (446 men, 70 guns)	124	0	40	2	16	8	17	9	1,066	1680	,,	,,	10,896

FOURTH-RATES.

	Length		Breadth		Depth		Draught of Water		Tonnage	When	Where	By Whom	Price of the Hull
WOOLWICH (274 men, 54 guns)	116	0	35	6	15	2	16	9	716	1675	Woolwich	Phin. Pett	5,728
OXFORD (274 men, 54 guns)	109	0	34	0	15	8	17	8	677	1674	Bristol	Mr. Bayley	4,837

Ship					Men	Built	Place	Builder	Tons
GREENWICH (274 men,) 54 guns,	110 0	33 6	14 6	17 0	659	1666	Woolwich	Mr. Chr. Pett	5,491
ST. DAVID	110 0	33 6	14 6	17 6	638	1666	Forrest	Dan. Furzar.	5,491
NEWCASTLE (274 men, 54 guns,)	108 0	31 1	13 4	15 0	625	1654	Ratcliff	Phin. Pett	4,101
HAPPY RETURN	104 0	33 2	13 2	18 0	623	1654	Yarmouth	Mr. Edgar	3,932
PORTLAND (226 men, 48 guns)	105 0	33 11	13 4	15 9	588	1649	Wapping	Capt. Taylor	3,932
ANTELOPE	101 0	30 0	12 6	16 0	576	1654	Woodbridge	Mr. Carew	3,139
SWALLOW	100 0	31 10	12 11	14 1	559	1653	Pitchouse	Mr. T. Taylor	3,529
JERSEY (226 men, 48 guns)	101 10	32 2	13 3	14 0	558	1654	Malden	Mr. Starling	—
ASSISTANCE (226 men, 48 guns)	102 0	31 0	12 4	15 0	558	1650	Deptford	Mr. Johnson	3,386
MARY ROSE	100 0	31 8	13 0	15 0	555	1654	Woodbridge	Mr. Monday	3,132
DIAMOND	105 0	31 3	12 7	16 0	550	1651	Deptford	Mr. Pett, sen.	4,360
BRISTOL (226 men, 48 guns)	104 0	31 1	13 0	15 0	549	1653	Portsmouth	Mr. Tippetts	4,256
ADVICE (226 men, 48 guns)	100 0	31 2	12 4	16 0	545	1650	Woodbridge	Comr. Pett	3,334
DOVER (226 men, 48 guns)	104 0	31 8	12 8	17 0	554	1654	Shoreham	Mr. Castle	3,601
RESERVE (226 men, 48 guns)	100 0	31 1	12 8	16 0	538	1650	Woodbridge	Comr. Pett	3,300
FORESIGHT	102 0	31 0	12 9	14 6	538	1650	Deptford	Mr. Shish	3,393
RUBY (226 men, 48 guns)	105 0	31 6	12 9	14 9	532	1651	"	Peter Pett, sen.	4,175
CENTURION (226 men, 48 guns)	104 0	31 0	12 6	16 6	531	1650	Ratcliff	" "	3,451
CROWN	100 6	31 8	12 6	14 6	530	1654	Redriff	Mr. Castle	3,486
BONAVENTURE (226 men, 48 guns)	100 0	29 0	12 8	15 0	510	1649	Deptford	Mr. Pett, sen.	3,375
KINGFISHER (216 men, 46 guns)	110 0	33 8	13 0	13 0	664	1675	Woodbridge	Mr. Phin. Pett	5,312
HAMPSHIRE (226 men, 48 guns)	101 0	29 9	12 8	14 10	470	1653	Deptford	" "	3,592
PORTSMOUTH (216 men, 46 guns)	99 0	28 4	12 3	15 0	468	1649	Portsmouth	Mr. Th. Eastwood	3,587
DRAGON (216 men, 46 guns)	96 0	28 6	12 6	15 0	479	1647	Chatham	Mr. Goddard	2,743

APPENDIX A.—FOURTH-RATES (*continued*).

	Length (ft. in.)	Breadth (ft. in.)	Depth (ft. in.)	Draught of Water (ft. in.)	Tonnage	When (A.D.)	Where	By Whom	Price of the Hull (£)
TIGER (226 men, 46 guns)	99 0	29 4	12 0	14 9	457	1647	Deptford	Peter Pett, sen.	2,912
ADVENTURE (190 men, 44 guns)	94 0	27 9	11 4	13 9	432	1646	Woolwich	Comr. Pett	2,618
SWEEPSTAKES	86 0	28 0	10 9	12 6	376	1666	Yarmouth	Mr. Edgar	2,327
CONSTANT WARWICK	85 0	26 0	11 2	12 0	374	1648	Ratcliff	Mr. Peter Pett	1,982
ASSURANCE	87 0	27 0	11 0	12 6	372	1646	Deptford	Old Peter Pett	2,379
PHŒNIX	90 0	27 10	11 0	13 0	368	1666	Portsmouth	Mr. Deane	2,379
FALCON	89 0	27 6	11 0	13 0	367	1666	Woolwich	Mr. Chr. Pett	2,527
NONSUCH (226 men, 48 guns)	88 3	27 8	12 10	12 8	345	1668	Portsmouth	Mr. Deane	2,692
CHARLES	122 0	29 4	10 2	11 2	526	1676	Woolwich	Mr. Phin. Pett	3,682
JAMES	104 0	27 8	12 9	12 3	433	1676	Blackwall	Mr. Deane	2,814
TIGER PRIZE	112 0	33 0	12 8	15 0	649	1678	Turks	Prize	—
GOLDEN HORSE	125 0	36 8	14 10		722	1681	,,	,,	—
HALF MOON	113 6	34 1	13 4		536	1682	,,	,,	—
TWO LIONS	115 0	33 6	13 6		552	1682	,,	,,	—
LEOPARD	109 0	33 9	15 0	17 0	676	1658	Deptford	Mr. Shish	5,482
MORDAUNT	101 9	32 4½	13 0	16 0	561	1683	Bought from	Lord Mordaunt	—
FIFTH-RATES.									
SAPPHIRE	89 0	26 10	10 0	12 8	346	1675	Harwich	Comr. Deane	—
SWAN (110 men, 24 guns)	74 0	25 0	10 0	11 0	305	1673	Dutch	Prize	—
MERMAID (135 men, 32 guns)	86 0	24 9	10 0	12 0	294	1651	Limehouse	Mr. Graves	—
DARTMOUTH	80 0	25 0	10 0	12 0	265	1655	Portsmouth	Mr. Tippetts	—
PEARL	86 0	25 0	9 11	12 0	260	1651	Ratcliff	Mr. Peter Pett	—
GARLAND	80 0	25 0	10 0	11 6	255	1654	Southampton	Mr. Furzar	—
GUERNSEY	80 0	24 0	10 0	12 0	255	1654	Walderock.	Mr. Shish	—
ORANGE	76 0	26 4	8 10	11 0	280	1677	Algeirs	Prize	—

Name									Tons	Built	Where	By whom	
ST. PAUL	74	0	25	9	11	2	14	0	260	1679	,,	,, Mr. Edgar	—
ROSE	75	0	24	0	10	0	12	6	234	1674	Yarmouth	Mr. Edgar	—
RICHMOND	86	0	24	0	9	10	11	0	223	1655	Portsmouth	Mr. Tippetts	—
SIXTH-RATES.													
LARK	75	0	22	6	9	9	10	0	199	1675	Blackwall	Sir Ant. Deane	—
SAUDADOES	51	2	16	0	9	0	10	0	199	1669	Portsmouth	,,	—
GREYHOUND	75	0	21	6	9	0	9	0	175	1672	,,	,,	—
DRAKE	85	0	18	0	7	0	8	0	151	1653	Deptford	Mr. Peter Pett	—
DEPTFORD	52	0	18	0	9	2	8	4	179	1665	,,	Mr. Shish	—
QUAKER	54	0	18	2	9	0	9	6	179	1671	Bought of Harwich	Mr. Moore	—
FAIRFAX	44	0	19	0	10	0	5	8	133	1666	,,	Mr. Deane	—
DUMBARTON	71	0	22	0	9	0	11	0	191	1685	Ships taken in Scotland	in Scotland	—
SOPHIA	65	0	20	1	9	6	11	0	145	1685	,,	,,	—
FIRE-SHIPS.													
EAGLE	85	0	25	8	9	10	12	0	305	1654	Wapping Bought	Captain Taylor	—
YOUNG SPRAGGE	96	0	18	0	9	0	8	6	80	1673	,,	—	—
PEACE	64	0	20	8	9	10	10	8	145	1678	,,	—	—
ANN AND CHRISTOPHER	76	0	25	5	10	0	11	0	261	1671	,,	—	—
CASTLE	85	0	27	0	11	0	11	6	240	1671	,,	—	—
SPANISH MERCHANT	79	0	26	3	10	2	11	6	250	1671	,,	—	—
SAMPSON	78	0	24	1	10	8	12	0	240	1678	,,	—	—
HULKS.													
ALPHERE	120	0	33	6	12	0	19	0	716	1673	Dutch	Prize	—
ARMS OF HORNE	106	0	30	3	12	0	18	0	516	,,	Bought	Prize	—
ARMS OF ROTTERDAM	119	0	39	0	18	9	18	6	987	,,	Dutch	—	—
FRENCH RUBY	112	0	37	0	16	6	17	10	968	1665	,,	,,	—
STATHOUSE	90	0	30	4	11	0	15	0	440	1667	,,	,,	—
YACHTS.													
ANN	52	0	19	0	7	0	7	0	100	1661	Woolwich	Chr. Pett	—
CHARLOTTE	61	0	20	2	8	0	9	3	143	1677	,,	Mr. Pett	—
CLEVELAND	53	4	19	0	7	9	7	0	107	1671	Portsmouth	Capt. Deane	—
KATHERINE	56	0	21	0	7	0	8	3	131	1673	Chatham	Mr. Page	—
KITCHEN	51	0	19	0	7	0	8	0	101	1670	Wivenhoe	Mr. Pett	—
MONMOUTH	66	4	21	0	8	0	8	7	155	1677	Chatham	,,	—
MARY	51	0	19	6	7	0	7	0	103	1666	Rotherhithe	Mr. Castle	—

Appendix A.—Yachts (*continued*).

| | Dimensions | | | | Ton- nage | Built | | | Price of the Hull |
	Length	Breadth	Depth	Draught of Water		When	Where	By Whom	
	ft. in.	ft. in.	ft. in.	ft. in.		A.D.			
MERLIN	54 0	19 6	6 6	6 6	109	1667	Rotherhithe	J. Shish	—
NAVY	48 0	17 6	7 7	7 6	74	1673	Portsmouth	Comr. Deane	—
PORTSMOUTH	57 0	20 6	7 6	7 4	133	1674	Woolwich	Mr. Pett	—
HENRIETTA	65 2	21 8	8 8	8 9	162	1679	Woolwich	Th. Shish	—
ISLE OF WIGHT	32 0	13 0	6 6	7 0	31	1673	Portsmouth	Mr. Furzar	—
BEZAN	34 0	14 0	3 6	7 0	35	1661	Dutch	Gift	—
QUEENBOROUGH	30 0	13 0	5 8	6 0	27	1671	Chatham	Mr. Pett	—
DEAL	32 0	13 0	5 3	6 0	24	1673	Woolwich	Mr. Pett	—
JEMMY	31 0	12 1	7 10	6 0	26	1662	Lambeth	Comr. Deane	—
FUBBS	63 0	21 1	7 9	9 6	148	1682	Greenwich	Sir Phin. Pett	—
ISABELLA	—	18 11	7 9	8 11	—	1683	"	"	—
HOYS.									
HARWICH	38 0	16 0	8 0	8 0	52	1660	Harwich	Sir John Tippetts	—
LIGHTER	38 0	18 0	6 6	7 6	65	1672	Portsmouth	"	—
MARYGOLD	32 0	14 0	7 0	7 0	33	1653	"	"	—
UNITY HORSE BOAT	—	—	—	—	—	—	—	—	—
TRANSPORTER	—	—	—	—	—	—	—	—	—
SLOOPS.									
BONETTA	61 0	13 0	4 6	5 0	67	1673	Woolwich	Phin. Pett	—
EXPERIMENT	35 6	11 6	5 0	6 4	24	1677	Greenwich	—	—
HOUND	57 6	12 10	4 6	5 0	50	1673	Chatham	Phin. Pett	—
HUNTER	60 0	12 0	4 6	5 0	46	1673	Portsmouth	Sir Anthony Deane	—
WOOLWICH	61 0	13 0	4 6	5 0	57	1673	Woolwich	Phin. Pett	—
SMACKS.									
LITTLE LONDON	26 0	11 0	4 0	5 8	16½	1672	Chatham	Phin. Pett	—
ROYAL ESCAPE	30 6	14 3	7 0	7 9	34	1660	Bought	—	—
SHEERNESS	28 0	11 0	5 6	6 6	18	1673	Chatham	Phin. Pett	—
SHISH	38 0	11 0	4 0	4 6	24	1673	Deptford	Joas. Shish	—

APPENDIX B.—A General State of the Royal Navy, from the 5th November, 1688, to 1st January, 1698.[1]

	Rates						Brigantines, Advice Boats, &c.	Fire-Ships	Bomb Vessels	Hoys	Ketches	Smacks	Yachts	Hulks and Store-Ships	Machines	Total is
	1	2	3	4	5	6										
Remains on the 5th November, 1688	9	11	39	41	2	6	—	21	3	6	3	5	14	8	—	169
INCREASE: Bought and built	—	4	23	44	33	22	22	32	33	8	11	—	3	10	16	261
Taken from the French	—	—	1	2	9	15	6	12	—	—	—	—	—	2	—	47
Total is	9	15	63	87	44	43	28	65	36	14	14	5	17	20	16	477
DECREASE: Burnt and blown up by disaster	1	—	2	—	—	—	—	5	—	—	1	—	—	—	—	9
Cast away	—	—	6	10	7	8	4	2	1	—	2	—	—	—	—	40
Taken or destroyed by the French	—	—	2	9	10	8	7	3	2	—	7	—	—	—	—	48
Burnt in service at La Hogue, St. Malos, Dieppe, Havre de Grace, and Dunkirk.	—	—	—	—	—	—	—	12	—	—	—	—	—	—	3	15
His Majesty's present to the Czar of Muscovy.	—	—	—	—	—	1	—	—	—	—	—	—	—	—	—	1
Cast on survey as irreparable, sold and old ships, broken up and laid to secure several docks and graving places	—	3	—	3	12	10	3	20	8	—	2	2	4	8	11	86
Total is	1	3	10	22	29	27	14	42	11	0	12	2	4	8	14	199
Remains	8	12	53	65	15	16	14	23	25	14	2	3	13	12	2	278
Forty-four ships are allowed in their rates and sorts, which are thus adjusted, viz. } Taken off	2	—	8	9	2	1	2	14	2	—	—	1	1	—	2	44
Set on	—	2	—	8	20	3	—	1	2	4	—	—	1	3	—	44
Remains on January 1st, 1698	6	14	45	64	33	18	12	10	25	18	2	2	13	15	0	278

[1] Miscellaneous Papers on Naval Affairs, 1576-1724. British Museum, Additional MS. No. 5439.

APPENDIX C.—*A List of the Navy of England in* 1699.
British Museum, *Additional MS. No.* 32,496.

Ships' Names	Men	Guns	Rate	Rate	Guns	Men	Ships' Names
BRITANNIA . .	760	110	1	3	70	420	YARMOUTH
ROYAL SOVEREIGN	760	110	1	3	70	420	ROYAL OAK
QUEEN . .	760	100	1	3	70	420	GRAFTON
VICTORY . .	760	100	1	3	70	420	HAMPTON COURT
ROYAL WILLIAM	760	100	1	3	70	420	EAGLE
ST. ANDREW .	750	100	1	3	70	420	NORTHUMBERLAND
LONDON . .	750	100	1	3	70	420	EXPEDITION
				3	70	420	STIRLING CASTLE
TRIUMPH . .	680	96	2	3	70	420	ELIZABETH
ASSOCIATION .	680	96	2	3	70	420	SUFFOLK
BARFLEUR . .	680	96	2	3	70	420	KENT
NAMUR . .	680	96	2	3	70	420	RESTORATION
NEPTUNE . .	680	96	2	3	70	420	BURFORD
DUKE . . .	680	96	2	3	70	420	ESSEX
DUCHESS . .	660	90	2	3	70	420	LENNOX
VANGUARD . .	660	90	2	3	70	420	BERWICK
OSSORY . .	660	90	2	3	70	420	CAPTAIN
ALBEMARLE .	660	90	2	3	70	420	CONTENT
SANDWICH . .	660	90	2	3	70	420	MONMOUTH
ST. MICHAEL .	660	90	2	3	70	420	RESOLUTION
ROYAL CATHERINE	660	90	2	3	66	390	SWIFTSURE
				3	66	390	DEFIANCE
SOMERSET . .	476	80	3	3	66	390	EDGAR
RANELAGH . .	476	80	3	3	66	390	WARSPIGHT
REVENGE . .	476	80	3	3	66	390	DREADNOUGHT
SHREWSBURY .	476	80	3				
CUMBERLAND .	476	80	3	4	60	330	PLYMOUTH
RUSSELL . .	476	80	3	4	60	330	MONTAGUE
CHICHESTER .	476	80	3	4	60	330	MARY
BOYNE . .	476	80	3	4	60	330	MONK
CAMBRIDGE. .	476	80	3	4	60	330	RUPERT
TORBAY . .	476	80	3	4	60	330	YORK
DEVONSHIRE .	476	80	3	4	60	330	DUNKIRK
LANCASTER . .	476	80	3	4	60	330	GLOUCESTER
CORNWALL . .	476	80	3	4	60	330	WINDSOR
NORFOLK . .	476	80	3	4	60	330	KINGSTON
DORSETSHIRE .	476	80	3	4	60	330	MEDWAY
HUMBER . .	476	80	3	4	60	330	EXETER
NEWARK . .	476	80	3	4	60	330	CANTERBURY
BEDFORD . .	420	70	3	4	60	330	PEMBROKE
OXFORD . .	420	70	3	4	60	330	SUNDERLAND
ALDBOROUGH .	420	70	3	4	50	260	WORCESTER
BREDA . .	420	70	3	4	50	260	HAMPSHIRE
IPSWICH . .	420	70	3	4	50	260	TRIDENT

LIST OF THE NAVY OF ENGLAND IN 1699—(continued).

Ships' Names	Men	Guns	Rate	Rate	Guns	Men	Ships' Names
COVENTRY . .	260	50	4	5	32	160	EXPERIMENT
ROMNEY . .	260	50	4	5	32	160	MERMAID
COLCHESTER .	260	50	4	5	32	160	POOLE
BLACKWALL .	260	50	4	5	32	160	SOUTHSEA CASTLE
GUERNSEY . .	260	50	4	5	32	160	SCARBOROUGH
HARWICH . .	260	50	4	5	32	160	RYE
PENDENNIS .	260	50	4	5	32	160	SHOREHAM
BURLINGTON .	260	50	4	5	32	160	DEAL CASTLE
WARWICK . .	260	50	4	5	32	160	WINCHESTER
LINCOLN . .	260	50	4	5	32	160	LOWESTOFT
ROCHESTER .	260	50	4	5	32	160	LYME
WEYMOUTH .	260	50	4	5	32	160	LOOE
LICHFIELD .	260	50	4	5	32	160	FOWEY
ANGLESEY .	260	50	4	5	32	160	MILFORD
NORWICH . .	260	50	4	5	32	160	RICHMOND
PORTLAND . .	260	50	4	5	32	160	NEWPORT
CHATHAM . .	260	50	4	5	32	160	REDBRIDGE
CENTURION .	260	50	4	5	32	160	SHEERNESS
BRISTOL . .	260	50	4	5	32	160	DOLPHIN
NEWCASTLE .	260	50	4	5	32	160	MORDEN
DRAGON . .	260	50	4	5	32	160	SOLEBAY
CHESTER . .	260	50	4	5	32	160	SPEEDWELL
RUBY . . .	260	50	4	5	32	160	ROEBUCK
OXFORD . .	260	50	4	5	32	160	LYNN
WOOLWICH .	260	50	4	5	32	160	SUSSEX
DEPTFORD .	260	50	4	5	32	160	ARUNDELL
GREENWICH .	260	50	4	5	32	160	HASTINGS
DOVER . .	260	50	4	5	32	160	JERSEY
FALMOUTH .	260	50	4	5	32	160	GOSPORT
PORTSMOUTH .	260	50	4				
SOUTHAMPTON .	260	50	4	6	24	126	QUEENBOROUGH
FORESIGHT .	260	50	4	6	24	126	FLAMBOROUGH
ASSISTANCE .	260	50	4	6	24	126	SEAFORD
SEVERN . .	260	50	4	6	24	126	SWAN
KINGFISHER .	260	50	4	6	24	126	LIZARD
TIGER . .	260	50	4	6	24	126	PENZANCE
NONSUCH . .	260	50	4	6	24	126	MARGARET
FALKLAND . .	260	50	4	6	24	99	GREYHOUND
CROWN . .	260	50	4	6	18	99	LARK
RESERVE . .	260	50	4	6	24	120	BIDEFORD
BONAVENTURE .	260	50	4	6	24	120	ELY
ADVICE . .	260	50	4	6	18	99	JULIAN
FARMERS' GOOD-WILL .	260	50	4	6	24	120	CONCEPTION
ASSURANCE . .	260	50	4				
SWEEPSTAKES .	260	50	4				BRIGANTINES
				6	6	40	EXPRESS
CHARLES GALLEY	190	40	5	6	6	40	INTELLIGENCE
MARY GALLEY .	190	40	5	6	6	40	DISCOVERY
ADVENTURE .	190	40	5	6	6	40	DILIGENCE
ST. LEWIS . .	190	40	5	6	6	40	DISPATCH

O 2

LIST OF THE NAVY OF ENGLAND IN 1699—(*continued*).

Ships' Names	Men	Guns	Rate	Rate	Guns	Men	Ships' Names
POSTBOY . .	40	6	6	—	—	—	LIGHTNING
MERCURY . .	40	6	6	—	—	—	THUNDERBOLT
FLY . . .	40	6	6	—	—	—	ROSE
SPY . . .	40	6	6	—	—	—	TERRIBLE
				—	—	—	VESUVIUS
YACHTS				—	—	—	PHŒNIX
				—	—	—	OWNERS' LOVE
HENRIETTA . .	30	8	6	—	—	—	ST. PAUL
FUBBS [1] . .	30	8	6	—	—	—	FIREBRAND
ISABELLA . .	30	8	6	—	—	—	CHARLES
WILLIAM . .	40	10	6	—	—	—	HUNTER
CATHERINE . .	30	8	6	—	—	—	HAWK
NOAH . . .	30	8	6				
MARY . . .	30	8	6	**BOMB VESSELS**			
MERLIN . .	30	8	6				
MONMOUTH . .	30	8	6	—	—	—	KITCHEN
CLEVELAND . .	30	8	6	—	—	—	MORTAR
				—	—	—	SOCIETY
KETCHES				—	—	—	STAR
				—	—	—	DRAKE
MARTIN . .	40	10	6	—	—	—	SALAMANDER
QUAKER . .	40	10	6	—	—	—	MACHINE
ROE . . .	40	10	6	—	—	—	FIREBALL
				—	—	—	OWNERS' GOOD-WILL
FIRE-SHIPS							
VULCAN . .	—	—	—	—	—	—	CARCASS
VULTURE . .	—	—	—	—	—	—	PORTSMOUTH
FLAME . .	—	—	—	—	—	—	EAGLET

[1] Fubbs was a pet name of the Duchess of Portsmouth *temp.* Charles II. The Fubbs yacht continued in the service till about 1770.

APPENDIX D.

LETTERS FROM STEPHEN MARTIN-LEAKE.[1]

1728.

SIR,—We embarked, as you know, with Commissioner Clevland[2] in the Charlotte. It is the first time I have sailed with him, and I hope the last. He is an ill-bred mere Scotch seaman, and nothing but a seaman ; covetous, mean-spirited, and fawning to his superiors, but a tyrant where he has the power ; without the least manners, good nature, or any one quality to make him tolerable. Though he is allowed his bill of expenses without limitation, he has kept a table we clerks should have been ashamed to have done at our own charge. He sent his boat a-begging for fish or what they could pick up by the way, and learnt us, for the first time, to eat fish without butter, which was our principal dish, and when he went away left us some mutton that had hung until it stank ; yet I don't doubt but he will bring in a bill as if he had entertained us with venison and Burgundy. But I have kept an account of our bills of fare, and am resolved to expose him to the whole office, which will be treating him as he did us. One would think a man might be generous at the public expense, as a favourable opportunity to seem generous and gain the good opinion of others ; but this requires some degree of good nature, of which he has no share. Hooke told me a story of his generosity that pleased me. It was upon an expedition to Chatham like this. He had a present made him of half a dozen bottles of Tokay ; he

---

[1] These letters are from copies in a letter book which belonged to the Garter. The name of the person to whom they were addressed is not given, nor the exact date.

[2] William Clevland belonged to the family of Clevlands or Clelands, in Lanarkshire. He was captain of the Montagu at the taking of Gibraltar, and was Commissioner of Navy Accounts from 1718 to 1732. He purchased the estate of Tapely, near Bideford, and died in 1735. His son, John Clevland, was M.P. for Saltash and Secretary to the Admiralty.

tasted it at dinner and did not like it, and therefore,
seeming open-hearted, told them if they liked it they
might drink it.   They knew what it was, and that evening
drank out five of the six bottles, leaving one to tantalise
him when he should know what it was.   The next day a
gentleman dined with him, and to save his other wine he
called for a bottle of that.   The gentleman drank a glass,
and commended it for as good Tokay as ever was drank,
and worth at least half a guinea a bottle.   'Zounds!' says
he, 'Tokay!   How much is there left, John?'   'No more
than this, sir.'   'By G—d, gentlemen,' says he, 'now you
have drank it, much good may it do ye; but had I known
what it was, the devil a drop should you have had of it;'
and ordered the rest of the bottle to be carried home, and
I believe he has remembered it ever since.   How opposite
to this selfish temper we have been speaking of is what we
call friendship, even in the least degree; for as to true and
perfect friendship, it is rather speculative than practical,
a mere enthusiasm, and nowadays as rare as the gift of
prophecy, if ever it was in the degree that some have supposed.   I was led into this subject by reading the story of
David and Jonathan (being Sunday), which seems to be as
remarkable an instance of it as any, for it is said Jonathan
loved him as his own soul, and yet not in that superlative
degree as some make it, which is to say there is no such
thing as friendship.   It seems to have been the prudence
of wise men in all ages to act with caution, even in friendship.   'Be not surety for a friend,' says Solomon; and the
prophet Micah, 'Trust not in a friend;' and we have an
old saying, 'Lend not money to a friend, lest you lose
both.'   But you'll say, Then what is friendship?   I reply,
A readiness to serve another to the utmost of my power,
according to my circumstances in life, without injury to
any.   It is with this limitation we must understand Solomon when he says, 'A friend loveth at all times;' that
there is a friend that sticks closer than a brother.   And
this was the friendship of Jonathan for David.   He was
ready to hazard his life and fortune to serve his friend,
consistent with the relation he bore to others.   But as for
an entire and lasting friendship, it is mere imagination, and
I question whether these notions of it have not done
more harm than good, making people more open than

was consistent with prudence, which has exposed them to great inconveniences when the friendship has been dissolved or broken. The relation a man stands in the world makes him incapable of perfect friendship upon earth. It is in reality what is expressed of David and Jonathan only figuratively, two persons to be animated by one soul, which is impossible in nature ; for two persons to be actuated in this manner must have the same fortunes, relations, inclinations, and even constitutions. And this sameness of inclinations will make a disagreement. If *one* were disposed with such an extraordinary nature, where shall be found two such, even though they were twins and counterparts of each other? If there were two such ! Do not circumstances and years alter us, that we differ from ourselves almost every seven years ? Shall we always live single ? If we do but think otherwise, the band is relaxed, if not broken ; and if we marry, we alter our whole scheme. And in any of these cases, upon a separation, we should wish to have had less friendship and been more reserved, for then, without any breach or strangeness, we might have continued the friendship in a suitable degree—that is, by a rational friendship, so as to promote the law and welfare of another, in all circumstances of life, consistent with what I owe to myself and others. Even between man and wife, which is the closest union next to soul and body, I conceive prudence requires some reserve ; much more with a friend, who is liable to be separated from us by various accidents and to create new friendships. A man would not, in that case, be so weak as to have laid open his whole heart. God only knows the heart of a wise man. Indeed, Solomon (Prov. xxvii. 10) seems to mean by a friend no more than a good neighbour, and I think it means no more. Most young men are apt to have notions of strict friendship, which they may search for, like Diogenes, with a candle at noon, but they will not find it. They may meet with something like it, and when they think they have found it they lose it to their cost, that is when they have laid open their heart and discovered their weakness. A good soldier, you know, will always secure a retreat ; and this prudent caution will no more impeach his courage than his friendship, especially as the world now goes. So that there is no such thing as perfect and lasting friendship, but good neighbours only with men of **family**, and a temporary friendship amongst bachelors. It may happen you may go one way and I another in different stations ; may marry and contract new friendships, as if **this had** never been ; but I hope you never will forget **that I** once was, as I really am, with reason,

Your Friend and Servant,
STEPHEN MARTIN-LEAKE.

Portsmouth : October 1728.

SIR,—I think I did not let grass grow under my feet. The 28th I left Chatham, and for expedition went to Gravesend, and in the tilt boat to London. I had only time to prepare for the next day, when at four in the morning I set out for Windsor, and performed **my** duty there upon his Majesty, at his assuming **his** stall ;[1] a duty not a little tedious and fatiguing, because **we** were standing **or** bowing the whole time. I had **but time** to get my **dinner** after the ceremony, and returned **to** London to the **Cross** Keys in Grace Church Street, by **ten at** night. Got my supper, took a **nap** in my **chair, and at two** the next morning set out in the stage coach **for** Portsmouth, and, what was worst of all, alone some hours before day, yet no possibility of sleeping, though tired and sleepy, carted about like a shuttle-cock, without rest or amusement. Thus I spent two tedious days that brought me hither where I find I shall have time enough to rest myself, for after all this hurry I don't think we shall have anything to do this fortnight. As I never was here before, I am glad of the opportunity to see the place, and that I am likely to **have so** much **time to** myself **to** satisfy my curiosity ; but **would have chosen** to have had a pleasanter journey and **less fatiguing. Now that I am** here I should be content **to stay longer than perhaps I** may, for he that relieved **me at Chatham, to give me** an opportunity to go to Windsor, **was to go to Portsmouth, and** when he has done at Chatham, **is to come hither to his post.** It is Mr. Philipson's scheme. **He has a malicious pride in** him that can't bear one that **he thinks equal to himself,** and above courting his favour, **which I have always been.** And since I have been a **Herald, he has put our** commissioner upon sending me to

---

[1] In St. George's Chapel, at Windsor, as Sovereign of the Garter.

pays, not because it is an advantage (for for that reason *you* shan't have it), but because he thinks I will refuse to go, or be mortified by going, having another office to attend, which he believes requires more attendance than it does. But herein he is mistaken in me, for these short trips I like well enough, and if they grow tedious I'll find means to evade them, or if there is too much business ; for when you come to long payments it is so tedious, and requires such an intense application, that it is the greatest slavery imaginable, and fatigues the mind beyond anything I ever experienced. But I must not complain ; I was ten years in the office and never went to a pay. It was a favour that no man in the office but myself ever desired, and therefore is, indeed, no favour at all at present, when there are junior clerks as well qualified that desire to go ; as you know one, I shall esteem their favour accordingly. There is no great danger of my coming often to this place, for Chatham and the Nore is my station, and I like it best, because it is nearest to London, to which I can presently return upon occasion, and they are generally short trips and easy payments. I must be pretty much with my father, who is alone. That is my first care, and I should be glad to spend some time at the Herald's Office, now I have fitted and furnished my lodgings there, where I could amuse myself in the library better than with muster books, and peruse my heraldic studies with more pleasure than my desk at the office, or even payments afford, and if ever I have an advance in that office, I will quit the Navy. I know they would have me do so now, but I won't—I can't afford it. When I can, I will. But I have got strangely out of the road. I intended to give you an account of my proceedings from Chatham to this place, and of my journey. I told you I came from Gravesend in the tilt boat. It was the first, and I believe will be the last time I shall come by that conveyance, though it is much preferable to the Gravesend boats. I won't trouble you with our dry ceremonial at Windsor, but it would have delighted you to have seen the great man[1] strutting from his stall to the altar to make his offering. Instead of a bow to the altar, or anything like it, he threw his right foot forwards, tossed back

[1] George II.

his head, and **turned short** upon his **left heel ; no mock**
majesty upon **the** theatre ever equalled it.   **As** to my
journey hither, **the** lone situation I was in **was** most apt
for observation.   I never broke silence but **now and then**
in a little chat with the coachman.   We breakfasted at
Kingston, dined at Cobham, and lay at Godalming, three
miles beyond Guildford.   Guildford, by what I observed
going through it, and by what I learnt from the coachman, is a large, compact town, and has three churches.
It has a fine broad street through it, and is well built,
clean **and** healthy by its situation upon a rising ground,
washed by the river Wey, a good air and a charming
country.   It is the county and a corporation and borough
town, has a market on Saturday, and very **good** inns,
with the ruins of an old castle.   Godalming **is upon** the
side of a hill, a little above the river.   There **is a** causeway of stone across the valley, and an old stone bridge
of five arches.   From thence is a narrow, ordinary street
up the hill, with a well about the middle, and an ex·
cellent spring **of water in it** that **runs continually over,**
making a rill **through the** middle **of the street to the**
river.   There is another street runs from this, in length **upon**
the hill, the two streets making the figure of a Roman **L.**
The town **is** but indifferently built, but populous, **and**
lately buried 120 persons of the small-pox in three **months.**
From Godalming is a mountainous, open country, with
furze, wild thyme, and some little grass, which serves to feed
sheep ; but at this season, the furze being withered, it has
a very disagreeable, barren look.   Nevertheless, some of
it they say is tolerable good land.   The soil, as it appeared
to me, was sandy and stony, and the valleys full of a fine
sand washed down from the hills.   In this wild place is a
lofty peaked, wild mountain, called Hind-head.   You pass
upon the ridge of the hill with a frightful chasm on either
side, a bad place to pass in bad weather, being so much
exposed.   The coachman **told** me he once passed that way
in a high wind, when he was obliged to **draw** back the
curtains of the coach **to** give the wind a free passage, lest
the coach should have **been** blown into **the** bottom.   On
the left he showed **me a** place between two hills, where
there is always found a strong wind, even on the calmest
day ; and the common people, it seems, believe it comes out

of the ground, and call the place 'Windy Gap.' But if it be
so, it must be owing to the situation that they are in, to
draw an air at any time, for he said it was observed that
which way soever the wind blew, it was much stronger in
the gap than anywhere else. It was some amusement to
me, having no other, to observe the gradual approaches of
the day in a foggy morning, as is usual at this time of year.
How from a thick fog it first began to break from the tops
of the highest hills, which, peeping above the surface, appeared like distant islands in the sea ; the even surface of
the fog then appeared to have deceived the sight so naturally that at first I took it for the sea. That part of the
fog on the side of the hills to the rising sun being first
rarefied, was lost imperceptibly, whilst that on the other
side being differently affected, as it was more or less shaded
from the sun, drove away in streams by a gentle wind, till
they likewise insensibly disappeared, or continued like
clouds ascending until they became real ones. The remaining part skulking behind the impending hills de-
scended in dewy tears. Pursuing our journey we came to
Petersfield, a small market town, which is all I can say of
it. The country from thence is mostly an open, hilly down,
the soil a hard chalk mixed with flint stone, with a mould of
about six inches upon it, and a fine turf that feeds innumer-
able flocks of sheep. This is a sort of country that delights
me much. After this, passing through Liphook, a village,
we come to the forest of Bear, where they say is good
timber, but none appeared in sight of the road. It is three
miles through, was formerly almost impassable, but now
there is a turnpike, and the road is well mended with chalk
and flint stones, which bind exceeding hard, and are here-
abouts in great plenty. After this, coming to a ridge of
hills called Portsdown, we had a fine prospect of the sea,
the Isle of Wight, the channel between the island and the
main leading to Southampton, and the whole harbour and
town of Portsmouth at about five miles distance, which I
beheld with more pleasure, as I was desirous to be at my
journey's end. From the hills, by a descent of about a mile,
we came to Portsea island, the channel that divides it from
the mainland being no more than a broad ditch at low
water. Here is a turnpike, and a bridge over to the island,
with a small guard. From this extremity of the island to

the other, where Portsmouth stands, is four miles by a very good road, all upon a flat, and not unpleasant, it being well cultivated and has some good farms upon it, and here and there a house of entertainment. To view Portsmouth from Portsdown, it seems to be in the very water, but when you come thither you are better reconciled to it. It was a new sight to me, and a pleasant one, for I love to see fortifications, and, according to the custom of fortified towns, there was a guard at the gate, who stopped the coach to know who was in it, which I thought ridiculous enough, being a stage, and that they suffer horsemen to pass without examination. But of this, more another time. I was glad to get to my lodgings at Mrs. Watermans, where I have a good bed, a neat, clean room and furniture, and excellent provision, and there is a glass of as good French claret at the tavern for three shillings a bottle as ever I drank. This letter is all the business I have undertaken these two days I have been here. As I shall have more leisure to satisfy my curiosity, you may expect to hear further from, &c.,

STEPHEN MARTIN-LEAKE.

Portsmouth : January 1728-9.

SIR,—We had a frozen journey hither, and made it three days, as they always do when they travel with money in the coach. Our guard was eight horse Grenadier Guards, with a subaltern officer. It snowed a great part of the way, and I think they had a bad time of it, for we could hardly keep ourselves warm with the glasses up ; yet the officer would not let the troopers put on their cloaks, to inure them (I suppose) to bad weather and discipline. Two of them rode before the coach, the rest followed. Thus we travelled in state, and gave way to nothing. We detached one of our troop before to bespeak our dinner and the soldiers', and the like at night to provide supper and accommodation ; by this means we had everything ready in due time and order. I observed the troopers both noon and night constantly had a plum pudding, besides a good joint of meat, and upon these occasions they are welcome guests, because they pay like others for what they have, besides what we spend. I assure you we live well, and do something extraordinary upon account of the figure we travel in, and entertain the officer at our table. At night the money is kept in the guard-room with the soldiers. I am at my old lodgings at Mrs. Watermans. As to business, we have only paid one ship at Spithead, and I believe shall do nothing else the short time we are like to continue here. I shall make the best use of that time to complete my account of Portsmouth, which you shall see when finished. I pace the works and take the angles as well as I can, without being taken notice of, in order to lay down a plan of the town and fortifications. The last time I was here I took a view of the town from the sea as well as I could in a boat. I don't know anything to communicate but what you'll see in my description of the place, unless it be the early club at Piles' Coffee House, which, indeed, is something singular. We have, indeed, clubs enough in London that deserve that name, never parting till early in the morning, but this don't meet till that time, and they consist of some of the most sensible men in the place. One of them is a doctor of physic. Their hour is four in the morning, when they meet without disturbing the coffee people or their own families. The fire is laid in the coffee room, and everything ready they may want over night. He that comes first lets himself in, strikes a light, lights the fire, and puts on the tea-kettle. When so many are met the coffee is made ; and after spending an hour drinking coffee, reading the news, and talking politics, they separate. This club would by no means suit me, I could sooner be reconciled to a late than an early club ; business or travelling makes it tolerable, I can then rise as well as others, but never by choice. It is neither pleasant nor wholesome to go abroad till the sun has blessed the earth and exhaled the vapours of the night. There is often the difference of summer and winter between the morning early and the noon of the same day, and sure no one can like such extremes. Pray dispatch the two enclosed to Mile End and the Herald's Office, and you'll oblige   Your Friend, &c.

Portsmouth is situated upon the little isle of Portsea, at the mouth of the harbour, about four miles from Portsea Bridge. The island is reckoned about fourteen miles round, and is separated from the main land only by a small channel, which at the bridge is almost dry at low water.

The whole island is of late pretty well cultivated, and has some good farms upon it. Portsmouth town is not inconsiderable. It has two principal streets from east to west, from the land gate to the sea, besides some other smaller and a great many cross streets and alleys or lanes. The form is irregular, but nearest a square, having four sides, west to the sea, north to the harbour, south and east to the land. The buildings are tolerably good, but none remarkable. The Town Hall in the High Street is one of the best. There is a large and commodious cooperage for use of the Navy, and handsome new barracks of brick designed in the form of a half H, but one wing is wanting to perfect it. The best house in the town is Mr. Ridge's, the brewer, and the only good one, for the governor's, though it be a large commodious old building, has but a mean appearance. There is but one church in the town, a very old building, but it has a very good tower and chimes, and in the upper part is a room where a man lives to give notice of all ships that appear off the harbour, which he does by striking a bell as many times as there are ships. They have a good peal of eight bells, which were brought from the church in Dover Castle by the interest of Sir George Rooke, one of their members. They are said to be the first ringers that struck their bells in slams (as they call it), that is, together at one stroke like a volley of muskets, which they do in the middle of a peal, as often as they please, without breaking off the peal ; and this they do upon rejoicing days in imitation of huzzas or volleys. Thursdays and Saturdays are their market days, where they have everything a plentiful country round about them can supply, and not a little is brought from the Isle of Wight ; amongst other things they have excellent fish, and French claret at 3*s.* per bottle in the taverns. They are a Corporation, governed by a mayor, &c., and send two members to Parliament. You may be sure that it is a Navy borough, for their whole dependance is upon the Navy. The mayor has the civil government within the walls, the governor the military, and commands the walls and gates ; if any soldier offends he is delivered over to the civil magistrate, indeed, they both act in aid of each other, it being the interest of the magistrate to agree with the governor, and the governor must be governed by law.

As a fortification it has been gradually improved, and grown up to what it is at present. Queen Elizabeth first made it a strong place according to the method of those times, but King Charles II. modernised and completed it, well knowing the importance of it, for the security and use of the Navy. The south side is defended by the sea bastion at the south-west corner, and the south-east bastion at the other corner, with a flat bastion in the middle, and casemates to the bastions. A broad ditch, and between the flat bastion and the bastion of the sea, which else would be very much exposed, is a ravelin. The east side has like bastions, with two ravelins and counterguards, and the northernmost of the two curtains on this side being longer than the other ; there is likewise a counterguard before that ravelin. Through this ravelin you pass to the land gate, first by a bridge to the counterguard, then by another to the ravelin, where you pass through two stone gates, and from thence by a third bridge over the main ditch to the town gate, a good stone building. From the north-east bastion the wall makes an angle to the westward, ending in a demi-bastion, the counterguard being continued all the way from the last bastion, and before the curtain and demi-bastion, till it communicates with a small neck of land (whereon is a water-mill) that joins to the harbour. Hereon is a mill which keeps up a large body of water on this side and supplies the ditch ; and on the opposite side to the mill in this water is a kind of lunette advanced before the counterguard of the last bastion. The mill field is on a small neck of land between the water and the harbour, and is the nearest communication with the dock, and is joined to the Water Gate of the town by a good stone covert way without the town ditch, between that and the harbour, having a ditch and drawbridge at each end, with flankers and a kind of flat bastion in the middle. This is a sufficient security next the harbour, but the mill at the end is secured to the land by a ditch, with a stone wall, gates, and drawbridge. The Water Gate of the town, at the other end of the causeway, is the communication with the harbour, and just without the gate is a wharf for vessels to unload, and a dock or basin for small vessels, made by a little peninsula of land called the Point, that runs within the harbour's mouth and joins to the town

by a very narrow isthmus, with a ditch through it from the
dock or basin to the sea ; and is joined to the Point by a
bridge and gate called Point Gate. All on this side next
the harbour, that is, from the demi-bastion by the mill to
the Water Gate, is a straight line without any bastions or
flankers ; but between the Water Gate and the Point Gate,
about the middle of the basin, is a ravelin, where is a
magazine. On the west side to the sea is, first, the sea
bastion at the south-west corner, mounted with whole
cannon ; thence a straight line runs to the platform ; another
battery, built all of stone, has a good guard-room, and is
mounted with cannon. About the middle of the line is a
small ravelin, close under the wall upon the beach, with a
communication to it underground ; the platform, which is
a large square building, projecting a little without the wall
into the sea. It commands both the sea and the harbour's
mouth, and a pleasant prospect to the Isle of Wight.
Here you see everything that passes in or out of the
harbour or at sea, and, therefore, serves as a look-out, as
well as a parade for the officers and gentry. From this
platform the line continues straight along shore, with a
high old stone wall, and ten portholes for guns, ending in a
square stone building with a tower, whereon they hoist the
flag ; and the building serves for a magazine. From thence
the line inclines inwards, with a stone wall, and soon joins
to the Point Gate. From the Point Gate the line slants
outwards upon the Point. It is a long stone building,
covered over like a gallery ; has fourteen ports for guns,
besides the gate called the Sally Port, where boats land
upon a good beach. At the end of this, which contracts
the harbour's mouth to a narrow space, is a small castle
which flanks it, and points right down the entrance of the
harbour. Answering this on the other side is another
small fort, and a long line of guns facing the south, on the
seashore, worth all the rest, for ships must come right
down upon it to enter the harbour ; nor can they bring
their guns to bear upon this battery without being equally
exposed to the cannon from the town. So that, I think,
there hardly can be a more secure harbour, considering
how easily the mouth may be secured, being so narrow you
may easily throw a stone across. The ditch of the town is
clean, full of water, and in good order, except to the south,

which is indeed very broad, but full of weeds, not being so
well supplied with water as the other. The walls are of
earth, in a very good condition, faced with stone at bottom
a little above the water. The ramparts are in good order,
a nd guns well mounted upon ship carriages, for it is found
by experience they do most service. The outworks are not
taken so much care of, though they are not bad. But the
counterscarp is wholly neglected. The garrison in war is
usually two regiments of foot, but in peace eight companies
of invalids, making 400 men. Besides the main guard,
which may consist of about thirty, with an officer, there is
a guard at the Land Gate and a small one at the Mill Gate ;
sentinels upon the corner bastions, the platform, and at the
governor's house, but nowhere else, for there are none at
the Water Gate nor Point Gate. Indeed, there is not much
need at the latter, because it is within sight of the main
guard at the west end of the High Street, and this guard
is very well situated, as it commands the gate, the High
Street, and is near the magazine, the platform, and the
governor. Opposite to the governor's house, which is
open to the south and west, is a spacious area, or place of
arms, taking up the south-west corner of the town, sufficient
to draw up 2,000 or 3,000 men. It is now a good field,
and serves the governor's use, that is, the deputy-governor,
for the governor never resides here. They observe the
same order here as in other garrison towns, as soon as it is
dusk a gun is fired from the platform, as a warning it is
time to shut the Land Gate, whereupon the tattoo is beat
round the town and in a moderate time after the Land Gate
is shut ; but the Water Gate is not shut till ten o'clock, and
the Point Gate not till eleven, when notice is given by ring-
ing a bell of the church. The invalids of the garrison have
many of them little houses on the south and east sides
next the wall, where they live with their families, the rest
in the barracks.

Besides the town itself, there are considerable suburbs
And first, the Point is more peculiarly so, and even a part
of the town, for there is no coming at it by land but
through the town. It makes one side of the harbour's
mouth, and is defended by the Sally Port, which entirely
covers it on that side, and is of a triangular form, the other
two sides lying within the harbour. It has one good street

through the middle, from the Point Gate to the water side,
is full built, and very populous and thriving, being the
Wapping of Portsmouth.   Here the Johns carouse, not
being confined to hours, and spend their money for the
good of the public, which makes ale **houses** and shops
thrive mightily upon this spot.   Some have compared it to
the Point at Jamaica that was swallowed by an earthquake,
and think, if that was Sodom this is Gomorrah ; but it is
by no means so bad as some would make it, though **bad**
enough.   On the land side, eastward (for there is none to
the south), a little way from the Land Gate, are very large
suburbs, extending to the dock, and joined by the Ordnance
to the Mill Gate, all which taken together is much more than
the whole town.   The Ordnance is a pretty neat place, it
runs west into the harbour, just beyond the Mill Gate,
flanking the covert way ; here they have a line of guns
upon land carriages, which they fire upon rejoicing days,
and hoist the union flag upon a tall flagstaff.   One day I
saw it flying, and could not help observing the St. Andrew's
or Scotch Cross **was** much broader, and the St. George's
Cross much narrower **than** they ought **to** have been, by
which one might know a Scotchman was **master** of the
Ordnance.   The Duke of Argyll **is** known **to be** very
national, but I could not have thought he would **have** dis-
played it so unwisely.   The dockyard is a fine place, but
I need not describe it, because it is like other yards which
you are well acquainted with.   I shall only observe of it,
that it is more compact than any other, and the docks are
stone, which in others are wood.   The officers' houses, I
think, are better than any other, though not so pleasantly
situated as those at Chatham, this being all a flat ; but the
officers are greater men here than anywhere, for they are
all commissioners.   The yard is walled in with a high wall.
They have a chapel for the use of the yard, and I do
assure you, a good dock regiment.   I saw them once perform an exercise very well, but if they are soldiers, what
pretence the officers have to be captains I don't understand.   If they could persuade the men to fight, I'm persuaded they could not fight themselves.

On the opposite side of the harbour is Gosport, a good
town dependent upon the town and harbour of Portsmouth, and therefore may be esteemed a part of it, as in

common speech it is taken to be. It is much the
pleasanter side to live on, having a fine country adjoining
which you are in as soon as you go out of the town ;
whereas from Portsmouth you must either cross the
water, be confined to the Isle of Portsea, or ride five or
six miles to come at a good country, which, with as many
back, is as far as most people ride for pleasure. Gosport
is likewise esteemed a better situation, and has good water
in plenty, which Portsmouth wants. But, then, for company and agreeable living, Portsmouth is best. The
garrison and corporation, the navy, ordnance and dockyard, and the company that is brought thither by business
or curiosity, besides what the sea brings, naval or mer-
cantile, makes as much difference almost between Portsmouth and Gosport as between town and country. Here
are two good coffee-houses, good taverns, and the fold of
business ; there you have provisions something cheaper,
and some, indeed, prefer the air of Gosport ; but they are
so near akin I see no reason for it, because it is found by
experience that Portsmouth is as healthy as most places,
notwithstanding its situation, which from Portsdown
appears to be much worse than it really is. For my part
I never was better anywhere ; and if I may judge by
myself, the sea air is the best of all airs, and I think it no
disagreeable place to live in. It is but stepping across the
water, and you have as good a country as you can wish,
either for walking or driving. And, considering you are
in a town, there are few places where you have pleasanter
walking than upon the walls round the town or without
the works.

The harbour is certainly one of the finest in the world,
safe and commodious for shipping, and secure against an
enemy. And it ought to be well secured, seeing it contains near one-third part of the British navy, and is so
conveniently situated for fleets or convoys to annoy the
enemy and protect our trade. It is surprising to see a
great ship sail into the harbour by so small an entrance,
and when you are through that narrow passage to see such
a spacious harbour, and the great ships lying at their
moorings for three or four miles up, and the harbour for
a mile at least on each side covered with buildings and
thronged with people ; the water covered with boats

P 2

passing and repassing like as on the Thames, and the
boats exactly like the wherries, only the head not so
pointed and sharp ; and these I have seen go off to ships
at Spithead full of passengers in very bad weather. The
prospect from the middle of the harbour gives you the
idea of a great city ; and, indeed, the whole, as it appears
on both sides taken together, is equal to most cities in
England, and in consequence equal to any but the metropolis. As I took some pleasure to view the place upon
the water both within and without the harbour, and have
laid down the plan of the town and fortification, I was
led to consider the strength of the place and how it might
be attacked or defended. In the case of an attack the first
opposition an enemy would meet with would be from a
castle called Southsea Castle upon the seashore about
half a mile from the sea bastion. The channel for ships
lies close to it, and there is a good battery of thirty guns
that lie low and might do great execution, but the misfortune of all batteries are that if they are high they do
less execution, if low they are so exposed to the greater
fire from a line of ships and their partridge and small shot
that after the first discharge it would be impossible to
stand to their guns. Then the castle itself is an old
building, not defensible to the land, and might be taken
by a party of seamen, unless a sufficient body of men were
detached from the town to oppose their landing. So that
I apprehend this castle would only serve to gain a little
time, but not be sufficient to stop a fleet in case of regular
attack ; and being taken, it is to be considered whether it
would not be an advantage to the enemy and facilitate the
taking of the town ; whereas, if it was fortified like a redoubt to the land, it would be capable of a good defence,
and entirely stop the progress of the enemy in the mean
time. But though an enemy were masters of Southsea
Castle, there is such a range of batteries that makes it
impracticable to force the harbour without being masters
first of the town. The sea bastion, the ravelin, and the
little ravelin upon the shore would give them a warm
reception, and if they got within them the ships would be
surrounded with batteries ; so situated, and within so
narrow a space, that it is like going into the mouth of a
cannon, or to certain destruction, especially if, besides

these, the harbour's mouth was strongly boomed, and ships sunk without and defended by others within. We could not have taken Vigo without the assistance of a land force, which took the batteries that defended the entrance. So in like manner must the town and batteries here be first secured before an enemy can hope to force the harbour ; and this must be by landing a good body of land forces sufficient, in conjunction with a fleet, to cut off the town from the land or take it before relief can be sent thither. In such a case the town could not hold out long. Having taken Southsea Castle, they would no doubt secure the passage to the island from the main ; they would cut off the town from the dock and make themselves masters of the mill, by which means they might draw off most of the water from the ditch. They must likewise endeavour to secure the battery on Gosport side by landing a body of men beyond it, near Gilkicker, which they may safely do. But then this would be no easy matter to do if the works were well defended and sustained from Gosport, the dock, and the ships in the harbour, which would give time for relief to come. Or they might carry on an attack against the face of the middle bastion on the south side, which could not hold out many days after the trenches were opened and the batteries began to play, because they could therein be assisted by the ships, and soon drive the defenders from the sea bastion and ravelin which flanks it. But the strongest place must yield to a superior force. And when this shall happen to Portsmouth, when our navy cannot defend it, in vain may they expect relief by land. England will then be no longer England. We must all submit to the conqueror, but in our present situation Portsmouth may be accounted strong and sufficient to answer the end—viz., to secure our navy and a good harbour, which as it effectually does ; it is undoubtedly a place of the utmost importance.

INDEX

Spottiswoode & Co. Printers, New-street Square, London